THIS BOOK BELONGS TO

Reader's Digest

BEST LOVED BOOKS
FOR YOUNG READERS

The Story of
King Arthur
and His Knights

A CONDENSATION OF THE FOUR-VOLUME WORK BY

Howard Pyle

Illustrated by Darrell Sweet

CHOICE PUBLISHING, INC.

New York

PRODUCED IN ASSOCIATION WITH MEDIA PROJECTS INCORPORATED

Executive Editor, Carter Smith
Managing Editor, Jeanette Mall
Project Editor, Jacqueline Ogburn
Associate Editor, Charles Wills
Contributing Editor, Lise Brenner
Art Director, Bernard Schleifer

Library of Congress Catalog Number: 88-63354
ISBN: 0-945260-31-8

This 1989 edition is published and distributed by Choice Publishing, Inc.,
Great Neck, NY 11021, with permission of The Reader's Digest Association, Inc.

Manufactured in the United States of America.

10 9 8 7 6 5 4 3 2 1

Foreword

LEGEND HAS NEVER produced a more romantic hero than King Arthur of Britain. Tales of his life were sung and narrated in medieval days long before they were written down; and over the intervening centuries many poets and writers have told and retold the tales in their own special words. We learn from them not only about Arthur, who unified Britain, defeated her enemies, and became her King sometime in the sixth century, but also about Arthur's Court and the Knights of his Round Table. Sir Launcelot, mighty in battles and in jousting; Queen Guinevere, the most beautiful lady in Christendom; chivalrous Sir Gawaine; churlish Sir Kay; Merlin, the Court magician; Sir Galahad, Launcelot's noble son who sought the Holy Grail; and Elaine, the lily maid of Astolat—all are part of Arthurian lore.

No one in this century has told the story of King Arthur more eloquently than Howard Pyle. The present selection, condensed from the four volumes of the original, brings to life all of Arthur's major adventures, and the splendid pageantry and color that fill these pages have the stylized beauty of an immense medieval tapestry.

Howard Pyle, who also wrote *The Merry Adventures of Robin Hood*, was known equally well as an illustrator. He taught at both the Drexel Institute in Philadelphia and at his own art school in Wilmington, Delaware. The vigor of his style had influenced a whole generation of illustrators by the time of his death in 1911.

Contents

PART I—ARTHUR AND GUINEVERE

CHAPTER I: THE SWORD IN THE ANVIL

IN ANCIENT DAYS THERE LIVED a very noble King, named Uther-Pendragon, and he became Overlord of all Britain. This King was greatly aided unto the achievement of the Pendragonship of the realm by the help of two men. The one of these men was a certain very powerful enchanter and prophet known as Merlin the Wise; and he gave very good counsel unto Uther-Pendragon. The other man was a renowned knight, hight Ulfius; and he gave Uther-Pendragon aid and advice in battle. So Uther-Pendragon was able to overcome all of his enemies and to become King of the entire realm.

After Uther-Pendragon had ruled his kingdom for a number of years he took to wife a certain beautiful lady, hight Igraine. This noble dame was the widow of the Duke Gerlois; by which prince she had had two daughters—one of whom was named Margaise and the other Morgana le Fay. And Morgana le Fay was a famous sorceress. These daughters the Queen brought with her to the Court of Uther-Pendragon, and there Margaise was wedded to King Urien of Gore, and Morgana le Fay was wedded to King Lot of Orkney.

Now after a while Uther-Pendragon and Queen Igraine had a son born unto them, and he was very beautiful and of great size and

I

strength of bone. And whilst the child still lay wrapped in his swaddling clothes, Merlin came to Uther-Pendragon with a spirit of prophecy strong upon him, and he said, "Lord, it is given unto me to foresee that shortly thou shalt die of a fever. Now, should such a dolorous thing befall, this child (who is, certes, the hope of this realm) will be in great danger of his life; for many enemies will rise up to seize his inheritance, and either he will be slain or else he will be held in captivity from which he shall hardly hope to escape. Wherefore, I beseech thee that thou wilt permit Sir Ulfius and myself to convey him away to some secret place where he may be hidden until he groweth to manhood."

When Merlin had made an end of speaking thus, Uther-Pendragon made reply: "Merlin, certes, if thy prophecy be true, then indeed this child should be conveyed hence to some safe place. Wherefore, I pray thee, perform thy will."

Merlin did as he had advised, and he and Sir Ulfius conveyed the child away by night. And shortly afterward Uther-Pendragon was seized with sickness and died, exactly as Merlin had foretold.

Then all the realm fell into great disorder. For each lesser king contended against his fellow for overlordship, and wicked knights and barons harried the highways and levied toll upon helpless wayfarers.

Thus there passed nearly eighteen years in great affliction, and then one day the Archbishop of Canterbury summoned Merlin to him and bespake him: "Merlin, men say that thou art the wisest man in the world. Canst thou not find some means to heal the distractions of this woeful realm? Canst thou not choose a king who shall be a fit overlord for us, so that we may enjoy happiness as we did in the days of Uther-Pendragon?"

Then Merlin lifted up his countenance upon the Archbishop, and he said: "My Lord, I do perceive that this country is soon to have a king who shall be wiser and greater and more worthy of praise than was even Uther-Pendragon. And he shall bring order and peace; and, moreover, this King shall be of Uther-Pendragon's own full blood royal."

To this the Archbishop said: "What thou tellest me, Merlin,

is a wonderfully strange thing. But many lesser kings would fain be overlord of this land. How then shall we know the real King from those who proclaim themselves to be the rightful king?"

"My Lord Archbishop," quoth Merlin, "if I have thy leave to exert my magic I shall set an adventure which, if any man achieve it, all the world shall know that he is the rightful King." And to this the Archbishop said, "Merlin, I bid thee do so."

So Merlin caused by magic that a huge marble stone, four square, should appear in an open place before the greatest church of London. And upon this block of marble there stood an anvil and into the anvil there was thrust a great sword midway deep of the blade. And this sword was the most wonderful that any man had ever seen, for the blade was of blue steel and extraordinarily bright, and the hilt was of gold, inlaid with a great number of precious stones. And about the sword were written these words in letters of gold:

Whoso pulleth out this sword from the anvil that same is rightwise king-born of England.

Then Merlin bade the Archbishop call together all the chief people of that land upon Christmastide; and he bade him command that every man should make assay to draw the sword out of the anvil, for that he who should succeed should be rightwise King of Britain.

Thus the mandate of the Lord Archbishop went forth, summoning people to the assay; and as Christmastide drew nigh, it appeared as though the entire world was wending its way to London Town. The highways and byways became filled with kings and lords and knights and ladies and esquires and pages and men-at-arms. Every inn and castle was full of travelers, and everywhere were tents and pavilions pitched for the accommodation of those who could not find shelter within doors.

Now among those who came unto London Town, there was a certain knight, very honorable, by name Sir Ector of Bonmaison. This knight had with him two sons; and the elder of these was Sir Kay, a young knight of great valor and promise; and the younger was a lad of eighteen years of age, by name Arthur. Sir

Ector had also with him a great number of retainers and esquires and pages.

And when he had come to London Town he went to a meadow where many other noble knights had already established themselves, and there he set up a fair pavilion of green silk, and erected his banner emblazoned with the device of his house; to wit, a gryphon, black, upon a field of green.

And upon this meadow were a multitude of pavilions of many colors, and above each was the pennant and the banner of that lord to whom the pavilion belonged. Wherefore, the sky was at places well-nigh hidden with the gaudy colors of the fluttering flags. And by now there were in London no less than twelve kings and seven dukes, so that, what with their courts of lords and ladies and esquires and pages in attendance, the town of London had never seen the like before.

Now the Archbishop of Canterbury, having in mind the extraordinary state of the occasion that had brought together so many kings and dukes and lords, had commanded that there should be a noble tournament proclaimed. Likewise he commanded that this contest at arms should be held in a certain field nigh to the great church, three days before assay should be made of the sword and the anvil. To this tournament were bidden all knights who were of sufficient birth and quality for to fit them to take part therein. Accordingly, so many exalted knights made application for admission that three heralds were kept busy looking into their pretensions unto the right of battle. For these heralds examined the escutcheons and the rolls of lineage of all applicants with great care.

Now Sir Kay went to that congress of heralds and submitted his pretensions unto them. And, after they had examined into his claims to knighthood, they entered his name as a knight-contestant. Sir Kay then chose his young brother Arthur for to be his esquire-at-arms on the field of battle, and Arthur was exceedingly glad because of the honor that had befallen him.

Now, the day having arrived when this tourney was to be held, not less than twenty thousand lords and ladies assembled at the field of battle, so that it appeared as though a solid wall of human souls surrounded that meadow. And in the center of this wonderful court there was erected the throne of the Lord Archbishop. Above the throne was a canopy of purple cloth emblazoned with silver lilies; and under this the Lord Archbishop sat in great estate.

Now when all that great assembly were in their places, a herald stood forth before the throne of the Archbishop and blew a very strong blast upon a trumpet. At that signal the turnpikes of the lists were opened and two parties of knights-contestant entered therein—the one party at the northern extremity of the meadow and the other party at the southern extremity thereof. Then all that field was aglitter with polished armor as each of these two parties took up its station.

Then the herald blew upon his trumpet a second time, and each of those parties of knights quitted its station and rushed forth against the other. This they did with such noise and fury that the earth groaned beneath the feet of the war-horses; and when the two companies met in the midst of the field, the roar of breaking lances was so terrible that those who heard it were appalled. Several fair dames swooned away with terror, and others shrieked aloud; for not only was there that great uproar, but the air was filled with splinters of ash wood that flew about.

In that famous assault threescore and ten honorable knights were overthrown; wherefore when the two companies withdrew each to its station the ground was covered all over with broken fragments of lances and of armor, and many knights were woefully lying in the midst of that wreck. To these ran divers esquires and pages, and lifted up the fallen men and bare them away. And attendants ran and gathered up the broken armor and the spears and bare them away, so that the field was cleared once more.

Then all those who gazed upon that meadow gave loud acclaim, for such a glorious contest at arms in friendly assay had hardly ever been beheld in that realm before.

Now in this assault Sir Kay had conducted himself with such credit that no knight who was there had done better than he. For, though two opponents at once had directed their spears against him, yet he had successfully resisted their assault. And one of those two he smote so violently that he lifted that assailant entirely over the crupper of the horse which he rode. So Sir Kay was wonderfully well satisfied and pleased at heart.

Now the two parties in array returned each to its assigned station. And when they had come there, each knight delivered up his spear unto his esquire. For the next assault was to be undertaken with swords.

Accordingly, when the herald again blew upon his trumpet, there was a great splendor of blades all flashing in the air at once. And when the herald blew a second time each party pushed forward to the contest.

In this affair likewise Sir Kay proved himself to be an extraordinary champion; for he violently smote down five knights, the one after the other, ere he was stayed in his advance. But when he struck a sixth knight, his sword blade snapped short at the haft with the fierceness of the blow. In this pass it would have gone very ill with Sir Kay but that three of his companions in arms thrust in betwixt him and his opponent. Thus Sir Kay was able to escape to the barriers.

Now when he reached the barrier, his esquire, young Arthur, came running to him. Sir Kay cried out: "Ho! Brother, get me another sword from our father's pavilion!" And Arthur said, "I will do so," and thereupon he leaped over the barrier and ran to his father's pavilion.

But when he came to the pavilion he found no one there, for all the attendants were at the tournament. Neither could he find any sword, wherefore he was put to a great pass to know what to do.

In this extremity he bethought him of that sword that stood thrust into the anvil before the church. Whereupon he ran thither with all speed. And when he had come there he discovered that no one was upon guard at the block of marble, for all were at the contest of arms. So young Arthur leaped upon the block of marble and laid his hands unto the hilt of the sword. And he bent his body and drew upon the sword, and, lo! it came forth from the anvil with wonderful smoothness. And he wrapped the sword in his cloak so that no one might see it (for it shone with exceeding brightness) and he hastened unto Sir Kay.

Now when Sir Kay beheld the sword he immediately knew it, and he wist not what to think. Then in a while he said, in a very strange voice, "Where got ye that sword?" And Arthur beheld that his brother's countenance was greatly disturbed. And he said, "Brother, I could find no sword in our father's pavilion, wherefore I bethought me of that sword that stood in the anvil before the church. So I went thither and drew it forth."

Then Sir Kay communed with himself thus: Lo! my brother is hardly more than a child, and he is exceedingly innocent. Therefore he knoweth not what he hath done nor what the doing thereof signifieth. Now, since he hath achieved this weapon, why should I not lay claim to that achievement? Whereupon he said to Arthur, "Give the sword and the cloak to me." And when Arthur had done so, Sir Kay said, "Tell no man of this, but go to our father where he sits at the lists and bid him come straightway unto our pavilion."

CHAPTER II: YOUNG ARTHUR'S BIRTHRIGHT

ARTHUR DID AS SIR KAY commanded him, greatly possessed with wonder that his brother should be so disturbed in spirit. For he wist not what he had done in drawing out that sword from the anvil, for so it is in this world that a man sometimes proves himself to be worthy of great trust, and yet, in lowliness of spirit, he is unaware that he is worthy thereof. And so it was with young Arthur. So he made haste to that part of the lists where his father, Sir Ector, sat, and he said, "Sire, my brother Kay hath sent me to bid thee come straightway unto our pavilion."

Then Sir Ector arose, and went with Arthur to the pavilion, and there, behold! Sir Kay was standing in the pavilion, and his face was as white as ashes and his eyes shone with a wonderful brightness. And Sir Kay said to Sir Ector, "Sire, here is a very wonderful matter." Therewith he took his father by the hand and brought him to a table, and, lo! there lay the sword of the anvil.

Sir Ector immediately knew that sword. Wherefore he was filled with astonishment, and he cried out, "How came you by that sword?"

And Sir Kay said, "Sire, I brake my sword in battle, whereupon I found me this sword in its stead."

Then Sir Ector was altogether bemazed. But after a while he said, "If so be that thou didst draw forth this sword from the anvil, then it must also be that thou art rightwise King of Britain. But if thou didst indeed draw it forth from the anvil, then thou shalt as easily be able to thrust it back again."

At this Sir Kay was troubled in spirit, and he cried out, "Who could perform so great a miracle as to thrust a sword into solid iron?" Whereunto Sir Ector made reply, "Such a miracle is no greater than that thou hast performed in drawing it out."

Then Sir Kay took comfort to himself, saying, If my young brother Arthur was able to perform this miracle, why should I not do a miracle of a like sort?

So he wrapped the sword in the cloak again, and he and Sir Ector and Arthur betook their way unto the marble stone and the anvil. And Sir Kay mounted upon the cube of marble and beheld the face of the anvil. And lo! it was without a scratch or scar of any sort. And Sir Kay said to himself, What man is there in life who could thrust a sword blade into a solid anvil of iron? Ne'ertheless, he set the point of the sword to the iron and bore upon it with all his strength. But yet did he not pierce the iron even to the breadth of a hair.

So he at last came down. And he said to his father, "Sire, no man in life may perform that miracle."

Unto this Sir Ector made reply, "How is it possible then that thou couldst have drawn out that sword as thou sayest?"

Then young Arthur lifted up his voice and said, "My father, have I thy leave to speak?" And Sir Ector said, "Speak, my son." And Arthur said, "I would that I might assay to handle that sword." Whereunto Sir Ector replied, "By what authority wouldst thou handle that sword?" And Arthur said, "Because it was I who drew that sword forth from the anvil for my brother."

Then Sir Ector gazed upon young Arthur in such a strange manner that Arthur cried out, "Sire, why dost thou gaze so upon me? Hast thou anger against me?" Whereunto Sir Ector made reply, "In the sight of God, my son, I have no anger against thee. If thou hast a desire to handle the sword, thou mayest assuredly do so."

So Arthur took the sword from Kay and he leaped upon the marble stone. And he set the point of the sword upon the anvil and bore upon it and lo! the sword penetrated smoothly into the center of the anvil, and there it stood fast. And after that he drew the sword forth swiftly and easily, and then thrust it back again.

Then Sir Ector cried out, "Lord! Lord! what is the miracle mine eyes behold!" And when Arthur came down from the cube of marble, Sir Ector kneeled down before him.

But when Arthur beheld what his father did, he cried like one in pain: "My father! why dost thou kneel to me?"

To him Sir Ector made reply, "I am not thy father, and now it is made manifest that the blood of kings flows in thy veins."

Then Arthur fell a-weeping and he cried out, "Father! what is this thou sayest? I beseech thee to arise!"

So Sir Ector arose and stood before Arthur, and he said, "Arthur, why dost thou weep?" And Arthur said, "Because I am afeard."

Then Sir Ector spake, saying, "Arthur, I trow the time hath come for thee to know the true circumstances of thy life. Now I do confess everything to thee in this wise: that eighteen years ago there came to me the Enchanter Merlin. And Merlin showed me the signet ring of Uther-Pendragon and he commanded me by virtue of that ring that I should be at the postern gate of Uther-Pendragon's castle at midnight of that very day.

"So I went to that postern gate at midnight, and there came unto me Merlin and Sir Ulfius, who was the chief knight of Uther-Pendragon's household. And Merlin bare in his arms a child not long born and wrapped in swaddling clothes. And I saw the child in the light of a lanthorn which Sir Ulfius bare, and he was very fair of face and large of bone—and thou wert that child.

"Then Merlin commanded me to take that child and rear him as mine own; and he said that the child was to be called Arthur;

9

and he said that no one was to know otherwise than that the child was mine own. And I told Merlin that I would do as he would have me. And that lady who was my wife took that secret with her unto Paradise when she died, and since then until now no one in all the world knew aught of this matter but I and those two afore-mentioned worthies.

"Nor have I until now known who was thy father; but now I do suspect that thy father was Uther-Pendragon himself. For who but his son could have drawn forth that sword from the anvil?"

Then Arthur cried out, "Woe! Woe!" And Sir Ector said, "Arthur, why art thou woeful?" And Arthur said, "Because I have lost my father, for I would rather have my father than be a king!"

Now there came unto that place two men, very tall and of noble appearance. And one was the Enchanter Merlin and the other was Sir Ulfius. And Merlin spake, saying, "What cheer?" And Sir Ector made answer, "Here is cheer of a very wonderful sort; for, behold, Merlin! this is that child that thou didst bring unto me eighteen years ago, and, lo! thou seest he hath grown unto manhood."

Then Merlin said, "Sir Ector, I know very well who is this youth, for I have kept diligent watch over him for all this time. Within the surface of an enchanted looking glass I have beheld all that he hath done today. And, lo! the spirit of prophecy is upon me and I do foresee that thou, Arthur, shall become the greatest King that ever lived in Britain; and I do foresee that many knights of extraordinary excellence shall gather about thee; and I do foresee that the most marvelous adventure of the Holy Grail shall be achieved by three of the knights of thy Court, and that to thy lasting renown.

"And, lo! the time is now at hand when the glory of thy House shall again be made manifest unto the world, and all the people of this land shall rejoice in thee and thy Kinghood. Wherefore, Sir Ector, for these three days to come, do thou guard this young man as the apple of thine eye, for in him doth lie the hope and salvation of this realm."

All this while Sir Kay had stood like unto one struck by thunder, and he wist not whether to be uplifted unto the skies or to be cast down into the depths, that his young brother should thus have been exalted unto that extraordinary altitude of fortune.

But then Sir Ector cried unto Arthur, "A boon! a boon!" And Arthur said, "Dost thou, my father, ask a boon of me when thou mayest have all in the world that is mine to give? Ask and it is thine!" Then Sir Ector said, "I do beseech this of thee: that when thou art King thy brother Kay may be Seneschal of the realm." And Arthur said, "It shall be as thou dost ask." And he said, "As for thee, it shall be still better, for thou shalt be my father unto the end!" Whereupon he took Sir Ector's head into his hands and he kissed Sir Ector, and so sealed his plighted word.

So WHEN THE MORNING of Christmas Day had come, many thousands of folk of all qualities, both gentle and simple, gathered in front of the church to behold the assay of that sword.

Now there had been a canopy of embroidered cloth spread above the sword, and nigh unto that place there had been a throne for the Archbishop established; for the Archbishop was to overlook the assay and to see that every circumstance was fulfilled with due equity. And after the Archbishop had established himself upon his throne, he commanded his herald to sound a trumpet, and to bid all who had the right to make assay of the sword to come unto that adventure.

Now unto that assay there had gathered nineteen kings and sixteen dukes. And when the herald had sounded his trumpet there immediately appeared the first of these kings, and he was King Lot of Orkney. King Lot mounted the platform, and first he saluted the Archbishop, and then he laid his hands to the sword. And he drew upon the sword with great strength, but he could not move the blade in the anvil even the breadth of a hair. And he tried four times more, but still he was altogether unable to move the blade. Then, filled with anger, he came down from that place.

And after King Lot there came his brother-in-law, King Urien of Gore; but neither did he succeed. And after King Urien there came King Fion of Scotland, and King Mark of Cornwall, and King Ryence of North Wales, and then came thirty other kings and dukes, and not one of all these was able to move the blade.

Now the people who were there were astonished, and they said to one another, "If all those kings and dukes have failed to achieve that adventure, who then may hope to succeed?"

And, likewise, those kings and dukes spoke together in the same manner. And there came six of the most worthy; and these stood before the Archbishop and spake in this wise: "Sir, here have all the kings and dukes of this realm striven to draw forth that sword, and lo! not one hath succeeded. What, then, may we understand but that the Enchanter Merlin hath set this adventure for to bring shame upon all of us and upon you, who are the head of the church?"

Then was the Archbishop much troubled in spirit, but he spake aloud, "Messires, I have yet faith that Merlin hath not deceived us, wherefore I pray your patience for a little while longer. For if, in the time a man may count five hundred twice over, no one cometh forward to perform this task, then will I choose one from amongst you and will proclaim him King and Overlord of all."

Now Merlin had bidden Arthur and his father and brother to abide in their pavilion until such time as he thought fit for them to come out. And now Merlin and Sir Ulfius went to the pavilion, and Merlin said, "Arthur, arise and come forth, for the hour is come." So Arthur did as Merlin bade him, and he came forth from the pavilion with his father and his brother, and he was like one who walked in a dream.

So they five went down toward the church and unto that place of assay. And when they had come there the people made way for them, saying to one another, "Who are these with the Enchanter Merlin and Sir Ulfius?" For all the world knew Merlin and Sir Ulfius. And Arthur was clad all in flame-colored raiment embroidered with silver, so that others of the people said, "Certes, that youth is fair to look upon; now who may he be?"

But Merlin said no word to any man, but he brought Arthur through the press unto that place where the Archbishop sat; and Merlin said, "Lord, here is one come to make the assay of yonder sword." And he laid his hand upon Arthur.

Then the Archbishop looked upon Arthur and he beheld that the youth was very comely of face, wherefore his heart went out unto Arthur. And the Archbishop said, "Merlin, by what right doth this young man come hither?" And Merlin made reply, "Lord, he cometh hither by the best right in the world; for he is the true son of Uther-Pendragon and of his lawful wife, Queen Igraine."

Then the Archbishop cried out aloud in amazement, and he said, "Merlin, what is this that thou tellest me? For who, until now, hath ever heard that Uther-Pendragon had a son?"

Unto this Merlin made reply: "Until now, only a very few have known of such a thing. For it was in this wise: When this child was born I foresaw that Uther-Pendragon would die before a great while. Wherefore I feared that the enemies of the King would lay violent hands upon the young child. So, at the King's behest, I and another took the child and gave him unto a third, and that man received the kingly child and maintained him as his own son. And there are others here who may attest the truth of these things—for he who was with me when the young child was taken from his mother was Sir Ulfius, and he to whom he was entrusted was Sir Ector of Bonmaison—and those two witnesses are without any reproach."

And Sir Ulfius and Sir Ector said, "All that Merlin hath spoken is true."

Then the Archbishop looked upon Arthur and smiled, and Arthur said, "Have I then thy leave, Lord, to handle yonder sword?" And the Archbishop said, "Thou hast my leave."

Thereupon Arthur went to the marble stone and he laid his hands upon the haft of the sword that was in the anvil. And he bent his body and drew and, lo! the sword came forth with great ease. And he swung the sword about his head so that it flashed like lightning. And after he had swung it thus thrice about his head, he set the point thereof against the face of the anvil and bore upon it, and, behold! the sword slid smoothly back into place.

Now when the people beheld this miracle performed, they lifted up their voices all together in a tumult of outcry. And all the kings and dukes who were there were filled with amazement. But some

13

of them were not willing to acknowledge Arthur. These withdrew; and they said among themselves: "Who can accredit such a thing that a beardless boy should be set above us all? Nay! we will have none of him."

But others of the kings and dukes came and saluted Arthur and paid him court, giving him joy of that which he had achieved; and all the multitude crowded around that place shouting so that it sounded like to thunder.

And when Arthur departed, great crowds followed after him, giving him loud acclaim as the chosen King of England; wherefore his heart was uplifted with great gladness, so that his soul took wing and flew like a bird into the sky.

Thus Arthur achieved the adventure of the sword and entered into his birthright of royalty. Wherefore, may God grant His Grace unto you all that ye too may likewise succeed in your undertakings. For any man may be a king in that life in which he is placed if so be he may draw forth the sword of success from out of the iron of circumstance. Wherefore when your time of assay cometh, I do hope it may be with you as it was with Arthur that day. Amen.

CHAPTER III: THE SABLE KNIGHT

NOW AFTER THESE THINGS had happened, the Archbishop ordained that Arthur should be anointed and crowned unto royal estate; and so it was done at the great church.

But when Arthur had thus been crowned, there were still those who were opposed unto his Kingship, and these withdrew themselves in anger, and set about to prepare war against him. But the people were with Arthur, and so also were several kings and many of the barons. And Arthur and his allies fought two great wars with his enemies and won both of these wars. And after that all the land was at peace such as it had not enjoyed since the days of Uther-Pendragon.

And King Arthur established his Court at Camelot (which some men now call Winchester). And he made Sir Kay his Seneschal as he had promised; and he made Sir Ulfius his Chamberlain; and Merlin he made his Counselor. These men greatly enhanced the glory and renown of his reign and established him upon his throne with entire security.

And meanwhile even as his reign was becoming thus established, many men of noble soul and of knightly prowess perceived that great credit and exaltation of estate were likely to be won under such a king. So there began to gather together such a Court of noble, honorable knights as men never beheld before that time, and shall haply never behold again.

Now when King Arthur had gathered together his Court, and when his reign was at peace, it fell upon a certain pleasant time in the springtide season that he and his Court made a royal progression through that part of Britain which lieth close to the Forests of the Usk.

The weather was exceedingly warm, and so the King and Court made pause within the forest under the trees in the cool and pleasant shade, and there the King rested late in the day upon a couch of rushes spread with scarlet cloth.

And the knights then present at that Court were Sir Gawaine, who was the son of King Lot, and Sir Ewaine, and Sir Kay, and Sir Pellias, and Sir Bedivere, and Sir Geraint, and Sir Mador de la Porte, and there was not to be found anywhere in the world a company of such exalted knights.

Now as the King and these worthies sat holding cheerful converse together, there came thitherward a knight, sore wounded, and upheld upon his horse by a golden-haired page. The knight's face was as pale as wax and hung down upon his breast, and his apparel, of white and azure, was all red with blood that ran from a great wound in his side.

Now King Arthur cried out, "Alas! hasten, ye my lords, and bring succor to yonder knight; and do thou, Sir Kay, bring that young page hither that we may hear what mishap hath befallen his lord."

So certain knights hastened and gave all succor to the wounded knight; and Sir Kay brought that young page before the King. And the King said, "I prithee tell me, Sir Page, who is thy master, and how came he to be in such a pitiable condition."

"Lord," said the youth, "know that my master is entitled Sir Myles of the White Fountain, and that he cometh from the country north of where we are. A fortnight ago (being moved thereunto by the lustiness of the springtime), he set forth with me for his esquire to seek adventure in such manner as beseemed a good knight. And my lord overcame six knights at various places and sent them all to his castle for to attest his valor unto his lady.

"At last, this morning, we came unto a bridge. Beyond the bridge was a lonesome castle with a tall tower, and before the castle was a wide lawn of grass. And immediately beyond the bridge was an apple tree hung over with a multitude of shields. And midway upon the bridge was a single shield, entirely of black; and beside it hung a hammer of brass; and beneath the shield was written these words:

"Whoso smiteth this shield doeth so at his peril.

"Now Sir Myles, when he read those words, went straightway to that shield, and, seizing the hammer, he smote upon it a blow. Thereupon the portcullis of the castle was raised, and a knight clad from head to foot in sable armor came riding swiftly across the bridge. And there he cried out, 'Sir Knight, I demand of thee why thou didst smite that shield. Now let me tell thee, because of thy boldness, I shall take away from thee thine own shield, and shall hang it upon yonder apple tree.'

"Unto this my master made reply. 'That thou shalt not do unless thou overcome me, as knight to knight.' And thereupon, immediately, he dressed his shield for an assault at arms.

"So my master and this Sable Knight, having made themselves ready, drave together with might and main. And they met in the middle of the lawn beyond the bridge, where my master's spear burst into splinters. But the spear of the Sable Knight held and it pierced through Sir Myles, his shield, and it penetrated his side, so that both he and his horse were overthrown into the dust; he being wounded so grievously that he could not arise again from the ground.

"Then the Sable Knight took my master's shield and hung it up in the apple tree with the other shields, and thereupon he rode away into his castle again, whereof the portcullis was dropped behind him. So, after that he had gone, I got my master to his horse with great labor, and straightway took him thence. And that, my Lord King, is our story."

"Ha! By the glory of Paradise!" cried King Arthur, "I do consider it great shame that in my kingdom strangers should be so discourteously treated. For it is certainly a discourtesy for to leave a fallen knight upon the ground, without tarrying to inquire as to his hurt. And still more discourteous is it for to take away the shield of a fallen knight who hath done good battle."

And it was at this time that Sir Myles died of his hurt. And all the knights of the King's Court exclaimed against the Sable Knight. And many wished to do battle with him, but King Arthur declared that he himself would go forth for to punish that knight. And, though the knights of his Court strove to dissuade him, yet he declared that he with his own hand would accomplish that proud knight's humiliation.

Now, the very next day, as soon as the birds began to chirp and the east to brighten with daylight, King Arthur summoned his two esquires, and, having with their aid donned his armor and mounted a milk-white war-horse, he took his departure upon that adventure.

And indeed it is a very pleasant thing for to ride forth in the dawning of a springtime day. For then the little birds do sing their sweetest song; then do the growing things of the earth smell freshest; then doth the dew bespangle all the sward; then is all the world as though it had been new created.

So King Arthur's heart expanded with great joy, and he chanted a quaint song as he rode through the forest upon the quest of that knightly adventure.

So, about noontide, he came to a part of the forest where charcoal burners plied their trade. For here were many mounds of earth, all asmoke with the smoldering logs within.

As the King approached this spot, he beheld three sooty fellows with knives in their hands, who pursued one old man, whose beard was as white as snow. And he beheld that the old man, who was clad richly in black, and whose horse stood at a little distance, was running hither and thither, and he appeared to be very hard pressed and in great danger of his life.

Pardee! quoth the young King to himself, here, certes, is one in need of succor. Whereupon he cried out in a great voice, "Hold, villains! What would you be at!" and set spurs to his horse and drove down upon them with a noise like to thunder for loudness.

When the three wicked fellows beheld the armed knight thus thundering down upon them, they straightway, with loud outcries of fear, ran away into the thickets of the forest.

Whereupon King Arthur rode up to him whom he had succored, thinking to offer him condolence. And behold! when he had come nigh to him, he perceived that the old man was the Enchanter Merlin. Yet what he did in that place, the King could in no wise understand. Wherefore he bespoke the Enchanter, "Ha! Merlin, it seemeth to me that I have saved thy life. For, surely, thou hadst not escaped from the hands of those wicked men had I not happened to come hither at this time."

"Dost thou think so, Lord?" said Merlin. "Now let me tell thee that I might have saved myself easily had I been of a mind to do so. But, as thou sawest me in this seeming peril, so may thou know that a real peril, far greater than this, lieth before thee. Wherefore, I pray thee, Lord, to take me with thee upon this adventure."

"Merlin," said King Arthur, "if such peril lieth before me, meseems it will be very well for me to take thee with me."

So Merlin mounted upon his palfrey, and King Arthur and he rode together through the forest, until the King perceived that they must be approaching nigh to the place where dwelt the Sable Knight. For the forest began to show an aspect more thin and open, as though a dwelling place of mankind was close at hand.

And, after a little, they beheld before them a violent stream of water, and across this stream of water was a bridge of stone, and upon the other side of the bridge was a lawn of green grass, and beyond this lawn was a tall and forbidding castle. And, midway upon the bridge, there hung a sable shield, exactly as the page had said; and upon the farther side of the stream was an apple tree, amid the leaves of which hung a great many shields of various devices.

"Splendor of Paradise!" quoth King Arthur, "that must be a valiant knight who hath overthrown so many other knights. For, indeed, Merlin, there must be a hundred shields hanging in yonder tree!"

Unto this Merlin made reply, "And thou, Lord, mayest be very happy an thy shield, too, hangeth not there ere the sun goeth down this eventide."

"That," said King Arthur, "shall be as God willeth. For, certes, I have a greater mind than ever for to try my power against yonder knight." Thereupon King Arthur pushed forward his horse and so, coming upon the bridge, he read that challenge:

Whoso smiteth this shield doeth so at his peril.

Upon reading these words, the King seized the heavy maul that hung there, and smote that shield so violent a blow that the sound thereof echoed back from the smooth walls of the castle.

In answer to that sound, the portcullis was immediately raised, and there issued forth a knight, very huge of frame, clad in sable armor. Likewise all the trappings of his horse were of sable, so that he presented a most grim aspect. This Sable Knight came across that meadow with a stately gait; and, reaching the bridge-head, he drew rein and saluted King Arthur haughtily. "Ha! Sir Knight!" quoth he, "why didst thou smite upon my shield? Now I do tell thee that, for thy discourtesy, either thou shalt deliver thy shield unto me without more ado or prepare for to defend it with thy person."

"Gramercy for the choice thou grantest me," said King Arthur. "But as for taking away my shield—I do believe that that shall be as Heaven willeth, and not as thou willest. Know, unkind knight, that I have come hither to do battle with thee and to redeem with my person all those shields that hang yonder upon that apple tree. So make thou ready straightway that I may have to do with thee."

"That will I do," replied the Sable Knight. And thereupon he turned his horse's head and, riding back a distance across the lawn, he took stand. And so did King Arthur ride forth also upon that lawn, and take his station.

Then each knight dressed his spear and shield for the encounter, and, having thus made ready, each shouted to his war-horse and drave his spurs into its flank.

Then those two noble steeds rushed forth, coursing across the ground with great speed, and those two knights met in the midst of the field, crashing together like a thunderbolt. And so violently did they smite the one against the other that the spears burst into splinters, and the horses of the riders staggered back from the onset, so that only because of the extraordinary address of the knights-rider did they recover from falling before that shock of meeting.

And indeed King Arthur was very much amazed that he had not overthrown his opponent, for at that time he was considered to be the very best knight in deeds of arms in all of Britain. Wherefore he now gave that knight greeting, and bespoke him with great courtesy: "Sir Knight, I know not who thou art, but I do pledge my knightly word that thou art the most potent knight that ever I have met. Now I do bid thee get down straightway from thy horse, and let us two fight this battle with sword and upon foot, for it were pity to let it end in this way."

"Not so," quoth the Sable Knight, "not until one of us twain be overthrown will I contest this battle upon foot." And upon this he shouted, "Ho!" in a loud voice, and straightway there came running forth from the castle two tall esquires clad in black. And each of these esquires bare in his hand a great new spear of ash wood. So King Arthur chose one spear and the Sable Knight took the other, and thereupon each returned to his station.

Then once again each knight rushed his steed to the assault, and once again did each smite so fairly in the midst of the defense of the other that the spears were again splintered.

But this time, so violent was the blow that the Sable Knight delivered upon King Arthur's shield that the girths of the King's saddle burst apart, and both he and his steed were cast violently backward. So King Arthur might have been overcast, had he not voided his saddle with extraordinary skill, wherefore, though his horse was overthrown, he himself still held his footing and did not fall into the dust.

At that, King Arthur was filled with anger and he ran to the Sable Knight, and catching the bridle rein of his horse, he cried out: "Come down, thou black knight! and fight me upon foot and with thy sword."

"That will I not do," said the Sable Knight, "for, lo! I have overthrown thee. Wherefore deliver thou to me thy shield."

"That will I not!" cried King Arthur, with passion, "neither will I yield myself until either thou or I have altogether conquered the other." Thereupon he thrust the horse of the Sable Knight backward by the bridle rein so that the other was constrained to void his saddle. And now each knight drew his sword and both rushed together like two wild bulls. They foined, they smote, they parried, and the sound of their blows, crashing and clashing, filled the surroundings with an extraordinary uproar. Whole cantles of armor were hewn from their bodies and many deep and grievous wounds were given and received, so that the armor of each was altogether stained red with blood.

At last King Arthur struck so fierce a blow that no armor could have withstood that stroke had it fallen fairly upon it. But with that stroke his sword broke at the hilt and the blade thereof flew in three pieces into the air. Yet was the stroke so wonderfully fierce that the Sable Knight groaned, and staggered, and ran about in a circle as though he had gone blind.

But presently he recovered himself, and perceiving King Arthur nearby, and not knowing that his enemy had now no sword to defend himself, he cast aside his shield and took his own sword into both hands, and smote so dolorous a stroke that he clave through King Arthur's shield and helmet and even to the bone of his brainpan.

Then King Arthur thought that he had received his death

wound, and he sank down to his knees, whilst the blood and sweat, commingled in his helmet, flowed down into his eyes. Thereupon, seeing him thus grievously hurt, the Sable Knight called upon him for to yield himself and to surrender his shield, because he was now too sorely wounded for to fight any more.

But King Arthur would not yield himself, but catching the other by the sword belt, he lifted himself to his feet. Then, being in a manner recovered from his amazement, he embraced the other with both arms, and cast him backward down upon the ground. And the Sable Knight was, awhile, entirely bereft of consciousness. Then King Arthur unlaced the helm of the Sable Knight and so beheld his face, and he knew that that knight was King Pellinore, one of the foremost kings of Britain, who had twice warred against him!

And King Arthur cried out aloud, "Ha! Pellinore, is it then thou? Now yield thee to me, for thou art at my mercy." And upon this he drew his misericordia, as his dagger was called, and set the point at King Pellinore's throat.

But by now King Pellinore had greatly recovered from his fall, and perceiving that the blood was flowing down in great measure from out of his enemy's helmet, he wist that that other must have been very sorely wounded. Wherefore he catched King Arthur's wrist in his hand and directed the point of the dagger away from his own throat.

And, indeed, what with his wound and with the loss of blood, King Arthur was now fallen exceedingly sick and faint. Accordingly, it was with no very great ado that King Pellinore suddenly heaved himself up from the ground and so overthrew his enemy that King Arthur was now underneath his knees.

And King Pellinore was so enraged that he wrenched the dagger out of his enemy's hand, and began to unlace his helm, with intent to slay him where he lay. But at this moment Merlin came in great haste, crying out, "Stay! Sir Pellinore; what would you be at? Stay your sacrilegious hand! For he who lieth beneath you is none other than Arthur, King of all this realm!"

At this King Pellinore was astonished beyond measure. And for a little he was silent, and then he cried out, "Say you so, old man? Then verily this is he who hath taken from me power, and king-ship, and honors, and estates. Wherefore he shall die!"

Then Merlin said, "Not so! For I, myself, shall save him." Whereupon he uplifted his staff and smote King Pellinore across the shoulders. Then immediately King Pellinore fell down and lay upon the ground like one who had gone dead.

Upon this, King Arthur uplifted himself upon his elbow and cried out, "Merlin! what hast thou done? Hast thou, by thy arts of magic, slain him?"

"Not so, my Lord King!" said Merlin; "for, in sooth, thou art far nigher to thy death than he. For he is but in sleep and will soon awaken; but thou art in such a case that it would take only a very little for to cause thee to die."

And indeed King Arthur was exceeding sick with the wound he had received, so that it was only with much ado that Merlin could help him up upon his horse. Having done the which and having hung the King's shield upon the horn of his saddle, Merlin straight-way conveyed the wounded man thence across the bridge, and, leading the horse by the bridle, so took him away into the forest.

Now there was in that part of the forest a certain hermit so holy that the birds of the woodland would rest upon his hand whiles he read his breviary, and so gentle that the wild does would come to the door of his hermitage. And this hermit dwelt so remote from the habitations of man that when he rang the bell for matins or for vespers, there was hardly ever anyone to hear the sound thereof excepting the wild creatures that dwelt thereabout. Yet to this lonely place folk of high degree would sometimes come, as though on a pilgrimage, because of the hermit's exceeding saintliness.

So Merlin conveyed King Arthur unto this sanctuary, and he and the hermit lifted the wounded man down from his saddle—the hermit giving many words of pity and sorrow—and together they conveyed him into the holy man's cell.

There they laid him upon a couch of moss and unlaced his armor and bathed his wounds and dressed them, for that hermit was a very skillful leech. So for all that day and part of the next,

King Arthur lay upon the hermit's pallet like one about to die; for he beheld all things about him as though through thin water, and the breath hung upon his lips and fluttered because of the weakness that lay upon him.

CHAPTER IV: THE WINNING OF EXCALIBUR

UPON THE AFTERNOON OF THE second day there fell a great noise of talk and laughter in that part of the forest. For it happened that the Lady Guinevere of Cameliard, with her court of ladies and of knights, had come upon a pilgrimage to that holy man. For that lady had a favorite page who was sick of a fever, and she trusted that the holy man might give her some charm by which he might be cured. And the Lady Guinevere rode in the midst of her damsels and her court, and her beauty outshone the beauty of her damsels as the splendor of the morning star outshines that of all the lesser stars. For then and afterward she was held by all the Courts of Chivalry to be the most beautiful lady in the world.

Now when the Lady Guinevere had come to that place, she perceived the milk-white war-horse of King Arthur nigh to the hermitage; and likewise she perceived Merlin. So of him she demanded whose was that war-horse. And unto her Merlin made answer, "Lady, it belongs to a knight who lieth within, sorely wounded."

"Pity of Heaven!" cried the Lady Guinevere. "Now lead me unto that knight. For I have in my court a skillful leech, who is used to the cure of hurts such as knights receive in battle."

So Merlin brought the Lady into the cell, and there she beheld King Arthur upon the pallet. And she wist not who he was. Yet it appeared to her that in all her life she had not beheld so noble-appearing a knight. And King Arthur cast his looks upward to where she stood beside his bed, and in the great weakness that lay upon him he wist not whether she whom he beheld was a mortal lady or whether she was not some angel who had descended from Paradise for to visit him in his pain. And the Lady Guinevere was filled with a great pity at beholding King Arthur's sorrowful estate. Wherefore she called to her that skillful leech who was with her court. And she commanded him for to search that knight's wounds and to anoint them with balsam.

So that wise leech did according to the Lady Guinevere's commands, and immediately King Arthur felt ease and great content. And when the Lady and her court had departed, he found himself much uplifted in heart, and three days thereafter he was entirely healed.

And this was the first time that King Arthur ever beheld the Lady Guinevere of Cameliard, and from that time forth she was almost always present in his thoughts. Wherefore he said to himself: I will cherish the thought of this Lady and will serve her faithfully as a good knight may serve his chosen dame.

And so he did, as ye shall hear later in this book.

In the meantime, however, he found himself to be moved by a most vehement desire to meet his enemy King Pellinore for to try issue of battle with him once more. Now, upon the morning of the fourth day, he walked for refreshment in the forest, listening to the cheerful sound of the wood birds singing their matins. And Merlin walked beside him, and King Arthur spake his mind concerning his intent to engage once more in knightly contest with King Pellinore.

Thereunto Merlin made reply, "How then, Lord, mayest thou hope to undertake this adventure? For, lo! thou hast no sword, nor spear, nor hast thou even thy misericordia for to do battle withal."

And King Arthur said, "Even an I have no better weapon than an oaken cudgel, yet would I assay this battle again."

"Ha! Lord," said Merlin, "I do perceive that thou art altogether fixed in thy purpose. Wherefore I must tell thee that in one part of this forest there is a certain woodland sometimes called Arroy, and other times called the Forest of Adventure. For no knight ever entereth therein but some adventure befalleth him. And close to Arroy there is a lake. And in the center of that lake there hath for some time been seen a woman's arm—exceedingly beautiful and clad in white samite, and the hand of this arm holdeth a sword of such beauty that no eye hath ever beheld its like. And the name of this sword is Excalibur—it being so named by those who have beheld it because of its marvelous beauty. Now several knights have endeavored to obtain that sword, but no one hath been able to touch it, and many have lost their lives. For when any man draweth near unto it, either he sinks into the lake, or else the arm disappeareth beneath the lake. Now I will conduct thee unto that Lake of Enchantment, and there thou mayest see Excalibur with thine own eyes. Then, an thou art able to obtain it, thou wilt have a sword very fitted for battle."

"Merlin," quoth the King, "this is a very strange thing which thou tellest me. Now I am desirous beyond measure for to attempt to obtain this sword."

So that morning King Arthur and Merlin took leave of the holy hermit (the King having kneeled to receive his benediction), and entered the deeper forest.

And after a while they came to Arroy, and traveled through these woodlands. And then about the middle of the afternoon they came, of a sudden, out from the forest and upon a fair and level plain, bedight all over with flowers. And lo! all the air appeared as it were of gold—so bright was it and so radiant. And here and there upon that plain were trees all in blossom; and in their branches were birds of many colors, and the melody of their singing ravished the heart of the hearer. And midway in the plain was a lake of water as bright as silver, and all around its borders were lilies and daffodils.

So, because of all the beauty of this place, and because of its strangeness and its solitude, King Arthur perceived that he must have come into a land of powerful enchantment where dwelt a fairy of very exalted quality; wherefore his spirit was enwrapped in a manner of fear, as he pushed his great milk-white war-horse through that long fair grass, and he wist not what strange things were about to befall him.

So when he had come unto the margin of the lake he beheld in the midst of the expanse of water a fair and beautiful arm, as of a woman, clad all in white samite. And the arm was encircled with bracelets of wrought gold; and the hand held a sword of marvelous workmanship aloft in the air above the water. And, behold! the sun of that strange land shone down upon the hilt of the sword, and it was of pure gold beset with jewels, and it glittered like to some star of exceeding splendor. And King Arthur sat upon his war-horse and gazed from a distance at the arm and the sword, and he greatly marveled thereat; yet he wist not how he might come at that sword, for the lake was wonderfully wide and deep. And as he sat pondering this thing, he was suddenly aware of a strange lady, who approached him through the tall flowers. And he quickly dismounted from his horse and went forward to meet her with the bridle rein over his arm. And he perceived that she was extraordinarily beautiful, and that her face was like wax for clearness, and that her hair was black and like silk, and that her eyes were black also, and bright and glistening as two jewels. And the lady was clad all in green; and around her neck there hung a beautiful necklace of opal stones and emeralds set in gold. So King Arthur kneeled as he said, "Lady, I do certainly perceive that thou art no mortal damoiselle, but that thou art Fay. Also that this place, because of its beauty, can be no other than some land of Faerie."

And the Lady replied, "King Arthur, I am indeed Faerie. I may tell thee that my name is Nymue, and I am the chiefest of those Ladies of the Lake of whom thou mayest have heard people speak. Also, that what thou beholdest yonder as a wide lake is, in truth, a plain like unto this, all bedight with flowers, and in the midst of that plain there standeth a castle of white marble. But my sisters and I have caused this appearance as of a lake to extend all over that castle so that it is hidden from sight. Nor may any mortal man cross that lake, saving in one way—otherwise he shall perish."

"Lady," said King Arthur, "I am afraid that in coming hither I intrude upon the solitude of your dwelling place."

"Nay, not so, King Arthur," said the Lady of the Lake, "for thou art very welcome. Moreover, I may tell thee that I have a great friendliness for thee and the noble knights of thy Court. But I do beseech thee to tell me what brings thee to our land?"

"Lady," quoth the King, "I fought of late a battle with a certain Sable Knight, in the which I was wounded, and wherein I lost my spear and my sword and even my misericordia. In this extremity Merlin, here, told me of Excalibur, and of how it is upheld by an arm in the midst of this lake. So I came hither. And, Lady, I would fain achieve that excellent sword, that by means of it I might fight my battle to its end."

"Ha! my Lord King," said the Lady of the Lake, "no man may win yonder sword unless he be without fear and without reproach."

"Alas!" quoth King Arthur, "that is indeed sad for me. For, though I may not lack in knightly courage, yet there be many things wherewith I do reproach myself. Ne'ertheless, I prithee tell me how I may best undertake this adventure."

"King Arthur," said the Lady of the Lake, "I will aid thee in this matter." Whereupon she lifted a single emerald that hung by a small chain of gold at her girdle and, lo! the emerald was cunningly carved into the form of a whistle. And she set the whistle to her lips and blew upon it. Then straightway there appeared upon the water a boat all of shining brass. And the prow of the boat was carved into the form of a head of a beautiful woman, and upon either side were wings like the wings of a swan. And the boat moved upon the water like a swan—very swiftly—and when it had reached the bank it rested there.

Then the Lady of the Lake bade King Arthur to enter the boat, and so he entered it. And the boat moved swiftly away from the bank. And Merlin and the Lady of the Lake stood upon the margin of the water, and gazed after King Arthur and the brazen boat. And the boat floated across the Lake to where was the arm uplifting the sword, and the arm and the sword moved not.

Then King Arthur reached forth and took the sword in his hand, and immediately the arm disappeared beneath the water, and King Arthur held the sword and the scabbard thereof in his hand and, lo! they were his own. Then verily his heart swelled with joy, for Excalibur was far more beautiful than he had thought possible.

Then the boat bare him back to land again and he stepped ashore. And he gave the Lady of the Lake thanks beyond measure for all that she had done for to aid him in this undertaking; and she gave him cheerful and pleasing words in reply. Then King Arthur mounted his war-horse, and Merlin having mounted his palfrey, they rode away thence upon their business—the King's heart still greatly expanded with pure delight at having for his own the most beautiful and the most famous sword in all the world.

Anon, about noontide of the next day, King Arthur and Merlin reached the valley of the Sable Knight.

"Now, Merlin," quoth King Arthur, "I do this time most strictly forbid thee for to exert any of thy arts of magic in my behalf."

Thereupon, straightway, the King rode forth upon the bridge and, seizing the maul, he smote upon the sable shield with all his might. Immediately the portcullis was raised as aforetold, and the Sable Knight rode forth therefrom, already bedight and equipped for the encounter. So he came to the bridgehead and there King Arthur spake to him: "Sir Pellinore, we do now know one another well, and each doth judge that he hath cause of quarrel with the other: thou, that I, for reasons as seemed to me to be fit, have taken away from thee thy kingly estate; I, that thou hast set thyself up here for to do injury and affront to knights and lords of this king-dom of mine. Wherefore, seeing that I am here as an errant knight, I do challenge thee for to fight with me, man to man, until either thou or I have conquered the other."

Thereupon King Pellinore wheeled his horse, and, riding a little distance, took his place where he had afore stood. And King Arthur also took his station where he had afore stood. At the same time there came forth from the castle a page clad in sable, and gave to King Arthur a stout spear of ash wood; and when the two knights were duly prepared, they shouted and drave their horses together; the one smiting the other so fairly that the spears again shivered in the hand of each. Then each of the two knights imme-diately voided his horse and drew his sword. And thereupon they fell to, so furiously that two wild bulls could not have engaged in a more desperate encounter. But now, having Excalibur for to aid him, King Arthur soon delivered so vehement a stroke that King Pellinore was entirely benumbed thereby, and he sank unto his knees upon the ground. Then he called upon King Arthur to have mercy, saying, "Spare my life and I will yield myself unto thee."

And King Arthur said, "I will spare thee. And now that thou hast yielded thyself unto me, lo! I will restore unto thee thy power and estate. For I bear no ill will toward thee, Pellinore; ne'ertheless, I can brook no rebels against my power in this realm. Only as a pledge of thy good faith toward me, I shall require that thou send me as hostage thy two eldest sons, to wit: Sir Aglaval and Sir Lamorac."

So those two young knights came to the Court of King Arthur, and they became very famous knights, and by and by were made fellows in great honor of the Round Table.

And King Arthur and King Pellinore went together into the castle of King Pellinore, and there King Pellinore's wounds were dressed and he was made comfortable. That night King Arthur abode in the castle, and when the next morning had come, he and Merlin returned unto the Court of the King, where it awaited him in the forest.

And forever after that King Arthur treasured Excalibur, and the sword remained with him for all of his life, wherefore the name of Arthur and of Excalibur are one.

So endeth the story of the winning of Excalibur, and may God give unto you in your life, that you may have His truth to aid you, like a shining sword, for to overcome your enemies; and may He give you Faith (for Faith containeth Truth as a scabbard containeth its sword). For with Truth and Faith girded upon you, you shall be as well able to fight all your battles as was that noble hero of old, whom men called King Arthur.

CHAPTER V: A NOBLE GARDENER'S LAD

Now UPON A CERTAIN DAY King Arthur proclaimed a high feast, which was held at Carleon upon Usk. An exceedingly splendid Court gathered at the King's castle, and all the great gathering of kings, lords, and knights were united in good-fellowship. Wherefore, when the young King looked about him and beheld such amity among all these noble lords where, aforetime, had been discord: Certes, quoth he to himself, it is wonderful how this reign of mine hath knit men together in good-fellowship!

Now while the King sat thus at feast, lo! there came a herald from the west country. And he came and stood before the King, and he said: "I come from King Leodegrance of Cameliard, who is in sore trouble. For thus it is: His enemy, King Ryence of North Wales, doth make demands which my master is loath to fulfill. And King Ryence threateneth to bring war into Cameliard. Now King Leodegrance hath no such array of knights as he one time had gathered about him; for, since thou in thy majesty hath brought peace to this realm, those knights who once made the Court of King Leodegrance famous have gone elsewhere for to seek better opportunities for their valor. Wherefore my master doth beseech aid of thee, who are his King and Overlord."

To these things King Arthur listened, and his countenance became overcast. "Well," he said, "I will give what aid I am able to King Leodegrance. But tell me, Sir Herald, what things are they that King Ryence demandeth of thy master?"

"Firstly," quoth the herald, "King Ryence demandeth a great part of those lands of Cameliard that border upon North Wales. Secondly, he maketh demand that the Lady Guinevere, the King's daughter, be delivered in marriage unto Duke Mordaunt of North Umber, who is kin unto King Ryence, and that duke, though a mighty warrior, is so evil of appearance, and so violent of temper, that I believe that there is not his like for ugliness in all the world."

Now when King Arthur heard this he was seized with such an anger that he rose from his chair and went into an inner room of the castle by himself, and there he walked up and down for a great while. And the reason of his wrath was this: that ever since he had lain wounded in the forest, he bare in mind how the Lady Guinevere had appeared before him like some shining angel. Wherefore, at thought of that wicked Duke Mordaunt making demand unto marriage with her, he was seized with a rage that shook his spirit like a mighty wind.

After a while, he gave command that Merlin and Sir Ulfius and Sir Kay should come to him. And when they had come thither he bade Merlin to make ready to go upon a journey with him, and he bade Sir Ulfius and Sir Kay to gather together a large army, and to bring that army into those parts coadjacent to the royal castle of Tintagalon, which standeth close to the borders of North Wales and of Cameliard.

So Sir Ulfius and Sir Kay went to do as King Arthur commanded; and the next day King Arthur and Merlin, together with Sir Gawaine and Sir Ewaine and Sir Pellias and Sir Geraint, set forth for Tintagalon.

They traveled for all that day and a part of the next, and so they came, at last, to that noble castle which guards the country bordering upon Cameliard and North Wales. Here King Arthur was received with great rejoicing; for whithersoever the King went the people loved him very dearly.

Now the morning after King Arthur had come unto Tintagalon, he and Merlin arose betimes to go abroad to enjoy the freshness of the early daytime. So, in the cool of the day, they walked in the garden. And here King Arthur opened his mind to Merlin, and he said: "Merlin, I do believe that the Lady Guinevere is the fairest Lady in the world; wherefore my heart seems to be filled with love for her, and I am not willing that any other man should have her for his wife.

"Now I know that thou art wonderfully cunning in the arts of magic. Wherefore I greatly desire it that thou wilt so disguise me that I may go, unknown of any man, into Cameliard, and that I may so dwell there that I may see the Lady Guinevere every day. For I desire to behold her in such a wise that she may not know of my regard. Likewise I would fain see for myself how great may be the perils that encompass my friend King Leodegrance."

"My Lord King," said Merlin, "it shall be as thou desirest."

So later that morning Merlin came unto the King and gave him a little cap. And when the King set the cap upon his head he assumed, upon the instant, the appearance of a rude and rustic fellow. Then the King commanded that a jerkin of rough frieze should be brought to him, and with this he covered his royal vestments and that golden collar which he continually wore about his neck. Whereupon, being thus disguised, he quitted Tintagalon unknown of any man, and took his way afoot unto Cameliard.

Now toward the slanting of the day he beheld before him a town of many comely houses all upon a high hill. And a great castle guarded the town, and all round about it were many fair gardens and meadows and orchards.

Thus came King Arthur unto the castle of Cameliard, in the guise of a poor peasant. And he made inquiries for the head gardener; and he besought the gardener that he be taken into service in that part of the garden that appertained to the dwelling place of the Lady Guinevere. Then the gardener looked upon him and saw that he was tall and strong, wherefore he liked him and took him into service.

Now the King was very glad to be in that garden; for in this summer season the Lady Guinevere came every day to walk with her damsels, and King Arthur, all disguised, beheld her many times.

Now it happened upon a day when the weather was warm, that one of the damsels who was in attendance upon the Lady Guinevere arose very early in the morning. This damsel, whose name was Mellicene of the White Hand, went into the anteroom and, opening the casement, looked forth into that garden of roses which adjoined the Lady Guinevere's bower.

Now there was at that place a carven marble fountain, where water as clear as crystal flowed into a basin of marble. And all around was a growth of roses, so that the place was entirely hidden, saving only from those windows of the castle that were above. So it befell that as the damsel looked down, she beheld a wonderful sight. For, lo! a strange knight kneeled beside the fountain and bathed his face in the water. And sunlight fell upon him, and his hair and his beard were of the color of red gold, and his brow and his throat were white like alabaster. And around his neck there hung a golden collar of marvelous beauty, so that when the sunlight shone upon it it flashed like pure lightning.

So the damsel Mellicine stood, all entranced, and wist not

whether that which she saw was a dream. But, by and by, recovering, she ran fleetly down the turret stairs, and so out into the garden. But King Arthur had heard her coming, and had set the cap upon his head again, so that she found no one by the fountain but the gardener's boy. Of him she demanded: "Who art thou, fellow?"

And he replied: "I am the gardener's lad."

"Then tell me, fellow," quoth she, "who was that young knight who was here beside the fountain but now?"

"Lady," he said, "there has been no one at this fountain this day, but only I."

At this the damsel looked upon him in perplexity and, because of her perplexity, she felt a great displeasure. "Truly," she said, "if thou art deceiving me, I shall have thee whipped."

Thereupon she went away. And that morning she told the Lady Guinevere all that she had seen, but the Lady Guinevere only laughed, telling her that she had been asleep and dreaming. And, indeed, the damsel herself had begun to think this must be the case.

Nevertheless, she thereafter looked out every morning from her window, albeit she beheld nothing for a while, for King Arthur came not soon to that place again. But, by and by, there befell a morning when lo! there sat that strange knight by the fountain once more. And he bathed his face. And he appeared as noble as before. And this time his collar of gold lay upon the brink of the fountain beside him. Then the damsel ran to where the Lady Guinevere lay, and she cried, "Lady! arouse thee! For that same young knight whom I beheld before is even now bathing himself at the fountain."

Then the Lady Guinevere, marveling, aroused herself, and, dighting herself, went with the damsel unto that casement window. And there she herself beheld the young knight. And she saw that his hair and his beard shone like gold; and she saw that beside him lay that collar of gold.

Then she commanded Mellicene to come with her, and therewith she descended the turret stairs, and went out into the garden; and she straightway hastened to the fountain. But behold! she found no young knight there, but only the gardener's boy. Then the Lady Guinevere marveled, and she demanded of the gardener's boy whither had gone the young knight. And unto her the gardener lad made answer as aforetime: "Lady! there hath been no one at this place this morning, but only I."

Now when King Arthur had donned his cap, he had, in his haste, forgotten his golden collar, and this Guinevere beheld beside the fountain. "How now!" quoth she. "Wouldst thou mock me? Now tell me, fellow, do gardeners' boys wear golden collars like unto that? Now, an I had thee whipped, it would be thy due. But take thou that bauble yonder and give it unto him to whom it doth belong, and tell him from me that it doth ill become a true knight for to hide himself away in the gardens of a lady." Then turned she with Mellicene, and went back into her bower.

Yet, indeed for all that day, as she sat over her 'broidery, she did never cease to wonder how that strange knight should so suddenly have vanished. Then, of a sudden, toward the cooler part of the afternoon, a thought came unto her. So she called Mellicene, and she bade her to go and tell the gardener's lad for to fetch her a basket of fresh roses to adorn her chamber.

So Mellicene went, and after considerable time the gardener's lad came bearing a basket of roses. And, lo! he wore his cap upon his head. And all the damsels in waiting upon the Lady Guinevere cried out, and Mellicene demanded of him: "What! How now, Sir Boor! Dost thou know so little of what is due unto a king's daughter that thou dost wear thy cap in her presence?"

And to her King Arthur made answer: "Lady, I cannot take off my cap."

Quoth the Lady Guinevere: "And why not, surly fellow?"

"Lady," said he, "I have an ugly place upon my head."

"Then wear thy cap," quoth the Lady Guinevere. "Only fetch thou the roses unto me."

And so he brought her the roses. But when he had come nigh unto the Lady, she, of a sudden, snatched at the cap and plucked it off. Then, lo! he was transformed; for instead of the gardener's boy there stood before the Lady Guinevere a noble young knight with hair and beard like gold. Then he let fall his basket of roses, and

35

he stood and looked at all who were there. And some of those damsels shrieked, and others stood still from pure amazement. But not one of those ladies knew that he was King Arthur. Nevertheless the Lady Guinevere remembered that this was the knight whom she had found wounded, lying in the hermit's cell.

Then she laughed and flung him back his cap again. "Take thy cap," quoth she, "and go, thou gardener's boy who hath an ugly place upon his head."

King Arthur did not reply to her, but, with great sobriety, set his cap upon his head again. So resuming his humble guise, he quitted that place, leaving roses scattered all over the floor.

And after that time, whenever the Lady Guinevere would come upon the gardener's lad in the garden, she would say unto her damsel in such a voice that he might hear her: "Lo! yonder is the gardener's lad who hath an ugly place upon his head!" Thus she spake, mocking at him; but privily she bade her damsels to keep unto themselves all those things which had befallen.

CHAPTER VI: THE WHITE CHAMPION

UPON A CERTAIN DAY at this time there came a messenger to King Leodegrance, with news that King Ryence of North Wales and Duke Mordaunt of North Umber were coming thither with a considerable Court. At this news King Leodegrance was much troubled; yet he went forth to greet them, desiring them that they should come into the castle so that he might entertain them according to their degree.

But to this courtesy King Ryence made reply: "Nay, King Leodegrance, just now we are, certes, no such good friends that we care to sit at thy table. Nor may we be aught but enemies of thine until thou hast satisfied our demands; to wit, that thou givest to me those lands which I demand, and that thou givest unto my cousin, Duke Mordaunt of North Umber, the Lady Guinevere to be his wife. Wherefore we shall abide here, outside of thy castle, for five days, in the which time thou mayest frame thine answer."

"And in the meantime," quoth the Duke of North Umber, "I do hold myself ready for to contest my right unto the hand of the Lady Guinevere with any knight of thy Court who hath a mind to deny my title thereto; and if thou hast no knight who can successfully assay a bout of arms with me, thou canst hardly hope to defend thyself against the great army of King Ryence."

Then King Leodegrance turned and walked back into his castle, beset with anxiety and sorrow. And King Ryence and Duke Mordaunt and their Court pitched their pavilions in those meadows over against the castle.

And when the next morning had come, the Duke of North Umber went forth clad in armor, and he rode up and down before the castle. "Ho!" he cried. "Knights of Cameliard! Is there no one to come forth to meet me? How then may ye hope to contend with the knights of North Wales, an ye fear to meet with one single knight from North Umber?" So he scoffed at them, and the people of Cameliard, gathered upon the walls, listened to him with shame and sorrow. For the Duke of North Umber was one of the most famous knights of his day, and there was now, in these times of peace, no one of King Leodegrance's Court who was able to face a warrior of his skill.

Now all this while King Arthur digged in the garden; but, nevertheless, he was well aware of everything that passed. So, of a sudden, it came to him that he could not abide this any longer. Wherefore he laid aside his spade and went out secretly by a postern way, and so into the town.

Now there was in Cameliard an exceedingly rich merchant, by name Ralph of Cardiff, and his renown had reached even unto King Arthur's ears. Accordingly it was unto his house that King Arthur directed his steps.

And while he was on the way, he took off his magic cap, for he was now of a mind to show his knightliness. Accordingly, when he stood before the merchant in his closet, the merchant wist not what to think to behold so noble a lord clad all in frieze. Then King Arthur opened the breast of his jerkin and showed the merchant his gold collar, and also he showed the man his signet ring, and the merchant knew it to be the ring of the King of Britain. Wherefore the merchant arose and doffed his cap.

"Sir Merchant," quoth the King, "know that I am a stranger knight in disguise in this place. Ne'ertheless, I am a good friend to King Leodegrance. Thou art surely aware of how the Duke of North Umber rides up and down before the King's castle, and challenges anyone within to come forth for to fight. Now I am of a mind to assay that combat. Wherefore I desire that thou shalt provide me with armor and weapons, so that I may assay this bout of arms. Moreover, I do pledge thee that thou shalt be fully recompensed for all that thou canst let me have."

"My Lord," said Master Ralph, "it is a very great pleasure to fulfill thy behests."

Upon this he rang a silver bell, and several attendants appeared. Into their hands he entrusted the King, bidding them to do all that he requested. And taking the King to an apartment of great state, they there clad him in a suit of Spanish armor, cunningly wrought and inlaid with gold. The jupon and the trappings of the armor were of white satin; and the shield was white, and without emblazonment. Then these attendants conducted the King into the courtyard, and there stood a war-horse, as white as milk, and all the trappings of the horse were of white cloth; and the bridle and the rein were studded with bosses of silver.

Then after the attendants had aided King Arthur to mount this steed, the merchant came and gave him words of good cheer, and so the King bade him adieu and rode away, all shining and glittering in full armor.

And as he drave through the town, the people turned and gazed after him, for he made a very noble appearance.

So King Arthur directed his way to the castle, and there he made demand that he should have speech with the Lady Guinevere. So an attendant delivered the message, and by and by the Lady Guinevere came, much wondering, and passed along a gallery with her damsels, until she had come above where King Arthur was. And when he looked up and saw her, he loved her exceeding well. And he said to her: "Lady, I go forth now to do combat

38

with the Duke of North Umber. Accordingly, I do beseech of thee some token, such as a lady may give unto a knight for to wear when that knight rides forth to do her honor."

Then the Lady Guinevere said: "Certes, Sir Knight, I would that I knew who thou art. Yet, though I know not, I am altogether willing for to take thee for my champion. Therefore, what thou desirest of me thou shalt have." And she took from her neck the necklace of pearls which she wore, and dropped the same down to King Arthur.

And King Arthur took the necklace and tied it about his arm, and he gave great thanks for it. Then he saluted the Lady Guinevere with knightly grace, and she saluted him, and he went forth, greatly expanded with joy that the Lady Guinevere had shown him such favor.

Now the report had gone about Cameliard that a knight was to go forth to fight the Duke of North Umber. Wherefore great crowds gathered upon the walls, and King Leodegrance and the Lady Guinevere and all the Court came to the castle walls overlooking the meadow which the Duke of North Umber defended. And then the portcullis was lifted, and the bridge let fall, and the White Champion rode forth. On that narrow bridge, the hoofs of his war-horse smote like thunder, and when he came out into the sunlight, lo! his armor flamed like unto lightning, and the people shouted aloud.

Then the Duke of North Umber rode straightway to him. "Messire," he said, "I perceive that thou bearest no device upon thy shield, wherefore I know not who thou art. Ne'ertheless, I do believe that thou art a knight of good quality. Therefore I bid thee make such prayers as thou art able, for I shall presently cast thee down from thy seat so that thou shalt never rise again."

To this King Arthur made answer: "That shall be according to the will of Heaven, Sir Knight, and not according to thy will."

So each knight saluted the other and rode to his station, and then each shouted to his war-horse, and launched forth. And so they met with a noise like unto a thunderclap. And lo! the spear of the Duke of North Umber burst into splinters; but the spear of King Arthur broke not, so that the Duke was cast out of his saddle like a windmill—whirling in the air. And indeed he rolled full three times over ere smiting the earth.

Then all the people upon the wall shouted with might and main; for they had hardly hoped that their champion should have proved so strong.

Meanwhile, those of King Ryence's Court ran to the Duke of North Umber where he lay, and unlaced his helm to give him air. And he lay in a swoon for full two hours.

Now whilst the attendants were thus busied about the Duke, King Arthur sat his horse very quietly, observing all that they did. Then, perceiving that his enemy was not dead, he turned about and rode away.

Nor did he return unto Cameliard at that time, for he deemed that he had not yet entirely done with these enemies to the peace of his realm. So he bethought him of how, coming to Cameliard, he had passed through an arm of the forest where woodchoppers were at work. Wherefore he thought that he would betake him thither and leave his horse and armor in the care of those rude folk.

So now he rode away into the countryside, to where those woodchoppers plied their craft, and he abided with them for that night; and the next morning he entrusted them with his horse and armor, and he took his departure to return unto Cameliard. And he was clad again in his jerkin of frieze, and when he had reached the outskirts of the forest, he set his cap of disguise upon his head once more.

So he returned to Cameliard for to be gardener's boy as he had been before. And there he found the gardener exceedingly filled with wrath. And the gardener had a long birchen rod; and he said: "Knave! wherefore didst thou quit thy work to go a-gadding?" And King Arthur laughed and said: "Touch me not."

At this, the gardener catched the King by his jerkin, saying: "Dost thou laugh at me, knave? Now I will beat thee well!"

Then, when King Arthur felt that man's hand laid upon him, his royal spirit waxed big within him and he cried out: "Ha, wretch! wouldst thou dare to lay hands upon my person?" So saying, he seized the gardener by the wrists, and took the rod away from him, and struck him with it across the shoulders. And that poor knave lifted up a great outcry, albeit the blow hurt him not a whit. "Now get thee gone!" quoth King Arthur, "and trouble me no more." Herewith he let the man go; and the gardener was so bemazed with terror, that he gat him away as quickly as might be, all trembling and sweating with fear.

So he went straight to the Lady Guinevere and complained to her. "Lady," quoth he, weeping, "my boy goeth away for a day or more, I know not whither; and when I would whip him for quitting his work he taketh the rod away from me and beateth me with it. Wherefore, now, I prithee, deal with him as is fitting, and let several men drive him away from this place with rods."

Then the Lady Guinevere laughed. "Let be!" she said, "and meddle with him no more, for, indeed, he appeareth to be a very saucy fellow. As for thee! take thou no heed of his coming or his going, and I will deal with him in such a way as shall be fitting."

Whereupon the gardener went his way, greatly marveling that the Lady Guinevere should be so mild in dealing with that knave. And the Lady Guinevere went her way, very merry. For she began to bethink her that there was some excellent reason why it should happen that when the White Champion, who did such wonderful deeds, should come thither, then that gardener's boy should go; and that when the Champion should go, then the gardener's boy should come thitherward again. Wherefore she suspected many things, and was wonderfully cheerful of spirit.

Now, meanwhile, Duke Mordaunt of North Umber had recovered from his hurts. Wherefore, the next morning, he appeared again before the castle clad in armor. But this time there rode before him two heralds, and when the Duke and the two heralds had come to that part of the meadows that lay before the castle of Cameliard, the heralds blew their trumpets. So at the sound many people gathered upon the walls; and King Leodegrance came, and took stand upon a tower. Then the Duke of North Umber cried out: "Ho! King Leodegrance! Thou shalt not think because I suffered a fall from my horse through mischance, that thou art quit of me. Yet, ne'ertheless, I do now make this fair offer unto thee.

Tomorrow I shall appear before this castle with six knights-companion. Now if thou hast any seven knights who are able to stand against me and my companions, then I shall engage myself for to give over all pretense whatsoever unto the hand of the Lady Guinevere. But if thou canst not provide such champions by set of sun tomorrow, then shall I not only lay claim to Lady Guinevere, but I shall likewise seize upon and shall hold for mine own, three castles of thine that stand upon the borders of North Umber, together with their lands."

Hereupon Duke Mordaunt turned his horse and went away. Then King Leodegrance also went his way, very downcast in his spirits. For he said to himself: Is it likely that another champion shall come unto me like that wonderful White Champion who came, I know not whence? And I know not where to seek that White Champion to beseech his further aid. Wherefore he went straight unto his own room, and there shut himself in; nor would he see any man nor speak unto anyone, but gave himself over entirely unto despair.

Now in this extremity King Arthur bethought him of Sir Gawaine, Sir Ewaine, Sir Geraint, and Sir Pellias, who awaited him at Tintagalon. So again he slipped away from the garden, and, dressed as the gardener's boy, he set forth on foot. And when afternoon came, he met all four of those knights, who were riding for their pleasure through the countryside near Tintagalon. And they, seeing only a rustic knave before them in the road, were about to pass him by, when of a sudden King Arthur took the cap from off his head, and, lo! they beheld that it was King Arthur who stood near them. Then a great silence fell upon them all, and each man sat as though he were turned into stone. And King Arthur said: "Ha! how now, Sir Knights! Have ye no words of greeting for me?"

Then those four knights cried out aloud; and they leaped from their horses and kneeled down in the dust of the road. And King Arthur laughed with great joy, and he bade them for to mount their horses again, for time was passing by when there was much to do.

So they mounted their horses and obtained a horse for King

Arthur at Tintagalon, and as they rode away the King told them all that had befallen him, so that they were amazed. And they rejoiced that they had a king to rule over them who was possessed of such a high and knightly spirit. So they rode to where King Arthur had left his white horse and his white armor, and there they passed the night, and then they rode on to Cameliard.

Now, that same morning, the Duke of North Umber and six knights-companion appeared upon the field in front of Cameliard. And in front of those seven champions rode seven heralds with trumpets, and behind them rode seven esquires. So they paraded up and down that field, and, meantime, a great crowd of people stood upon the walls and gazed at the spectacle. But King Leodegrance was so cast down with shame that he hid himself away. Nevertheless, the Lady Guinevere went unto his closet, and spake to him through the door, saying: "My Lord King and father, I prithee look up and take cheer. For there is a glorious champion who hath our cause in his hands, and he shall assuredly come ere this day is done."

Still King Leodegrance opened not the door; but whilst he came not forth, yet he was comforted at that which she said.

Thus passed that morning; and yet no one appeared to take up that challenge with the seven knights. Then, whilst the sun was three or four hours high, there suddenly appeared at a distance a cloud of dust. And in that cloud there presently appeared five knights riding thitherward. And when these had come nigh unto the walls, lo! the people beheld that he who rode foremost was the White Champion. Moreover, they perceived that the four knights who rode with him were very famous knights of great glory of arms. For they knew the insignia of those four knights. So the people upon the walls shouted aloud with a mighty voice.

Now, when King Leodegrance heard the people shouting, he came forth to see what was ado. And the Lady Guinevere came forth likewise. And when she beheld that White Knight and his four companions, her heart was like to break within her for pure joy, wherefore she wept for the passion thereof. And she waved her kerchief unto those five noble lords and kissed her hand unto them, and the five knights saluted her as they rode past her and into the field.

Now, the Duke of North Umber rode forth for to meet those five knights. And he said unto the White Champion: "Sir Knight, I have once before condescended unto thee who art altogether unknown to me. Now this quarrel is more serious than that other, wherefore I and my companions will not run a course with thee until I first know who thou art and what is thy condition."

Then Sir Gawaine opened his helmet, and he said: "Sir Knight, know that I am Gawaine, the son of King Lot. Wherefore thou mayest perceive that my condition and estate are even better than thine own. Now I do declare that yonder White Knight is of such a quality that he condescends unto thee when he doeth combat with thee."

"Ho, Sir Gawaine!" quoth the Duke of North Umber. "What thou sayest is strange, for, indeed, there are few in this world who may condescend unto me. Ne'ertheless, since thou dost avouch for him, I may not gainsay that which thou sayest. Yet there is still another reason why we may not fight with ye. For, behold! we are seven well-approved knights, and ye are but five; so, consider how unequal are our forces, and that you stand in great peril."

Then Sir Gawaine smiled right grimly. "Gramercy for the tenderness which thou showeth concerning our safety, Sir Duke," quoth he. "But I consider that the peril in which ye seven stand is fully equal to our peril. Moreover, wert thou other than a belted knight, a simple man might suppose that thou wert more careful of thine own safety in this matter, than thou art of ours."

Now at these words the countenance of the Duke of North Umber became altogether red, for he wist that he had, indeed, no great desire for this battle. So each knight closed his helmet, and all turned their horses, and the one party rode unto one end of the field, and the other party rode to the other, and there each took stand. Then King Arthur and Duke Mordaunt each shouted aloud, and the one party hurled upon the other party.

And so they met in the middle of the field with an uproar so dreadful than one might have heard the crashing thereof for more than a mile. And when the dust of the encounter had arisen, lo! three of the seven had been overthrown, and not one of the five had lost his seat.

And one of those who had been overthrown was Duke Mordaunt. And behold! King Arthur's spear had pierced the shield of the Duke of North Umber, and had pierced his body armor; and so violent was the stroke, that the Duke of North Umber had been lifted entirely out of his saddle, and had been cast a full spear's length behind the crupper of his horse. Thus died that wicked man, for as King Arthur drave past him, the evil soul of him quitted his body with a weak noise like to the squeaking of a bat, and the world was well rid of him.

Now when King Arthur turned him about at the end of the course and beheld that there were but four knights left upon their horses of all those seven, he drew rein and bespake his knights: "Messires, I do not care to fight any more today, so engage ye those knights in battle. And I will abide here, and witness your adventure."

So those four good knights did as he commanded. And King Arthur sat with the butt of his spear resting upon his instep, and looked upon the field with great content of spirit.

As for those four knights-companion that remained of the Duke of North Umber's party, they came not forth to this second encounter with so much readiness. Nevertheless, they prepared themselves, and came forth as they were called upon to do. Then Sir Gawaine drave straight up to the foremost knight, who was a well-known champion hight Sir Dinador. And lifting himself up in his stirrups he smote Sir Dinador so fierce a blow that he cleft the shield of that knight, and he cleft his helmet, and a part of the blade of his sword brake away and remained therein.

And when Sir Dinador felt that blow, a great terror fell upon him, so that he drew rein violently to one side. So he fled away from that place with the terror of death hanging above him like to a black cloud of smoke. And his companions also drew rein to one side and fled away. And Sir Gawaine and Sir Ewaine and Sir Geraint and Sir Pellias pursued them. And they chased them straight

45

through the Court of King Ryence, so that the knights and nobles of that Court scattered hither and thither like chaff at their coming; and when they had chased those knights entirely away, they returned to that place where King Arthur still held his station, steadfastly awaiting them.

Now the people of Cameliard shouted with might and main. Nor did they stint their shouting when those four knights returned unto the White Champion again. And still more did they give acclaim when those five knights rode across the drawbridge and into the town.

Thus ended the great bout at arms, which was one of the most famous in all the history of King Arthur's Court.

CHAPTER VII: THE ESTABLISHMENT OF THE ROUND TABLE

WHEN KING ARTHUR HAD THUS accomplished his purposes, he sent his knights to stay with King Leodegrance, and he himself went unto that merchant of whom he had obtained the armor that he wore, and he returned that armor.

Then, having set his cap of disguise upon his head, he came back into the Lady Guinevere's garden.

Now when the next morning had come the people of Cameliard looked forth and, lo! King Ryence had in the night departed entirely away from before the castle. At this the people of Cameliard were exceedingly rejoiced, and made merry.

Now that same morning Lady Guinevere walked into her garden, and with her walked Sir Gawaine and Sir Ewaine, and lo! there she beheld the gardener's boy again.

Then she laughed aloud, and she said, "Messires, behold! Yonder is the gardener's boy, who weareth his cap because he hath an ugly place upon his head."

Then those two knights, knowing who that gardener's boy was, were exceedingly abashed at her speech, and wist not what to say or whither to look. And Sir Gawaine spake aside unto Sir Ewaine: "'Fore Heaven, that lady knoweth not what manner of man is yonder gardener's boy; for, an she did, she would be more sparing of her speech."

And the Lady Guinevere said unto Sir Gawaine: "Haply it doth affront thee that that gardener's boy should wear his cap before us, and maybe thou wilt take it off from his head."

And Sir Gawaine said: "Peace, Lady! Thou knowest not what thou sayest. Yonder gardener's boy could more easily take my head from off my shoulders than I could take his cap from off his head."

At this the Lady Guinevere made open laughter; but secretly she pondered that saying and marveled what Sir Gawaine meant.

Then King Leodegrance sent, privily, for the Lady Guinevere and said to her: "My daughter, a knight clad all in white, and bearing no crest or device of any sort, hath twice come to our rescue. Now it is said by everybody that he is thine own particular champion and that he weareth thy necklace as a favor. Now I prithee tell me who that White Champion is, and where he may be found."

Then the Lady Guinevere was overwhelmed with confusion, and she said: "Verily, my Lord, I know not who that knight may be."

Then King Leodegrance took the Lady Guinevere by the hand and spake very seriously: "My daughter, thou art now of an age when thou must consider being mated unto a man who may duly cherish and protect thee. Now, it doth appear to me that thou couldst not hope to find anyone who could so well safeguard thee as this White Knight. Wherefore it would be well if thou didst feel thyself to incline unto him as he appeareth to incline unto thee."

Then the Lady Guinevere became all rosy red, and she said: "My Lord and father, an I give my liking unto anyone in the manner thou speaketh of, I will give it only unto the poor gardener's boy."

At these words, the countenance of King Leodegrance became contracted with anger, and he cried: "Ha, Lady! Wouldst thou make a jest of my words?"

Then the Lady Guinevere said: "Indeed, my Lord! I jest not. Moreover, I tell thee that that same gardener's boy knoweth more concerning the White Champion than anybody else in the world."

Then King Leodegrance said: "What is this that thou tellest me?"

And the Lady Guinevere said: "Send for that gardener's boy and thou shalt know." And King Leodegrance said: "Verily, there is more in this than I may at present understand." So he called to him his page, hight Dorisand, and he said: "Go and bring hither the gardener's boy from the Lady Guinevere's garden."

So in a little while the gardener's boy was brought to the table where King Leodegrance sat. And the King looked upon him, and said: "Ha! wouldst thou wear thy cap in my presence?"

Then the gardener's boy said: "I cannot take off my cap."

But the Lady Guinevere, who stood beside King Leodegrance, said: "I do beseech thee, Messire, for to take off thy cap unto my father."

Whereupon the gardener's boy said: "At thy bidding I will take it off."

So he took the cap from off his head, and King Leodegrance beheld his face and knew him. And he made a great outcry from pure amazement, saying: "My Lord and my King! What is this!" Thereupon he arose and kneeled down before King Arthur. And he set the palms of his hands together and he put his hands within the hands of King Arthur, and he said: "My Lord! Is it then thou who hast done all these wonderful things?"

Then King Arthur said: "Yea; such as those things were, I have done them." And he lifted King Leodegrance up unto his feet.

And lo! the Lady Guinevere understood of a sudden all these things. Wherefore a great fear fell upon her so that she trembled exceedingly, and said unto herself: What things have I said unto this great King, and how have I made a mock of him! And she set her hand upon her side for to still the extreme disturbance of her heart. So, whilst King Arthur and King Leodegrance gave to one another words of royal greeting, she withdrew herself and stood against the window nigh to the corner of the wall.

Then, by and by, Arthur beheld her where she stood afar off. So he went unto her and he took her by the hand, and he said: "Lady, what cheer?"

And she said: "Lord, I am afeard of thy greatness." And he said: "Nay, Lady. Rather it is I who am afeard of thee. For thy kind regard is dearer unto me than anything in the world, else had I not served as gardener's boy in thy garden all for the sake of thy good will." And she said: "Thou hast my good will, Lord." And he said: "Have I thy good will in great measure?" And she said: "Yea, thou hast it in great measure."

Then he stooped his head and kissed her, and thus their troth was plighted.

Then King Leodegrance was filled with such an exceeding joy that he wist not how to contain himself therefore.

And King Arthur remained for a while in Cameliard with an exceedingly splendid Court of noble lords and of beautiful ladies. And there were feasting and jousting and many famous bouts at arms. And King Arthur and the Lady Guinevere were altogether happy together.

Now, one day, whiles King Arthur sat at feast with King Leodegrance, King Leodegrance said: "My Lord, what shall I offer thee for a dowry when thou takest my daughter away for to be thy Queen?"

Then King Arthur turned to Merlin, who stood nigh, and he said: "Ha, Merlin! What shall I demand of my friend by way of dowry?"

Unto him Merlin said: "My Lord King, thy friend King Leodegrance hath one thing, the which, should he bestow it upon thee, will singularly increase the glory and renown of thy reign."

And King Arthur said: "I bid thee tell me what is that thing."

So Merlin said: "My Lord King, in the days of thy father, Uther-Pendragon, I caused to be made for him a certain Table in the shape of a ring, wherefore men called it the Round Table. Now, at this Table were seats for fifty men, and these seats were designed for the fifty knights who were the most worthy knights in all the world. These seats were of such a sort, that whenever a worthy knight appeared, then his name appeared in letters of gold upon that seat that appertained unto him; and when that knight died, then would his name suddenly vanish from that seat.

"Now, forty and nine of these seats, except one seat, were altogether alike (saving only one that was set aside for the King himself, which same was elevated above the other seats), and the one seat was different from all the others. This seat was all cunningly inset with gold and silver of curious device; and it was covered with a canopy of satin, and no name ever appeared upon it, for only one knight in all of the world could hope to sit therein with safety. For, if any other dared to sit therein, either he would die a violent death within three days' time, or else a great misfortune would befall him. Hence that seat was called the Seat Perilous.

"Now, when King Uther-Pendragon died, he gave the Round Table unto his friend, King Leodegrance. And in the beginning of King Leodegrance's reign, there sat four and twenty knights at the Round Table. But times have changed, and the glory of King Leodegrance's reign hath paled. So now that Round Table lieth beneath its pavilion unused.

"Yet if King Leodegrance will give that Round Table unto thee, my Lord King, for a dower with the Lady Guinevere, then will it lend unto thy reign its greatest glory. For in thy day every seat of that Table shall be filled, even unto the Seat Perilous, and the fame of the knights who sit at it shall never be forgotten."

"Ha!" quoth King Arthur. "That would indeed be a dower worthy for any king to have with his queen."

"Then," King Leodegrance said, "that dower shalt thou have with my daughter; and if it bring thee great glory, then shall thy renown be my renown. For if my glory shall wane, and thy glory shall increase, behold! is not my child thy wife?"

And King Arthur said: "Thou sayest well and wisely."

Thus that famous Round Table was set up at Camelot on the day when King Arthur and Queen Guinevere were wed. For on that day, after those two noble souls had been married in the Cathedral at Camelot, and after a great feast had been held, the King and Queen, preceded by Merlin and followed by their Court, made progression to that place where Merlin had caused to be builded a pavilion above the Round Table.

And when the King and the Queen and the Court had entered in thereat they were amazed at the beauty of that pavilion; for the walls were all richly gilded and painted, and overhead the roof, like the sky, was all of cerulean blue sprinkled over with stars. And in the midst of the pavilion was the Round Table with seats thereat for fifty persons, and at each of the fifty places was a chalice of gold filled with fragrant wine, and at each place was a paten of gold bearing a manchet of fair white bread.

And King Arthur said unto Merlin: "Lo! that which I see is wonderful beyond telling."

Then Merlin pointed to a high seat, wonderfully wrought in precious woods, and gilded, and he said, "Behold, Lord King, that seat is thine." And as Merlin spake, lo! there suddenly appeared sundry letters of gold upon the back of that seat, and the letters of gold read the name:

Arthur, King

Then King Arthur was seated; and he desired that Merlin should choose those knights who were to fill the Round Table.

"Lord," said Merlin, "I may not fill the Round Table at this time, for there are but two and thirty knights here present who may be considered worthy to sit at the Round Table." And so Merlin did name, one by one, two and thirty knights.

To begin, there were Sir Pellinore and his sons, Sir Aglaval and Sir Lamorac; there were Sir Gawaine and Sir Ewaine, who were nephews unto the King; there was Sir Ulfius; there was Sir Kay the Seneschal, foster brother unto the King; and there was Sir Baudwain of Britain, Sir Pellias and Sir Geraint, and two and twenty others as well.

And as each of these knights was chosen by Merlin, lo! the name of that knight appeared in golden letters, very bright and shining, upon the seat that appertained to him.

And then the Archbishop of Canterbury blessed each and every seat, progressing from place to place surrounded by his Holy Court; and when the Archbishop had thus blessed every seat, the chosen knight took each his seat, and his esquire stood behind him, holding the banneret with his coat of arms above the knight's head. And all those who stood about that place, both knights and ladies, lifted up their voices in loud acclaim.

Then all the knights arose, and each knight held up before him the cross of the hilt of his sword, and each knight spake word for word as King Arthur spake.

And this was the covenant of their knighthood: That they would be gentle unto the weak; that they would be terrible unto the wicked; that they would defend the helpless; that all women should be held unto them sacred; that they would stand unto the defense of one another; that they would be merciful unto all men; that they would be gentle of deed, true in friendship, and faithful in love. Each knight sware unto this upon the cross of his sword.

Then all the knights of the Round Table seated themselves, and each knight brake bread from the golden paten, and quaffed wine from the golden chalice that stood before him, giving thanks unto God for that which he ate and drank.

So endeth these first stories about King Arthur. And now it is time for me to turn to the history of some of the noble knights who were the companions of King Arthur. The first of the noble knights is Sir Launcelot of the Lake, who was held by all men to be the most excellent, noble, perfect knight-champion who was ever seen in the world from the very beginning of chivalry unto the time when his son, Sir Galahad, appeared like a bright star.

PART II—LAUNCELOT

CHAPTER I: THE LADY OF THE LAKE

𝕹ow it chanced upon the day before Saint John's Day in the fullness of young summertime, that King Arthur looked forth from his chamber very early one morning and beheld how exceedingly fair was the world out-of-doors. For the sun was about to rise, and the sky was like to pure gold for brightness; all the grass and leaves and flowers were drenched with dew, and the birds were singing so vehemently that the heart of any man could not but rejoice.

There were two knights with King Arthur at that time, and one was Sir Ewaine, the son of Morgana le Fay (and he was King Arthur's nephew), and the other was Sir Ector de Maris, the son of King Ban of Benwick and of Queen Helen—this latter a very noble, youthful knight. These stood by King Arthur and looked forth out of the window with him, and unto them King Arthur spake, saying: "Messires, meseems this is too fair a day to stay withindoors. So let us three take our horses and our hounds and certain huntsmen, and let us go forth a-hunting into the forest."

So they rode forth from the castle, and it was yet so early in the morning that none of the castle folk were astir to know of their departure.

All that day they hunted in the forest with much joy, nor did they turn their faces toward home again until the day was so far spent that the sun had sunk behind the tops of the trees.

Now this time, being the Eve of Saint John, fairies and those folk who are Fay come forth, as is very well known, into the world. So when King Arthur and his party came to a certain outlying part of the forest, they were suddenly aware of a damsel and a dwarf waiting by the road, and they perceived that the damsel was very likely Fay. For she and her dwarf sat each upon a milk-white horse, very strangely still; and the damsel was wonderfully fair of face, and clad all in white samite from top to toe. And this damsel hailed King Arthur in a voice that was both high and clear, crying: "Welcome, King Arthur! I come from a lady who is your friend. She hath sent me here to meet you and to beseech you to come with me, and I shall lead you unto her."

"Damsel," said King Arthur, "I and my knights shall be right glad to go with you."

By this time the sun had set and the moon had risen, making a great light above the silent treetops. Everything now was embalmed in the twilight, and all the world was enshrouded in the mystery of the midsummer eve.

So the damsel and the dwarf led the way, and King Arthur and the two knights, and all their party of huntsmen and hounds followed them, until they came to where there was an open meadow in the forest. And here the King and his knights were aware of a great bustle of many people, some setting up pavilions of white samite, and others preparing a table as for a feast. And then King Arthur beheld that at some distance there were two people sitting upon a couch especially prepared for them, and these people were the chief of all that company.

The first was a lady clad all in white raiment embroidered over with silver in the pattern of lily flowers. Her face was covered by her wimple so that her countenance was not to be seen clearly. And the second was a youth of eighteen years, so beautiful of face that King Arthur thought he had never beheld so noble a being. And his hair curled and was as soft as silk and as black as it was possible to be; and his eyes were large and bright and extraordinarily black. This youth was clad altogether in white satin with no ornaments saving only a chain of shining silver set with opals and emeralds that hung about his neck.

Then when King Arthur had approached near enough he paid court to the lady, saying: "Lady, it seems that you were aware of my name when you sent for me. Now I should be exceedingly glad if you would enlighten me as to yourself."

"Sir," she said, "you have seen me aforetime and have known me as your friend." Therewith she lowered the wimple from her face and King Arthur perceived that it was the Lady of the Lake.

Upon this he kneeled upon one knee and took her hand and set it to his lips. "Lady," quoth he, "I have indeed cause to know you very well, for you have, as you affirm, been a friend to me." Then, rising, he asked: "And now, I prithee tell me, who is this fair youth who is with you?"

"Lord," said the Lady Nymue, "who he is, and of what quality, shall, I hope, be made manifest in time; just now I would not wish that he should be known even unto you. It was for his sake that I sent my damsel to meet you a while ago. But of that, more anon; for see! our feast is spread. So let us eat and make merry, and then we shall speak further of this matter."

So they all went and sat down to the table that had been spread for them. For the night was warm and a full moon shone down upon them with a marvelous luster, and there was a pleasant air from the forest, and, what with the scores of bright waxen tapers that stood upon the table, the night was made all illuminate like to some singular midday. There were set before them divers savory meats and excellent wines, and they ate and they drank and they made merry with talk and laughter.

Then the Lady of the Lake said to King Arthur: "Sir, I would ask you to look upon this youth who sits beside me. He is not Fay, but wholly mortal. Yet all his childhood has been spent with us. His father died when he was yet an infant, and I brought him to our land that he might be brought up to manhood as you see him now. He is so dear to me that I cannot very well make you know how dear he is. I have brought him hither now from our dwelling place that you should make him knight. And to this intent I have brought armor and all the appurtenances of knighthood."

"Lady," quoth King Arthur, "I will make him knight with much pleasure and gladness."

Now there was in that part of the forest border a small abbey of monks, and in the chapel of that abbey the youth watched his armor for that night and Sir Ewaine with him. Meantime King Arthur and Sir Ector de Maris slept each in a silken pavilion provided for them by the Lady of the Lake.

In the morning Sir Ewaine took the youth to the bath and bathed him, for such was the custom of those who were being prepared for knighthood. Now, whilst Sir Ewaine was bathing the youth, he beheld that on his shoulder was a mark in the likeness of a golden star. He made no mention of it at that time; only he marveled very much thereat.

Then Sir Ewaine clothed the youth, and brought him to King Arthur, and King Arthur knighted him with great ceremony, and buckled the belt around him with his own hands. After he had done this Sir Ewaine and Sir Ector set the golden spurs to his heels, and Sir Ector wist not that he was performing such office for his own brother. For indeed this was he who was to become the most famous of all knights, Launcelot, the youngest son of King Ban of Benwick and of Queen Helen, and younger brother to Sir Ector. Upon the death of King Ban, he had been carried away by the Lady of the Lake, who had raised him from infancy that he might one day be a glory to his father's house and to the world.

Now after King Arthur had dubbed Sir Launcelot knight, and the party of King Arthur was about to leave, the Lady of the Lake took Sir Launcelot aside and spake to him:

"Launcelot, forget not that you are a king's son, and see to it that your worthiness shall be as great as your beauty. Today you shall go unto Camelot with King Arthur to make yourself known unto that famous Court of Chivalry. But do not tarry there, but, ere the night cometh, go forth into the world to prove your knighthood. For I would not have you declare yourself to the world until you have proved your worthiness. Wherefore do not yourself proclaim your name, but wait until the world proclaimeth it."

Then the Lady of the Lake kissed Sir Launcelot upon the face, and gave him a ring set with a wonderful purple stone, which ring had such power that it would dissolve every enchantment. Then she said: "Launcelot, wear this ring and never let it be from off your finger." And Launcelot said: "I will do so." So Sir Launcelot set the ring upon his finger and it never left his finger whilst he drew the breath of life.

Then King Arthur and his party laid their ways toward Camelot. And, as they journeyed, Sir Ewaine communicated privily to Sir Ector how that the youth had a mark as of a golden star upon the skin of his shoulder, and upon this news Sir Ector fell very silent.

They reached Camelot whilst it was still quite early in the morning and all they who were there made great joy at the coming of so fair a young knight as Sir Launcelot.

Then King Arthur said: "Let us go and see if, haply, this youth's name is marked upon any of the seats of the Round Table." So all they of the Court went to the pavilion of the Round Table, and they looked; and lo! upon one seat was the name:

The Knight of the Lake

So the name stood at first, nor did it change until the name of Sir Launcelot of the Lake became so famous in all the world. Then it became changed to this:

Sir Launcelot of the Lake

So SIR LAUNCELOT REMAINED at Camelot for that entire day and was made acquainted with many of the lords and ladies of King Arthur's Court. And he was like one that walked in a dream, for he had never before beheld anything of the world of mankind since he had been carried away into the Lake as an infant, wherefore he wist not whether what he saw was real or whether he beheld it in a vision of enchantment. And he took great delight in it because that he was a man and because this world was the world of mankind.

Nevertheless, Sir Launcelot did not forget what the Lady of the Lake had said. Wherefore when it drew toward evening he besought leave of King Arthur to depart in search of adventures, and King Arthur gave him leave to do as he desired.

And whilst Sir Launcelot was in his chamber making ready to

depart, there came in Sir Ector de Maris. And Sir Ector said: "Sir, is it true that you bear upon your right shoulder a mark like unto a golden star?" And Sir Launcelot made reply: "Yea, that is true." Then Sir Ector said: "I beseech you to tell me if your name is Launcelot." And Sir Launcelot said: "That is my name."

Upon this Sir Ector broke out into great weeping and he catched Sir Launcelot in his arms and he cried out: "Launcelot, thou art mine own brother! For that mark was there when thou wert an infant, before thou wert carried away. And we are both sons unto King Ban of Benwick and Queen Helen." Therewith he kissed Sir Launcelot with great passion. And Sir Launcelot kissed Sir Ector with great joy that he had found a brother in this strange world into which he had so newly come. But Sir Launcelot charged Sir Ector that he should say nothing of this to any man; and Sir Ector pledged his knightly word to that effect. (Nor did he ever tell anyone who Sir Launcelot was until Sir Launcelot had performed such deeds that all the world spake his name.)

For when Sir Launcelot went out into the world in that wise he successfully undertook several very weighty achievements. First he removed an enchantment that overhung a castle, hight Dolorous Gard; and he freed that castle and liberated all the sad, sorry captives that lay therein. (And this castle he held for his own and changed the name to Joyous Gard and the castle became very famous afterward as his best-loved possession. For this was the first of all the possessions he won by the prowess of his arms, and he loved it and considered it always his home.) After that Sir Launcelot, at the bidding of Queen Guinevere, took the part of the Lady of Nohan against the King of Northumberland, and he made the King of Northumberland subject unto King Arthur. Then he overcame Sir Gallehaut, King of the Marches, and sent him captive to the Court of King Arthur. So in a little while all the world spoke of Sir Launcelot, for it was said of him, and truly, that he always succeeded in every adventure which he undertook.

So it was as the Lady of the Lake desired it to be, for Sir Launcelot's name became famous, not because he was the son of a king, but because of the deeds which he performed.

AFTER SIR LAUNCELOT had performed all these adventures, he returned to the Court of King Arthur crowned with the glory of his successful knighthood, and there he was duly installed in that seat of the Round Table that was his. And in that Court he was held in the greatest honor and esteem. For King Arthur spake many times concerning him to this effect: that he knew not any honor or glory that could belong to a king greater than having such a knight for to serve him as Sir Launcelot of the Lake.

And now I must needs mention that friendship that existed betwixt Sir Launcelot and Queen Guinevere, for after he returned to the Court of the King, they two became such friends that no two people could be greater friends than they were.

Now there have been many scandalous things said concerning that friendship, but I do not choose to believe any such evil things of others. And no one hath ever said with truth that the Lady Guinevere regarded Sir Launcelot otherwise than as her very dear friend. Wherefore I choose to believe only good of such noble souls as they.

Yet, though Sir Launcelot abided at the Court of the King, he ever loved the life of adventure, and he had lived so long in the Lake that the sturdy life of out-of-doors never lost its charm for him. So though he found, for a while, great joy in being at the Court (for there were many jousts held in his honor, and, whithersoever he rode forth, men would say to one another: "Yonder goeth Sir Launcelot, who is the greatest knight in the world"), yet from time to time he would beseech King Arthur for leave to go forth in search of adventures; and King Arthur would give him leave to do as he desired.

Now it happened one time when Launcelot was thus away from Camelot that Queen Guinevere was of a mind to take gentle sport; for it was that very joyous season, the month of May; wherefore one day she ordained that on the next morning certain knights of the Court should ride with her a-Maying into the woods and fields.

Of this May party it stands recorded in the histories of chivalry that the knights she chose were ten in all. And the Queen further ordained that each of these knights should choose him a lady for the day, and that each lady should ride behind the knight upon the horse which he rode. And she ordained that all those knights and ladies and their attendants should be clad entirely in green, as was fitting for that pleasant festival.

So the next morning they all rode forth in the freshness of dewy springtide; what time the birds were singing joyously from every hedge; what time the soft wind was blowing great white clouds across the blue canopy of heaven, each cloud casting a soft shadow that moved across the hills; what time all the trees and hedgerows were abloom with fragrant blossoms; and meadowlands were spread with a wonderful carpet of flowers.

For in those days the world was young and gay, and the people who dwelt therein had not yet grown aweary of its freshness of delight. Wherefore that fair Queen and her court took great pleasure in all the world that lay spread about them, as they rode two by two, gathering the blossoms of the May, chattering like merry birds, and now and then bursting into song because of the pure pleasure of living. And when noontide had come they took their rest in a flowery meadow about three miles from the town. And seated in the grass they ate and drank and made them merry; and whilst they ate, minstrels sang songs and recited tales for their entertainment. And meanwhile each fair lady wove wreaths of flowers and bedecked her knight, until all those noble gentlemen were entirely bedight with blossoms.

Now whilst the Queen and her party were thus sporting together, there suddenly came the sound of a bugle horn winded in the woodlands, and whilst they looked with some surprise to see who blew that horn, there suddenly appeared at the edge of the woodland an armed knight followed by more than fourscore men-at-arms clad as though prepared for battle.

This knight and his companions stood regarding that May party from a distance; then after a little they rode across the meadow to where the Queen and her court sat looking at them.

When that knight and his men had come nigh, Queen Guinevere and those with her wist that he was Sir Mellegrans, who was the son of King Bagdemagus, and they wist that his visit was not likely to bode any very great good to them. For Sir Mellegrans was not like his father, who was a worthy king, and a friend of King Arthur's. Contrariwise, Sir Mellegrans was malcontented and held bitter enmity toward King Arthur, and that for this reason:

A part of the estate of Sir Mellegrans marched upon the borders of Wales, and there had at one time arisen great contention between Sir Mellegrans and the King of North Wales concerning the ownership of a certain strip of forest land.

This contention had been submitted to King Arthur and he had decided against Sir Mellegrans and in favor of the King of North Wales; wherefore Sir Mellegrans had great hatred toward King Arthur. Wherefore it was that when the Lady Guinevere beheld that it was Sir Mellegrans who appeared before her thus armed, she was ill at ease.

When Sir Mellegrans had come near he drew rein to his horse and sat regarding that gay company scornfully (albeit at the moment he knew not who the Queen was). Then he said: "What party of jesters are ye, and what is this foolish sport ye are at?"

Then Sir Kay the Seneschal, who was of the party, spake up sternly: "Sir Knight, it behooves you to be more civil in your address. Do you not perceive that this is the Queen and her court unto whom you are speaking?"

Then Sir Mellegrans was filled with great triumph to find the Queen thus, surrounded only with unarmored knights. Wherefore he cried out: "Ha! Lady! It appears to me that Heaven hath surely delivered thee into my hands!"

To this a knight hight Sir Percydes replied very fiercely: "Do you dare, Sir Knight, to make threats to your Queen?"

Quoth Sir Mellegrans: "I tell you this, I do not mean to throw aside the good fortune that hath thus been placed in my hands. For here I find you all undefended, wherefore I seize upon you for to take you to my castle and hold you there as hostages until such time as King Arthur shall return to me my forest lands. So if you go with me in peace it shall be well for you, but if you go not in peace it shall be ill for you."

Then all the ladies that were of the Queen's court were seized with great terror; but Queen Guinevere, albeit her face was like to wax for whiteness, spake with great courage and anger, saying: "Wilt thou be a traitor to thy King, Sir Knight? Wilt thou dare to do violence to me and my court?"

"Lady," said Sir Mellegrans, "I will so dare."

At this Sir Percydes drew his sword and said: "Sir Knight, this shall not be while I have any life in my body!"

Then all those other gentlemen drew their swords also, and one and all spake to the same purpose, saying: "Sir Percydes hath spoken; sooner would we die than suffer that affront to the Queen."

"Well," said Sir Mellegrans, "if ye who are naked will to do battle with us who are armed, then let it be as ye elect." And Sir Mellegrans gave command that his men should make them ready for battle.

Then in a moment all that pleasant May party was changed to dreadful and bloody uproar; for men lashed fiercely at men with sword and glaive, and the Queen and her ladies shrieked and clung in terror together.

And for a long time those ten unarmed worthies fought against the armed men. But they could not shield themselves from the blows of their enemies, wherefore they were soon wounded in many places, and what with loss of blood they began to wax weak and faint. Then at last Sir Kay fell down to the earth and then six others, so that all who were left standing upon their feet were three, Sir Brandiles and Sir Ironside and Sir Percydes. Still these three set themselves back to back and thus fought on. As for their gay attire of green, lo! it was all ensanguined with the red that streamed from many wounds.

Then when Queen Guinevere beheld her knights how they stood bleeding, she cried out: "Sir Mellegrans, have pity! Slay not my knights! and I will go with thee. Only this covenant I make with thee: suffer the lords and ladies of my court and all of those attendant upon us, to go with me into captivity."

Then Sir Mellegrans said: "Well, Lady, it shall be as you wish, for these men of yours fight like devils, wherefore I am glad to end this battle. So bid your knights put away their swords, and there shall be peace between us."

Then the Lady Guinevere gave command that those three knights should put away their swords, though all three besought her that she should suffer them to fight a little longer for her. After that these three knights went to their fallen companions, and found that they were all alive, though sorely hurt. And they dressed their wounds in such ways as might be. After that they helped lift the wounded knights up to their horses, supporting them in such wise that they should not fall. So they all departed, a doleful company, from that place, which was now no longer a meadow of pleasure.

THEY RODE FOR ALL THAT DAY. And they continued to ride after the night had fallen, passing through a deep forest. From this forest, about midnight, they came out into an open stony place where they beheld a grim and forbidding castle, standing very dark against the starlit sky. And this was the castle of Sir Mellegrans.

Now the Queen had riding near to her throughout that journey a page named Denneys, and as they had ridden, she had whispered to him: "If thou canst find a chance of escape, do so, and take news of our plight to someone who may rescue us." So just as they came out thus into that stony place, Denneys drew rein a little to one side. Then, seeing that he was unobserved, he set spurs to his horse and rode away into the forest whence they had come, and so was gone before anybody had gathered thought to stay him.

Then Sir Mellegrans was very angry, and he sent several parties of armed men to hunt for Denneys; but Denneys got safe away into the cover of the night.

And after that he wandered through the dark and gloomy woodland, not knowing whither he went, for there was no ray of light. Yet ever he went onward until, at last, the dawn came shining through the tops of the trees. After that, Denneys journeyed on for the entire day, until the light began to wane once more and the sun set. Then lo! God succored him at last, for as the darkness fell, he heard the sound of a little bell ringing. He turned his horse toward that sound, and so in a little he perceived a light shining from the dwelling place of a hermit of the forest.

As Denneys drew nigh to the hut a great horse neighed from close by, and therewith he was aware that some other wayfarer was there, and at that his heart was glad. So he rode up to the door of the hut and knocked, and there came one and opened to him, and that one was a most reverend hermit with a long white beard and a face very calm and gentle. (And this was the hermit who once succored King Arthur.)

When the hermit beheld before him that young lad, all haggard and faint, he took great pity and lifted him down from his horse and helped him into the hermitage and went to fetch food. Then Denneys gazed about him with heavy eyes, and then he heard a voice speak with wonderment, saying: "Denneys, is it thou? What ails thee? Lo! I knew thee not when thee entered."

Then Denneys lifted up his eyes, and he beheld Sir Launcelot. At that, Denneys ran to Sir Launcelot and fell down upon his knees before him. And he embraced Sir Launcelot about the knees, weeping, and he told Sir Launcelot all that had befallen.

Then Sir Launcelot cried, "How is this!" and he cried again very vehemently: "Help me to mine armor!"

At that moment the hermit came in, bringing food. And Denneys and the hermit helped Sir Launcelot don his armor, and Sir Launcelot mounted his war-horse and rode away into the night.

So Sir Launcelot rode all night, and shortly after the dawning of the day he heard the sound of rushing water. So he followed a path that led to this water and by and by he came to an open space, stony and rough. And he saw that here was a great torrent of water that came roaring down from the hills, and a bridge of stone spanned the torrent, and upon the farther side of the bridge were at least five and twenty men-at-arms. And chief among them was a man clad in green armor.

Then Sir Launcelot rode out upon the bridge and he called to those men: "Can you tell me whether this way leads to the castle of Sir Mellegrans?"

Upon this the Green Knight said: "Messire, are you Sir Launce-lot of the Lake?" Sir Launcelot said: "I am he." "Then," said the Green Knight, "you can go no farther, for we are the people of Sir Mellegrans, and we are here to stay you or any of your fellows from going forward upon this way."

Then Sir Launcelot laughed and said: "Messire, how will you stay me?" The Green Knight said: "We will stay you by force of our numbers." "Well," quoth Sir Launcelot, "I have made my way against greater odds than those I now see before me."

Therewith he rode straight in amongst them, lashing right and left with his sword, so that at every stroke a man fell out of his saddle. So direful were the blows that Sir Launcelot delivered that terror fell upon them, wherefore, after a while, they fell away and left him standing alone in the center of the way.

Now there were a number of the archers of Sir Mellegrans lying hidden in the rocks at the sides of that pass. These straightway fitted arrows to their bows and began shooting at the horse of Sir Launcelot. Wherefore the steed was presently sorely wounded and began plunging and snorting in pain. And still the archers shot arrow after arrow until after a while the good steed fell down and rolled over into the dust.

But Sir Launcelot did not fall, but voided his saddle so that he kept his feet, wherefore his enemies were not able to take him at a disadvantage.

So Sir Launcelot stood there at the end of the bridge, and he waved his sword so that not one of his enemies dared to come nigh to him. And although the Green Knight commanded them to fight, they would not, so the Green Knight had to give orders for them to depart, and this they did.

Thus Sir Launcelot with his single arm won a battle against all that multitude.

But though Sir Launcelot had thus won, yet he was in a very sorry plight. For there he stood, a full-armed man with such a great weight of armor upon him that he could hardly walk. Nor knew he what to do in this extremity, for where could he hope to find a horse in that thick forest?

As he stood there a-doubt as to what to do in this sorry case, he heard upon one side from out of the forest the sound of an axe, and thereat he was very glad for he wist that help was nigh. So he took up his shield on his shoulder and his spear in his hand and slowly directed his steps toward where he heard the axe. Soon he came into a glade of the forest where he beheld a fagot maker chopping fagots. And he beheld the fagot maker had there a cart and a horse for to fetch his fagots from the forest.

But when the fagot maker saw an armed knight come thus like a shining vision out of the forest, walking afoot, he stood staring with his mouth agape. Then Sir Launcelot said to him, "Good fellow, I would have thee do me a service with thy cart. I would have thee take me to some place where I may get a fresh horse for to ride; for mine own horse hath been slain in battle."

Now in those days it was not thought worthy of anyone of degree to ride in a cart, for they would take lawbreakers to the gallows in just such carts as that one in which Sir Launcelot made demand to ride. Wherefore that poor fagot maker knew not what to think. "Messire," quoth he, "this cart is no fit thing for one of your quality to ride in."

But Sir Launcelot replied: "Sirrah, there is no shame in riding in a cart for a worthy purpose. And contrariwise, as my purpose is worthy, I shall, certes, be unworthy if I go not to fulfill that purpose, even if in so going I travel in thy poor cart. So do as I bid thee, and I will give thee five pieces of gold."

Now the fagot maker ran to make ready his cart with all speed. And Sir Launcelot entered it, and rode forth through the forest.

So it was that Sir Launcelot of the Lake came to ride errant in a cart, wherefore, for a long time after, he was called the Chevalier of the Cart. And many ballads and songs were made concerning that matter, which same were sung in several Courts of Chivalry by minstrels and jongleurs.

NOW TURN WE TO THE castle of Sir Mellegrans, where Queen Guinevere and her court were held prisoners.

Now that part of the castle wherein they were held overlooked the road which led up to the castle gate. Wherefore it came about that a damsel of the Queen, looking out of the window, beheld a knight riding thither in a cart. Beholding this, she fell to laughing, and cried out: "Look see! Yonder is a knight riding in a cart!"

Then Queen Guinevere came to the window and looked out, and several came and looked out also, including Sir Percydes. And Sir Percydes said: "Lady, I believe yonder knight is none other than Sir Launcelot." And Queen Guinevere said, "It is assuredly he." Sir Percydes said: "I take it to be a great shame that the chiefest knight of the Round Table should ride so in a cart as though he were a lawbreaker. For the world will assuredly hear of this, and it will be made a jest in every Court of Chivalry. And we who are his brethren of the Round Table will be made a laughingstock along with him." And the other knights and ladies agreed with him.

But the Queen said: "Messires and ladies, I take no care for the manner in which Sir Launcelot cometh, for I believe he cometh for to rescue us, and if he be successful in that undertaking, it will not matter how he cometh to perform so worthy a deed."

Thus they were put to silence by the Queen's words; but those knights who were there still held amongst themselves that it was great shame for Sir Launcelot to come thus to rescue the Queen.

CHAPTER III: THE CHEVALIER OF THE CART

Now when news was brought to Sir Mellegrans that Sir Launcelot was there in front of the castle in a cart, Sir Mellegrans cast about in his mind for some scheme whereby he might destroy Sir Launcelot. And at last he hit upon a scheme that was unworthy of him both as a knight and as a gentleman. He went down to the barbican of the castle and beheld Sir Launcelot. And he said, "Sir Launcelot, is it thou who art there in the cart?"

Sir Launcelot replied: "Yea, thou traitor knight, it is I, and I come to tell thee to set free the Queen and her court."

To this Sir Mellegrans spake in a very humble tone, saying: "Messire, I have taken thought, and I much repent me of all that I have done. Yet I know not how to make reparation without bringing ruin upon myself. If thou wilt intercede with me before the Queen, I will take thee to her. And after I have been forgiven what I have done, then ye shall all go free."

At this repentance of Sir Mellegrans, Sir Launcelot was greatly astonished; wherefore he said: "Sir Knight, how may I know that that which thou art telling me is the truth?"

"Well," said Sir Mellegrans, "I will prove my faith to thee in this: I will come to thee unarmed, and I will admit thee into my castle. And as thou art armed, thou mayest easily slay me if thou seest that I make any sign of betraying thee."

Still Sir Launcelot was a-doubt; but after he had considered for a space, he said: "If all this that thou tellest me is true, Sir Knight, then let me into this castle. But if I see that thou hast a mind to deal falsely by me, then I will indeed slay thee." And Sir Mellegrans said, "I am content."

So Sir Mellegrans commanded that the gates of the castle be opened. And Sir Launcelot descended from the cart and followed Sir Mellegrans deep into the castle with his sword in his hand.

Now there was in a certain part of that castle a trapdoor that opened through the floor of the passageway into a pit. And this trapdoor was controlled by a cunning latch; and when Sir Mellegrans would touch the latch with his finger, the trapdoor would immediately fall open.

So to that place Sir Mellegrans led the way. And Sir Mellegrans passed over that trapdoor in safety, but when Sir Launcelot had stepped upon the trapdoor, Sir Mellegrans touched the spring that controlled the latch, and the trapdoor opened and Sir Launcelot fell into the pit. And the pit was very deep and the floor was of stone, so that when Sir Launcelot fell he smote the stone floor so violently that he was bereft of his senses and lay there like to one who was dead.

Then Sir Mellegrans laughed and he closed the trapdoor and went away, and he said to himself: Now indeed have I such hostages in my keeping that King Arthur must needs make such terms with me as I shall determine.

NOW WHEN SIR LAUNCELOT AWOKE from his swoon he found himself to be in a very sad, miserable case. For he lay there upon the hard stones and all about him there was darkness. So for a while he knew not where he was; but by and by he remembered all that had befallen him, and he cried out: "Woe is me that I should have placed any faith in a traitor such as this knight."

Now as Sir Launcelot lay there in despair of spirit, he was suddenly aware that there came a crack of light shining in a certain place; and he heard the sound of keys and immediately afterward a door opened and there entered into that place a damsel bearing a lighted lamp in her hand.

And lo! this damsel was the Lady Elouise the Fair, the daughter of King Bagdemagus and sister unto Sir Mellegrans.

So Elouise the Fair came into that dismal place, and Sir Launcelot beheld that her eyes were red with weeping. And she said: "Woe is me that mine own brother should have brought thee to this pass, Sir Launcelot! I cannot bear to see so noble a knight lying thus in duress, so I have come hither. Now if I set thee free wilt thou show mercy unto my brother?"

"Lady," said Sir Launcelot, "this is a hard case thou puttest to me. Because this knight hath dealt treacherously with my Lady the Queen, I must seek to punish him if ever I can escape from this place. But if I do escape, this much mercy will I show to Sir Mellegrans: I will meet him in fair field, as one knight may meet another. Meseems that is all that may rightly be asked of me."

Then Elouise the Fair wept afresh, and she said: "Alas, Launcelot! I fear that my brother will then perish at thy hands!"

"Lady," said Sir Launcelot, "the fate of battle lieth ever in the hands of God and not in the hands of men. It may befall any man to die who doeth battle. So, whilst I may not pledge myself to avoid an ordeal of battle with Sir Mellegrans, yet it may be his good hap that he may live and that I may die."

"Alas, Launcelot," quoth the Fair Elouise, "and dost thou think that it would be any comfort to me to have thee die at the hands of mine own brother? Yet let it be as it may hap, I will set thee free, and do my duty by thee as the daughter of a king and of a true knight. As to that which shall afterward befall, that will I trust to the mercy of God."

So saying, the damsel bade Sir Launcelot to arise and to follow her, and he did so. And she led him up a long flight of steps and so to a fair large chamber in a tower of the castle. And Sir Launcelot beheld that here there was a table set with bread and meat and wine for his refreshment.

And the Lady Elouise said: "Here shalt thou rest at ease tonight, and in the morning I shall bring thy sword and thy shield to thee." Therewith she left Sir Launcelot, and he ate and he drank with great appetite, and then he laid him down upon a couch spread with flame-colored linen and slept.

The next morning the Lady Elouise fetched unto him his sword and his shield. And she said: "Sir Knight, I know not whether I be doing evil or good in the sight of Heaven in thus purveying thee with thy weapons; ne'ertheless, I cannot leave thee unprotected in this place without the wherewithal for to defend thyself against thine enemies."

Sir Launcelot gave thanks to the Lady Elouise. And after that he went down into the courtyard of the castle, and everyone was greatly astonished at his coming, for they deemed him to be still a prisoner in the dungeon. So all these, when they beheld him coming, fled away. So Sir Launcelot reached the courtyard, and there he set his horn to his lips, and blew a blast that sounded loud and shrill throughout the entire place.

Meantime, several messengers ran to where Sir Mellegrans was and told him that Sir Launcelot had escaped out of that pit. At that Sir Mellegrans went to a certain place whence he could look down into the courtyard, and there he beheld Sir Launcelot where he stood shining in the sunlight. And Sir Launcelot lifted up his eyes and espied Sir Mellegrans. Thereupon he cried out in a loud voice: "Sir Mellegrans, thou traitor knight! Come down and do battle, for I await thee."

But when Sir Mellegrans heard those words he withdrew hastily from the window, and he went away in great terror, saying to himself: Fool that I was, to bring this knight into my castle, when I might have kept him outside! Then he called a messenger and he said: "Go down to yonder knight in the courtyard and tell him that I will not do battle with him."

So the messenger went to Sir Launcelot and delivered that message. And Sir Launcelot laughed with great scorn, and said, "Doth the knight of this castle fear to meet me?" The messenger said, "Yea, Messire." Sir Launcelot said: "Then take thou this message to him: that I will lay aside my shield and helm and that I will unarm all the left side of my body, and thus will I fight him if only he will come and do battle with me."

So the messenger came to Sir Mellegrans and delivered that message. Then Sir Mellegrans said: "Now I will go down and do battle with this knight, for never will I have a better chance of overcoming him than this." Therewith he commanded that messenger: "Go! Hasten back to yonder knight, and tell him that I will do battle with him upon those conditions."

So after the messenger had delivered that message, Sir Launcelot laid aside his shield and his helm, and he removed his armor from his left side.

And after a while Sir Mellegrans appeared, clad all in armor from top to toe, and bearing himself with great confidence, for he felt well assured of victory. Thus he came very proudly nigh to Sir Launcelot, and he said: "Here am I, Sir Knight, come to do you service since you will have it so."

Sir Launcelot said: "I am ready to meet thee thus or in any other way, so that I may come at thee at all."

After that each knight dressed himself for combat, and all those who were in the castle gathered in the galleries above, and looked down upon the two knights.

Then they two came slowly together, and when they were pretty nigh to one another Sir Launcelot offered his left side so as to allow Sir Mellegrans to strike at him. And Sir Mellegrans straightway lashed a great blow at Sir Launcelot's unarmed side.

But Sir Launcelot dexterously turned himself so that he received the blow upon the side which was armed. So that blow came to naught.

But so violent was the stroke that Sir Mellegrans had lashed that he overreached himself. And ere he could recover himself, Sir Launcelot lashed at him a great buffet that cut deep through the helm and into the brainpan of Sir Mellegrans, so that he fell down upon the ground and lay there without motion. Then Sir Launcelot called to those who were near to look to their lord, and thereat several came running. These lifted Sir Mellegrans and removed his helmet. And they looked upon his face, and lo! even then the spirit was passing from him, for he never opened his eyes to look upon the sun again.

Then those of the castle lifted up their voices with lamentation. But Sir Launcelot cried out: "This knight hath brought this upon himself because of the treason he hath done." And then he said: "Fetch hither the porter of this castle!"

So the porter came, and Sir Launcelot demanded of him: "Where are the Queen and her court held prisoners? Bring me to them, Sirrah!"

So the porter brought Sir Launcelot to where the Queen was, and those others with her. Then all these gave great joy and acclaim that Sir Launcelot had rescued them. And Queen Guinevere said: "Did I not say to you that it mattered not how Sir Launcelot came hither even if it were in a cart?"

After that Sir Launcelot commanded them that they should make ready such horses as might be needed. And after that they all departed from that place and turned their way toward Camelot.

But Sir Launcelot did not again see that damsel Elouise the Fair, for she kept herself close shut in her own bower because of her grief and her shame.

And Sir Launcelot was much grieved that he should have brought trouble upon one who had been so friendly with him. Yet he wist not how he could have done otherwise.

After that time there was still much offense taken that Sir Launcelot had gone upon that adventure riding in a cart, for many jests were made of it. Wherefore Sir Lionel and Sir Ector, the kinsmen of Sir Launcelot, came to Sir Launcelot and Sir Ector said: "That was a very ill thing you did to ride to that adventure in a cart. Dost thou not know that thou art now called everywhere the Chevalier of the Cart and that songs are made of this adventure?"

To this Sir Launcelot made reply with much heat: "I know not why you should meddle in this affair. For that which I did, I did of mine own free will, and it matters not to any other man."

And he went and took his shield and laced a sheet of leather over the face. Thereafter he painted the leather covering of the shield a pure white so that it might not be known what was the device thereon, nor who was the knight who bare that shield. Then he armed himself and took horse and rode forth errant and alone, suffering his horse to wander upon whatsoever path it chose.

After that Sir Launcelot was not seen in the Court of King Arthur for the space of two years, during which time there was much sorrow at the Court because he was no longer there.

Here endeth, for a time, the story of Sir Launcelot. And here followeth the story of Sir Tristram of Lyonesse, who was deemed to be one of the most worthy and perfect knights-champion of his day. Likewise herein shall be told the story of the Lady Belle Isoult, who, next to Queen Guinevere, was reckoned to be the most fair, gentle lady in all of the world.

PART III—TRISTRAM AND ISOULT

CHAPTER I: THE BROKEN SWORD

TRISTRAM OF LYONESSE was the son of King Meliadus of Lyonesse, and of the Lady Elizabeth, who died when Tristram was born. As a child he was very large and robust of form and of extraordinary strength of body and beauty of countenance. And he grew to manhood well taught in knighthood and wonderfully excellent in arms; and also he became so skillful with the harp that no minstrel in the world was his equal.

So when he had reached the age of eighteen his father would have made him a knight, but Tristram said: "Lord, think not ill of me if I do not yet accept knighthood. For I would fain wait until the chance for some large adventure cometh; then I would be made a knight for to meet that adventure, so that I might immediately win renown. For what credit could there be to our house if I should be made knight, only that I might sit in hall and feast and make merry?"

So spoke Sir Tristram, and his words sounded well to King Meliadus, wherefore from thenceforth King Meliadus refrained from urging knighthood upon him.

So time went by, and then a time came when King Mark of Cornwall, who was uncle to Tristram, had great debate with the King of Ireland concerning an island that lay in the sea betwixt Cornwall and Ireland. For though that island was held by Cornwall, yet the King of Ireland claimed it and demanded that the King of Cornwall should pay him tribute for the same. This King Mark refused to do.

But the King of Ireland said: "Let there not be war betwixt us

74

but let us each choose a champion and let those two champions decide the rights of this case by combat. For so the truth shall be made manifest." Thereupon the King of Ireland chose for his champion Sir Marhaus of Ireland, who was one of the greatest knights in the world.

Now in those days there was not any knight of repute in all of Cornwall to stand against Sir Marhaus. Nor could King Mark easily find any knight outside of Cornwall; for Sir Marhaus being a knight of the Round Table, no other knight of the Round Table would fight against him.

In this strait, King Mark sent a letter to Lyonesse, asking if there was any knight at Lyonesse who would stand against Sir Marhaus. And when young Tristram heard of this letter he went to his father and said: "Sire, some whiles ago you desired that I should become a knight. Now I would that you would let me go to Cornwall, and when I come there I will beseech my uncle King Mark to make me a knight, and then I will go out against Sir Marhaus. For if I should overcome Sir Marhaus in battle, there would, certes, be great glory to our house through my knighthood."

Then King Meliadus looked upon Tristram and loved him very dearly, and he said: "Tristram, thou hast assuredly a great heart to undertake this adventure. So I bid thee go in God's name, if so be thy heart bids thee to go."

That very day Tristram departed for Cornwall, taking with him as his companion only one man, Gouvernail, a noble and honorable older lord who had been his tutor. So, by ship, he and Gouvernail reached Cornwall, and the castle of Tintagel, where King Mark was holding court.

It was at the sloping of the afternoon when they so came, and at that time King Mark was sitting in hall with many of his lords about him.

So those two were admitted and brought before the King. And Tristram stood forth before Gouvernail and Gouvernail bare the harp of Tristram, and the harp was of gold and shone most brightly. Then King Mark looked upon Tristram, and marveled at his size and beauty; for Tristram stood above any man in that place.

His hair was as red as gold and like the mane of a young lion, and his neck was sturdy and straight like to a white stone pillar, and he was clad in garments of blue silk embroidered with gold and set with gems of divers colors.

So King Mark marveled, and then he spoke, saying: "Fair youth, who are you, and what would you have of me?"

"Lord," said Tristram, "my name is Tristram, and I come from Lyonesse, where your sister was one time Queen. Having heard that you are in need of a champion, I come hither to say that if you will make me a knight, I will take it upon me to meet Sir Marhaus upon your behalf."

King Mark said: "Fair youth, are you not aware that Sir Marhaus is a knight well set in years and of great and accredited deeds of arms? How then can you, who are new to the use of arms, hope to stand against so renowned a champion?"

"Lord," quoth Tristram, "I am well aware of the danger of this undertaking. Yet if one who covets knighthood shall fear danger, what virtue would there then be in knighthood? So, Messire, I put my trust in God, and I have hope that He will lend me strength in my time of need."

Then King Mark said: "Tristram, I believe that you do stand a chance of success in this undertaking; wherefore I will make you a knight, and I will fit you with armor and accouterments."

The next day with all solemn ceremony Tristram was made knight. And in the afternoon of that day King Mark purveyed a ship, and in the ship Tristram and Gouvernail set sail for that island where Sir Marhaus was known to be abiding.

Now upon the second day of their voyaging they came to the land which they were seeking, and there made a safe harbor; and a gangway was set to the shore, and Sir Tristram and Gouvernail drave their horses across the gangway to the dry land. Thereafter they perceived in the distance three other ships drawn up to the shore. And a knight clad in full armor was under the shadow of those ships, and they wist that that must be Sir Marhaus.

Then Tristram gazed very steadily at Sir Marhaus, and by and by he said: "Gouvernail, go now and leave me alone, for I do not choose for anyone to be by when I have to do with yonder knight. For if he overcomes me and I yield to him, then mine uncle must pay tribute to the King of Ireland; but if I die without yielding, then mine enemy must yet do battle with another champion. So I am determined either to win this battle or to die therein."

When Gouvernail heard this, he cried out: "Sir, let not this battle be of that sort!" To him Sir Tristram said steadfastly: "Say no more, Gouvernail, but go as I bid thee." Whereupon Gouvernail went away, weeping bitterly.

Now by this time Sir Marhaus had caught sight of Sir Tristram, and so he came riding thitherward and he said: "Who art thou, Sir Knight?"

Unto this Sir Tristram made reply: "Sir, I am Sir Tristram of Lyonesse, and I am come to do battle upon behalf of the King of Cornwall."

Quoth Sir Marhaus: "Messire, are you a knight of approval and of battles?"

"Nay," said Sir Tristram, "I have only been created knight these three days."

"Alas!" said Sir Marhaus, "I am sorry. Thou art not fit to have to do with me. So I advise thee, because of thy youth, to return to King Mark and bid him send another champion."

"Sir," said Sir Tristram, "I give thee gramercy for thy advice. But I may tell thee that I was made knight for no other purpose than to do battle with thee; so I may not return without having fulfilled mine adventure."

"Alas!" said Sir Marhaus, "that is certes a pity. But as thou hast foreordained it, so it must needs be." Therewith he saluted Sir Tristram and rode to a distance where he made ready for battle. Nor was Sir Tristram behind him in making preparation.

Then each gave shout and drave spurs into his horse and rushed toward the other. And Sir Marhaus smote through Sir Tristram's shield and gave Sir Tristram a great wound in his side. Then Sir Tristram felt the blood gush out of that wound in such abundance that he thought he had got his death wound. But he held his seat and was not overthrown. Then he voided his horse and drew his sword; and Sir Marhaus likewise voided his horse and made ready for battle upon foot. So straightway they came together, lashing at each other with fearful strength. Whole pieces of armor were hewn off from their bodies; and the armor that still hung to them became red as though it were painted. Yet neither gave any thought to quitting.

Now by and by Sir Tristram perceived that he was stouter than Sir Marhaus and better winded; wherefore hope uplifted him. Then presently Sir Marhaus fell back a little, and then Sir Tristram ran in upon him and smote Sir Marhaus a great blow with his sword upon the helmet. So direful was that blow that the sword of Sir Tristram pierced through the helm of Sir Marhaus and into the brainpan. And Sir Tristram's sword stuck fast so that he could not pull it out again.

Then Sir Marhaus, half aswoon, fell down upon his knees, and therewith a part of the edge of the blade brake off from Sir Tristram's sword and remained in the wound.

Then Sir Marhaus rose staggering to his feet, and he began going about in a circle, crying most dolorously. Then, stumbling like one who had gone blind, he went on down to his ships. Then those who were aboard the ships met him and bare him away to his own ship. Thereafter they hoisted sail and departed.

Then by and by came Gouvernail and several others of Sir Tristram's party; and they found Sir Tristram leaning upon his sword and groaning sorely because of the wound in his side. So they lifted him upon his shield and bare him thence to his ship. There they laid him upon a couch and stripped him of his armor. Then they beheld his great wound, and they lifted up their voices in sorrow, for they all believed that he would die.

So they set sail, and in two days brought him back to King Mark in Cornwall.

And when King Mark saw how weak Sir Tristram was, he wept and grieved very sorely. But Sir Tristram smiled upon King Mark, and he said: "Lord, have I done well for thy sake?" And King Mark said, "Yea."

"Then," quoth Tristram, "it is time for me to tell thee that my father is King Meliadus of Lyonesse, and my mother was the Lady Elizabeth, who was thine own sister till God took her to Paradise."

When King Mark heard this he went into his own chamber. There he fell upon his knees and cried out: "Alas, that this should be! Rather would I lose my entire kingdom than that my sister's son should come to his death in this wise!"

Now it remaineth to say that, back in Ireland, Sir Marhaus died of the wound that Sir Tristram had given him. But ere he died, and whilst they were dressing that hurt, the Queen of Ireland, who was his sister, discovered the broken piece of the blade still in that wound.

This she drew forth and set aside, saying to herself: If ever I meet that knight to whose sword this piece of blade fitteth, then it will be an evil day for him.

CHAPTER II: HOW SIR TRISTRAM WENT TO IRELAND

Now THAT GRIEVOUS HURT which Sir Tristram had received grew ever more rankled and sore, so that many thought that the spear-head had been poisoned.

Then King Mark sent for the most learned leeches and chirur-geons to come and search the wound of Sir Tristram, but of these no one could bring him any ease.

Now one day there came to the Court a very wise lady, who had traveled much and had great knowledge of wounds. She too searched Sir Tristram's wound. And when she had done that, she said unto King Mark: "Lord, I can do nothing to save his life, nor do I know of anyone who may save it unless it be the daughter of the King of Ireland, who is known as the Belle Isoult because of her beauty. She is the most skillful leech in the world."

Then King Mark said to Sir Tristram: "Wilt thou go to the daughter of the King of Ireland and let her search thy wound?"

Sir Tristram groaned, and he said: "Lord, this is a great under-taking for one who is so sick. Moreover, if I go to Ireland, and if it be found that I am he who slew Sir Marhaus, then I may never escape from that country with my life. Ne'ertheless, I would rather die than live as I am living; wherefore I will go."

Accordingly, King Mark provided a ship to carry Sir Tristram to Ireland, and Sir Tristram was carried down to the ship in a litter; and Gouvernail was with Sir Tristram all the while in attendance upon him.

So they set sail, and on the third day, about the time of sunset, they came to a part of the coast of Ireland where there was a castle built upon the rocks.

Now there were several fishermen in boats near that castle, and of one of these the pilot of Sir Tristram's boat made inquiry what castle that was. The fisherman replied: "That is the castle of King Angus, where dwell the King and Queen and their daughter, Belle Isoult."

At this Sir Tristram gave orders that the pilot should let go anchor. And by that time the sun had set and all the air was illuminated with a golden light; and in this sky of gold the moon hung like a shield of silver above the towers of the castle. And there came from the land a pleasing perfume of blossoms; for it was then in the fullness of the springtime, and all the fruit-bearing trees were luxuriant with bloom.

Then there came a great content into the heart of Sir Tristram, wherefore he said to Gouvernail: "Bring me hither my harp, that I may play upon it."

So Gouvernail brought to Sir Tristram his shining harp, and Sir Tristram struck it and sang, and his voice sounded marvelously clear and sweet across the water. The Lady Belle Isoult who sat at the window of her bower enjoying the evening heard it, and she said to those damsels who were with her, "Meseems that must be the voice of some angel that is singing." Then she said to a page: "Bid the King and Queen come hither, that they may hear this singing also."

In a little the King and Queen came to the bower of Belle Isoult, and she and they leaned upon the window ledge and listened to Sir Tristram.

Then by and by King Angus said: "Now I will have yonder

minstrel brought hither to do us pleasure, for I believe that he must be the greatest minstrel in the world."

So King Angus sent a barge to that ship, and besought that he who sang should be brought to the castle. And the King's attendants brought Sir Tristram to the castle, where they laid him upon a bed in a fair room.

Then King Angus came to Sir Tristram where he lay, and finding how it was with him, he said: "Messire, what can I do for you to put you more at ease?" "Lord," said Sir Tristram, "I pray you to permit the Lady Belle Isoult to search a wound in my side that I received in battle, for I hear that she is the most skillful leech in the world."

"Messire," said King Angus, "I perceive that you are somebody of high nobility, and it shall be as you desire. And now I pray you, tell me your name and whence you come."

Upon this, Sir Tristram communed within his own mind, saying: Haply someone here will know that I was the cause why the brother of the Queen of this place hath died. So he said: "Lord, my name is Sir Tramtris, and I am come from Lyonesse."

Quoth King Angus, "Well, Sir Tramtris, tomorrow the Lady Belle Isoult shall search your wound to heal it if possible."

And so it was as King Angus said, for the next day the Lady Belle Isoult came with her attendants to where Sir Tristram lay. And when she beheld his wound she felt a great pity for Sir Tristram, and she said: "Alas, that so young and fair a knight should suffer so sore a wound!" Therewith she searched the wound with very gentle touch (for her fingers were like to rose petals for softness) and lo! she found a part of a spearhead embedded deep in the wound.

This she drew forth very deftly (albeit Sir Tristram groaned with a great passion of pain) and therewithafter came forth an issue of blood like a crimson fountain, whereupon Sir Tristram swooned away like one who had gone dead. But he did not die, for she quickly stanched the flow, and set aromatic spices to his nostrils, so that in a little he revived in spirit to find himself at great peace.

Now it came about that in a little while Sir Tristram waxed almost entirely hale and strong, so that he was able to come and go whithersoever he chose. But always he would be with the Lady Belle Isoult, for Sir Tristram loved her with a wonderfully passionate regard. And so likewise the lady loved Sir Tristram. So they two fair and noble creatures were always together in bower or in hall, and no one in all that while wist that Sir Tramtris was Sir Tristram.

So Sir Tristram was in Ireland for a year, and in that time he grew to be altogether sturdy again.

Now it was in those days that there came to that place Sir Palamydes the Saracen knight, who was held to be one of the foremost knights in the world.

And when Sir Palamydes beheld Belle Isoult, he came to love her with almost as passionate a regard as that with which Sir Tristram loved her, so that he also sought ever to be with her whenever the chance offered.

Belle Isoult felt no regard for Sir Palamydes, but she did not dare to offend him; wherefore she smiled upon him.

This Sir Tristram beheld and it displeased him a very great deal. But Belle Isoult said to him: "Tramtris, be not displeased, for what am I to do? I do not love this knight, but I am afraid of him because he is so fierce and strong."

To this Sir Tristram said: "Lady, it would be a great shame to me if I should suffer any knight to come betwixt you and me."

She said: "What would you do? Would you give challenge? Lo, you are not yet healed, and Sir Palamydes is in perfect strength."

"Lady," quoth Sir Tristram, "I am entirely recovered. Wherefore I have a mind to deal with this knight in your behalf. Now I will devise it in this way: tell your father, King Angus, to proclaim a jousting. In that jousting I will seek out Sir Palamydes, and with God's aid I shall overcome him."

So therewith Lady Belle Isoult besought her father to proclaim a jousting in honor of Sir Palamydes, and the King said that he would do so.

So came the day of that tournament, and there began to gather together in the two parties those who were to contest the one against the other. Of one of these parties, Sir Palamydes was the chiefest knight. Of the other the chiefest knight was the King of Scots, and Sir Tristram joined himself to this latter party.

And the armor of Sir Tristram was provided by the Lady Belle Isoult, and it was white, shining like to silver, and the horse was altogether white, so that Sir Tristram glistened with extraordinary splendor.

So in a little while that friendly battle began. And Sir Palamydes made at the King of Scots and he struck that knight so direful a blow that both horse and man fell to the ground. Then he struck down, one after another, seven other knights, so that all those who looked thereon cried out, "Is he a man or he is a demon?"

All this time Sir Tristram was also possessed with a great joy of battle, so that in a short time he too had struck down eight knights.

And as Sir Palamydes beheld this he said: "Ha! Now if I do not presently meet yonder knight, and that to my credit, he will have more honor in this battle than I."

So therewith Sir Palamydes pushed straight against Sir Tristram, and when Sir Tristram beheld that he was very glad. Then immediately Sir Palamydes smote Sir Tristram such a buffet that Sir Tristram thought a bolt of lightning had burst upon him, and for a little while he was altogether bemazed. But when he came to himself he rushed upon Sir Palamydes and smote him again and again with such fury that Sir Palamydes was altogether stunned. Thereupon Sir Tristram rose up in his stirrups and struck Sir Palamydes upon the helmet so dreadful a buffet that Sir Palamydes rolled off his horse into the dust beneath its feet.

Then the Lady Belle Isoult was so filled with the glory of Sir Tristram's prowess that she wept for joy thereof.

Now after that assault Sir Tristram withdrew to one side. Thus he perceived when the esquires attendant upon Sir Palamydes came to him and took him away. Then by and by he perceived that Sir Palamydes had mounted his horse, and he saw Sir Palamydes ride away with his head bowed down. Thereupon Sir

Tristram also took his departure, going in that same direction as Sir Palamydes.

By and by he perceived Sir Palamydes upon the road before him, at a place where there were several stone windmills with great sails swinging slowly around.

Now this was a lonely place, and one very fit to do battle in, wherefore Sir Tristram cried out to Sir Palamydes: "Sir Palamydes! Turn you about! Here is the chance for you to recover the honor that you have lost to me."

Thereupon Sir Palamydes turned him about. And he ground his teeth with rage, and drave his horse at Sir Tristram, drawing his sword. And when he came nigh to Sir Tristram, he lashed a blow at him with all his might. But Sir Tristram put aside that blow, and, recovering himself, he gave Sir Palamydes such a blow upon the head that Sir Palamydes fell down off his horse. Then Sir Tristram voided his own horse, and running to Sir Palamydes he plucked off his helmet and cried out: "Sir Knight, yield thee to me, or I will slay thee." And he lifted up his sword as though to strike off the head of Sir Palamydes.

Then Sir Palamydes said: "Sir Knight, I yield me to thee to do thy commands."

Thereupon Sir Tristram said, "Arise," and at that Sir Palamydes got him up.

"Now," said Sir Tristram, "this shall be my commandment upon you. That you forsake the Lady Belle Isoult, and that you do not come near her for the space of a year."

"Alas!" said Sir Palamydes, "would that I had died instead of yielding!" And he mounted his horse and rode away, weeping like one altogether brokenhearted.

So Sir Tristram rode back to the castle of the King of Ireland once more. And lo! he found a great party waiting for him before the castle, crying, "Welcome, Sir Tramtris!" And King Angus came forward and took the hand of Sir Tristram, and they went into the castle.

There the Queen of Ireland said to him: "Tramtris, one so nigh to death as you have been should not so soon have done battle.

84

Now I will have a bath prepared and you shall bathe therein, so that no ill may come to you from this battle."

So she had that bath prepared of tepid water and spices and herbs of divers sorts. And then Sir Tristram undressed and entered the bath, and the Queen and the Lady Belle Isoult were in the adjoining chamber which was his bedchamber. And they beheld the sword of Sir Tristram, for he had laid it upon the bed when he had unlatched the belt.

Then the Queen said to Belle Isoult, "See what a great huge sword this is," and she drew the blade out of its sheath. Then she saw where, within about a foot and a half from the point, there was a piece in the shape of a half-moon broken out of the sword; and she looked at that place for a long while. Then she felt a great terror, and she laid aside the sword and went very quickly to her own chamber. There she opened her cabinet and took thence the piece of sword blade which she had drawn from the wound of Sir Marhaus. With this she hurried back to the chamber of Sir Tristram, and fitted that piece of the blade to the blade; and lo! it fitted exactly.

Upon that the Queen shrieked out, "Traitor! Traitor!" and she snatched up the sword of Sir Tristram and she ran into the room where he lay naked, in his bath, and therewith she lashed at him with his sword. But Sir Tristram threw himself to one side and so that blow failed. Then the Queen would have lashed at him again; but at that Gouvernail ran in and held her back, struggling and screaming very violently, and so they took the sword away from her.

Then as soon as Gouvernail loosed her, she ran out of that room and to King Angus, crying out: "Justice! Justice! I have found that man who slew my brother!"

Then King Angus said: "Where is that man?" And the Queen said: "It is Tramtris."

King Angus said: "Lady, I cannot believe it!" Upon this the Queen cried: "Go yourself, Lord, and inquire."

Then King Angus went to the chamber of Sir Tristram. And there he found that Sir Tristram had very hastily dressed and armed himself. Then King Angus said: "How is this, that I find thee armed? Art thou an enemy to my house?"

And Tristram wept, and said: "Nay, Lord, I am your friend, for I have great love for you and for all that is yours. But I know not whether you be friends or enemies unto me; wherefore I have prepared myself."

Then King Angus said: "Thou speakest in a very foolish way, for how could a single knight hope to defend himself against my whole household? Now I bid thee tell me who thou art, and why thou camest hither knowing that thou hadst slain my wife's brother?"

Therewith Sir Tristram confessed everything to King Angus, to wit: who was his father and his mother; why he had fought Sir Marhaus; and how he had come hither to be healed of his wound, from which else he must die.

So King Angus listened, and when Sir Tristram had ended, quoth he: "As God sees me, Tristram, I cannot deny that you did with Sir Marhaus as a true knight should. But though this is true, if I keep you here I shall greatly displease not only the Queen and her kin, but many of those lords and knights who were friends to Sir Marhaus. So you must leave here straightway, for I may not aid you in any way."

Then Sir Tristram said: "Lord, I thank you for your great kindness unto me, and I know not how I shall repay the great goodness that my Lady Belle Isoult hath showed to me. She hath the entire love of my heart; so if my life be spared, I give you my knightly word that whithersoever I go I shall be your daughter's servant. Now, Lord, I beseech you that I may take leave of my lady your daughter. And then I may take leave of all your knights and kinsmen as a right knight should. And if there be any among them who chooses to challenge my going, then I must face that one at my peril."

"Well," said King Angus, "that is a knightly way to behave, and so it shall be as you will have it."

So Sir Tristram went to a certain chamber where Belle Isoult was. And he took her by the hand, and he said: "Lady, I am to go away from this place; but before I go I must tell you that I shall ever be your own true knight in all ways. For no other lady shall my heart ever have but you. Even though I shall haply never see your face again, the thought of you shall always abide with me withersoever I go."

At this the Lady Belle Isoult fell to weeping, and thereat the countenance of Sir Tristram was all writhed with passion, and he said, "Lady, do not weep so!"

She said, "Alas, I cannot help it!" Then he took her face into his hands and kissed her upon the forehead, and the eyes, and the lips. Therewith he turned and went away, all bedazed with his sorrow, and feeling for the latch of the door ere he was able to find it and go out from that place.

After that Sir Tristram went straight unto the hall of the castle, and there he found a great many lords and knights, and many of them were angry. But Tristram came in very boldly and he spoke, saying: "If there be any man here whom I have offended in any way, let him speak, and I will give him entire satisfaction."

At this all those knights stood still and held their peace, for the boldness of Tristram overawed them.

So after a while Sir Tristram left, without turning his head to see if any man followed him.

So he left that castle and Gouvernail went with him, and so he sailed away from Ireland. But though his body was very whole and sound, the heart of Sir Tristram was full of sorrow.

CHAPTER III: KING MARK SEEKS A BRIDE

So SIR TRISTRAM CAME BACK again to Cornwall, and King Mark and all his knights and lords made much joy over him.

But Sir Tristram took no joy in their joy. And he made many songs about Belle Isoult: about her beauty and her graciousness; about how he was her sad, loving knight; and how he was pledged to be true to her all his life.

These words he would sing to the music of his harp, and King

Mark loved to listen. And sometimes King Mark would sigh and say: "Messire, that lady must in sooth be a very wonderful, beautiful lady."

And Sir Tristram would say, "Yea, she is that."

At that time King Mark had great love for Sir Tristram. But in a little while his love was turned to bitter hate.

Sir Tristram undertook several knightly adventures, and as his fame grew, and he became known as a very great champion, King Mark began to wax jealous.

Then one day King Mark lay down upon his couch after his midday meal for to sleep a little; and by chance the window nearby was open. And three knights of the Court sat in the garden beneath the window. These knights talked to one another of what honor it was to have Sir Tristram in Cornwall. They said that if only the King of Cornwall were such a knight as Sir Tristram, then there would be even greater honor for Cornwall, and plenty of good knights would come to that Court. And they said: "Would God our King were such a knight as Sir Tristram!"

All this King Mark overheard, and the words that they said were like a bitter poison in his heart. After that day he ever pondered upon them, and the longer he pondered, the more he hated Sir Tristram.

But always the King dissembled this hatred, so that no one suspected him thereof, least of all Sir Tristram.

Now one day Sir Tristram was playing upon his harp and singing of Belle Isoult, and the King sat brooding as he gazed at Tristram. And whilst King Mark listened, a thought entered his heart and he smiled. So when Sir Tristram had ended his song, King Mark said: "Nephew, I would that you would undertake a quest for me."

Sir Tristram said, "What quest is that, Lord?" "Nay," said King Mark, "I will not tell you what quest it is unless you will promise me upon your knighthood to undertake it." Sir Tristram suspected no evil, wherefore he smiled and said: "Dear Lord, if the quest is a thing that it is in my power to undertake, I will undertake it, and unto that I pledge my knighthood." And King Mark said: "I

And the boat floated across the Lake to where was the arm uplifting the sword, and the arm and the sword moved not.

And she took from her neck the necklace of pearls which she wore, and dropped the same down to King Arthur.

*And the Queen further ordained that each of these knights should choose him
a lady for the day, and that each lady should ride behind the knight upon
the horse which he rode.*

*For the next day the Lady Belle Isoult came with her attendants to where
Sir Tristram lay.*

And he beheld that the Lady Belle Isoult and Sir Tristram sat at a game of chess, and that they played not at the game but that they sat talking together very sadly; and he beheld that Dame Bragwaine sat in a window to one side.

And catching the haft of his sword in both of his hands, he stabbed with his sword into the gaping mouth of the creature and down into its gullet.

Sir Galahad went to the table and lifted the cloth; and lo! beneath it was the Holy Chalice.

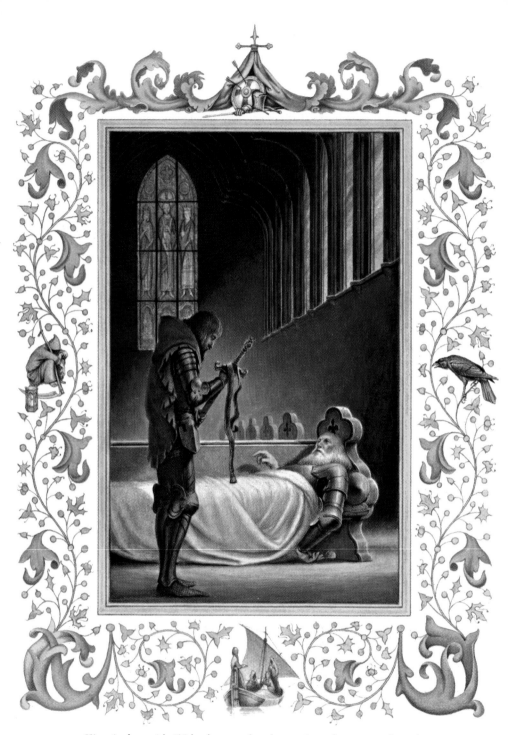

King Arthur said, "Take that sword and carry it to the water and cast it
into the water; then return thou hither and tell me what thou seest."

have listened to your singing for this long while concerning the Lady Belle Isoult. So I would have you go to Ireland, and bring her hence to be my Queen. For because of your songs and ballads I have come to love her." And therewith he smiled upon Sir Tristram very strangely.

Then Sir Tristram perceived how he had been betrayed. He rose, and he gazed for a long while at King Mark, and his countenance was white like that of a dead man. Then by and by he said: "Sir, I have ever served you truly as a worthy knight and kinsman. Wherefore I know not why you have done this unto me, for you know well that if I return to Ireland I shall likely be slain. Yet I would rather lose my life than succeed in this quest. For truly I love the Lady Belle Isoult; wherefore that which you bid me fulfill is more bitter to me than death."

"Well," said King Mark, "I know nothing of all this—only I know that you have given me your knightly word to fulfill this quest."

"Very well," said Sir Tristram, "if God will give me His help, then I will do that which I have pledged my knighthood to undertake." Therewith he went out from the King's Court, and it was as though his heart had been turned into ashes.

Sir Tristram went straightway into a small castle that King Mark had given him some while since, and there he abided for several days in despair, for it seemed to him as though God had deserted him entirely. There Gouvernail alone was with him, but after a while eighteen knights came to him and gave him condolence and offered to join him as knights-companion.

And they said to Sir Tristram: "Sir, you should not lend yourself to such travail of soul, but should bend yourself as a true knight should to assume that burden that God hath assigned you to bear."

So they spoke, and by and by Sir Tristram aroused himself and said to himself: Well, what these gentlemen say is true. So after a day or two Sir Tristram and the knights all took their departure from that castle. Then they took ship with intent to depart from Cornwall for Ireland.

But, upon the second day of their voyaging, there arose a great storm of wind. So the ship fled away before that tempest; and they were forced to seek haven, and they cast anchor under the walls of a castle and a town. And, lo! the town was Camelot.

So they went ashore, and visited with King Arthur and his knights, and even when the storm had passed they stayed on for several days. And at this time Sir Tristram met Sir Launcelot, and they became the best of friends. And there was much friendly jousting and feasting, and, for the while, Sir Tristram forgot the mission he was upon and was happy in heart and glad of that storm that had driven him thitherward.

Now, when they had been at Camelot for several days, as Sir Tristram and King Arthur and Sir Launcelot sat together one day in friendly discourse, there came Gouvernail of a sudden to Sir Tristram, and leaning over his shoulder he said: "Sir, I have just been told that King Angus of Ireland is at this very time at Camelot."

Upon this Sir Tristram turned to King Arthur and said: "Lord, I pray you tell me, is that true?" "Yes," said King Arthur, "that is true; but what of it?" "Well," said Sir Tristram, "I know not whether King Angus may look upon me as a friend or as an unfriend."

"Ha," said King Arthur, "King Angus is at this time in such anxiety that he needs to have every man his friend who will be his friend. One of my best knights, Sir Blamor de Ganis, hath accused him of having murdered Sir Bertrand de la Rivière Rouge, who was found dead at a certain pass in Ireland some time ago. Now King Angus is here upon my summons for to answer that charge, and Sir Blamor offers his body to defend the truth of his accusation. As for the King of Ireland, he can find no knight to take his part in that contention."

"Lord," said Sir Tristram, "what you tell me is very excellent news, for now I know that I may have talk with King Angus, and that he will no doubt receive me as a friend."

So Sir Tristram and Gouvernail went to that place where King Angus had taken up his lodging. And when King Angus saw Sir

Tristram, he gave a great cry of joy, and ran to him and flung his arms about him; for he was rejoiced beyond measure to find a friend in that unfriendly place.

"Lord," quoth Sir Tristram, "I know what trouble overclouds you, and because of that I am come hither. For I have not forgotten how you spared my life in Ireland. So if you will satisfy me upon two points, then I myself will stand for your champion."

"Ah, Tristram," quoth King Angus, "what you say is very good news to me. So tell me what are those two matters concerning which you would seek satisfaction."

"Lord," said Sir Tristram, "the first is that you shall satisfy me that you are innocent of the death of Sir Bertrand. And the second is that you shall grant me whatsoever favor I shall ask."

Then King Angus arose and drew his sword and he said: "Tristram, behold; here is my sword—and the blade and the handle thereof make the sign of the cross. See! I kiss that holy sign, and swear upon it that I am altogether guiltless of the death of that knight aforesaid. Now, Messire, art thou satisfied?"

And Sir Tristram said, "I am satisfied."

Then King Angus said: "As to the matter of granting you a favor, let me hear what it is that you have to ask."

"Lord," cried out Sir Tristram, "the favor is one I had liefer die than ask. It is this: that you give me your daughter, the Lady Belle Isoult, for wife unto mine uncle, King Mark of Cornwall."

Upon these words, King Angus gazed very strangely upon Sir Tristram. Then he said: "Messire, I can in no wise understand why you do not ask for her in your own name."

Then Sir Tristram cried out in despair: "Messire, I love that lady more than my life; but I am fulfilling a pledge made upon the honor of my knighthood. Yet I would liefer die than fulfill it."

"Well," said King Angus, "I will fulfill your boon as I have promised. But as for yourself, you must answer to God and to the honor of your knighthood whether it is better to keep that promise which you made to the King of Cornwall or to break it."

Then Sir Tristram cried out again: "Lord, you know not what you say, nor what torments I am at this present moment enduring."

And therewith he went forth from that place, for he was ashamed that anyone should behold the passion that moved him.

And now it is to be told that, on the following day, Sir Tristram did battle with Sir Blamor de Ganis, and indeed he defeated Sir Blamor, and Sir Blamor withdrew his accusations against King Angus. So all were reconciled and, as they sat at feast in the castle, there came one with news that the name of Sir Tristram had appeared upon one of the seats of the Round Table. So they all immediately went to the pavilion of the Round Table and there, behold! was his name indeed upon a seat:

Sir Tristram of Lyonesse

So the next day Sir Tristram was duly installed as a knight-companion of the Round Table with great pomp and circumstance, and a day or two after that he set sail with King Angus.

And when they reached Ireland, because Sir Tristram had aided the King in his extremity, the Queen forgave him all that she held against him, so that he was received at the Court of the King and Queen with great friendship and honor.

For a while Sir Tristram dwelt in Ireland and said nothing concerning that purpose for which he had come. Then one day he said to King Angus: "Lord, thou art not to forget to fulfill that promise which thou madest to me concerning the Lady Belle Isoult."

To this King Angus made reply: "I had hoped that now you had changed your purpose. Are you yet of the same mind?"

"Yea," said Sir Tristram, "for it cannot be otherwise."

"Well, then," said King Angus, "I shall go to prepare my daughter, though indeed it doth go against my heart to do such a thing."

So King Angus went away, and he was gone a long while. When he returned he said: "Sir, go you that way and the Lady Belle Isoult will see you."

So Sir Tristram went to a great chamber in a tower of the castle up under the eaves of the roof.

The Lady Belle Isoult stood upon the farther side of this chamber so that the light from the windows shone full upon her face, and she was clad altogether in white and her face was like to wax for whiteness and clearness. Her eyes shone very bright like one with a fever, and Sir Tristram beheld that tears stood upon her cheeks like to shining jewels.

So, for a while, Sir Tristram stood without speaking and regarded her from afar. Then after a while she said, "Sir, what is this you have done?"

"Lady," he said, "I have done what God set me to do, though I would rather die than do it."

She said: "Tristram, I beseech you to break this promise you have made, and let us be happy together."

At this Sir Tristram cried out: "Lady, did you put your hand into my bosom and tear my naked heart, you could not cause me so much pain as that which I this moment endure. Were it but myself I might consider, I would freely sacrifice both my life and my honor for your sake. But if I should violate a pledge given upon my knighthood, then would I dishonor that entire order to which I belong."

Then Belle Isoult looked upon Sir Tristram for some little while, and by and by she smiled very pitifully and said: "Ah, Tristram, I believe I am more sorry for thee than I am for myself."

"Lady," said Tristram, "I would God that I lay here dead before you." And therewith he turned and left that place. Only when he had come to a place where he was entirely by himself, he hid his face in his hands and wept as though his heart were broken.

After that, King Angus furnished a very beautiful ship with sails of satin, and he fitted the ship in all ways such as became the daughter of a king. And that ship was intended for the Lady Belle Isoult and Sir Tristram in which to sail to Cornwall.

And it was ordained that a certain excellent lady, who had been attendant upon the Lady Belle Isoult ever since she was a child, was to accompany her to Cornwall. And the name of this lady was the Lady Bragwaine.

Now the day before the Lady Belle Isoult was to take her departure from Ireland, the Queen of Ireland came to the Lady

Bragwaine and she bare with her a curiously wrought flagon of gold. And the Queen said: "Bragwaine, here is a flask of a singular elixir; for that liquor is of such a sort that when a man and a woman drink it together, they two shall thereafter never cease to love one another. Now when the Lady Belle Isoult and King Mark have been wedded, then give them both to drink of this elixir; for then they shall forget all else in the world and cleave only to one another. This I give you to the intent that the Lady Isoult may forget Sir Tristram and become happy in the love of King Mark."

Soon thereafter the party set sail. And one day, whilst they were upon that voyage, the Lady Bragwaine came into the cabin and beheld Belle Isoult lying upon a couch weeping. Dame Bragwaine said, "Lady, why do you weep?" Whereunto Belle Isoult made reply: "Alas, how can I help but weep, seeing that I am to be parted from the man I love and married unto another whom I do not love?"

Dame Bragwaine laughed and said: "Do you then weep for that? See! Here is a wonderful flask as it were of wine. When you are married to the King of Cornwall, then you are to quaff of it and he is to quaff of it and after that you will forget all others in the world, for it is a wonderful love potion."

When the Lady Belle Isoult heard these words she wept no more but smiled strangely. Then by and by she arose and went to where Sir Tristram was. And she said, "Tristram, will you drink of a draught with me?" He said, "Yea, Lady, though it were death in the draught." She said, "There is not death in it, but something very different," and thereupon she fetched the flagon and poured the elixir into a chalice. And she said, "Tristram, I drink to thee," and therewith she drank half of the elixir. Then she said, "Now drink thou the rest to me."

Upon that Sir Tristram took the chalice and drank all the rest of that liquor. Then Sir Tristram felt that elixir run like fire through every vein in his body, and he cried out, "Lady, what is this you have given me?" She said: "Tristram, that was a love potion intended for King Mark and me. But now thou and I have drunk it and never can either of us love anybody but the other."

Then Sir Tristram catched her into his arms and he cried out: "Isoult! Isoult! was it not enough that I should have been unhappy, but that thou shouldst have chosen to be unhappy also?"

Thereat Belle Isoult both wept and smiled, looking up into Sir Tristram's face, and she said: "Nay, Tristram; I would rather be sorry with thee than happy with another." He said, "Isoult, there is much woe in this for us both." She said, "I care not, so I may share it with thee."

Thereupon Sir Tristram kissed her thrice upon the face, and then immediately put her away from him; and he left her and went away by himself in much agony of spirit.

Thereafter they reached Cornwall in safety, and the Lady Belle Isoult and King Mark were wedded with much pomp, and after that there was much feasting and every appearance of rejoicing.

CHAPTER IV: THE MADNESS OF SIR TRISTRAM

AFTER THESE HAPPENINGS, Sir Tristram abode for more than a year at the Court of Cornwall, for so King Mark commanded him to do. And he sought to distract his mind from his sorrows by deeds of prowess. So he performed several adventures of which there is not now space to tell you. But these adventures won him such credit that all the world talked of his greatness.

And ever King Mark hated him more and more. For he could not bear to see Sir Tristram so noble and so sorrowful with love of the Lady Belle Isoult.

In time, not only King Mark but also many of his people hated Sir Tristram at heart; for there were many mischief-makers about the Court who were also jealous of Tristram and who were ever ready to blow the embers of the King's wrath into a flame.

Now the chiefest of all these mischief-makers was Sir Andred, who was nephew unto King Mark, and cousin-german unto Sir Tristram. Sir Andred was a fierce, strong knight, and very dextrous at arms; but he was as mean and as treacherous as Sir Tristram was generous and noble, wherefore he hated Sir Tristram with great bitterness and sought for every opportunity to do Sir Tristram a harm.

So one day Sir Andred came to Sir Tristram and said: "Sir, the Lady Belle Isoult wishes to talk with you in her bower." And Sir Tristram said, "Very well, I will go to her."

So Sir Tristram departed to find the lady; and therewith Sir Andred hurried to King Mark, and said: "Lord, arise, for Sir Tristram and the Lady Isoult are holding converse together in the bower of the Queen."

At that King Mark's rage and jealousy blazed up, so that he was like one seized with a frenzy. So he took a great sword, and ran with all speed to the bower of the Lady Isoult. There he flung open the door and found Sir Tristram and the Lady Isoult sitting together in the seat of a deep window. And he perceived that the Lady Isoult wept and that Sir Tristram's face was very sorrowful. Then King Mark cried out: "Traitor!" And he ran at Sir Tristram and struck furiously at him with the great sword.

Now Sir Tristram was at that time altogether without armor. Accordingly, he was able to be very quick in his movements. So he leaped aside and avoided King Mark's blow. Then he rushed in upon King Mark and wrenched the sword out of his hand.

Then Sir Tristram smote King Mark with the flat of the sword, so that King Mark howled like a wild beast. And King Mark fled, striving to escape, but Sir Tristram pursued him, smiting the King as he ran, over and over, with the flat of the sword.

Then many of the knights of Cornwall came running to defend the King, and with them came Sir Andred. But when Sir Tristram saw them, he struck at them so fiercely that they were filled with terror, and fled. So Sir Tristram cried out, "Certes, these are not knights, but swine!"

Thereafter he went to his chamber and armed himself, and after that he took horse and rode away from that place. And only his favorite hound, hight Houdaine, followed him into the forest.

Then, some little while after Sir Tristram had gone, Gouvernail also took horse and rode into the forest, and he searched for a long while until he came upon Sir Tristram seated under a tree. And

Houdaine lay beside Sir Tristram and licked his hand, but Sir Tristram was so deeply sunk in his sorrow that he was unaware that Houdaine licked his hand.

Then Gouvernail said: "Messire, look up and take cheer, for there must yet be joy for thee in the world."

Then Sir Tristram raised his eyes very slowly and he looked at Gouvernail as though not seeing him. Then by and by he said: "Gouvernail, what evil have I done that I should have so heavy a curse laid upon me?"

Gouvernail said, weeping: "Lord, thou hast done no ill, but art in all wise a noble gentleman. Let us go hence, I care not where, so be it that I am with you."

Then Sir Tristram said: "Gouvernail, it is great joy to me that you should love me so greatly. But you may not go with me, for the Lady Belle Isoult hath few friends at the Court of Cornwall, and many enemies, wherefore I would have you return unto her. And take this dog Houdaine with you and bid the Lady Belle Isoult for to keep him by her to remind her of me. For even as this creature is faithful unto me under all circumstances, so am I faithful unto her."

Then Gouvernail wept again, and he said, "Lord, I obey." Therewith he mounted his horse and rode away, and Houdaine followed after him.

After that Sir Tristram wandered for several days in the forest, he knew not whither, for he was bewildered with that which had happened; so that he ate no food and took no rest of any sort. Wherefore he became distraught in his mind. So, after a while, he forgot who he was, and what was his condition, or whence he came. And he took off his armor and cast it away, and roamed half naked through the woodlands.

So he wandered until he failed with faintness, and sank down into the leaves; and I believe that he would then have died, had not certain swineherds of the forest chanced to come that way. These found Sir Tristram lying as though dead, and they gave him to eat so that he revived once more. After that they took him with them, and he dwelt with them in those woodlands. These forest folk played with him and made merry with him, and he made them great sport. For he was ever gentle and mild like a little child.

Now Sir Andred of Cornwall very greatly coveted the possessions of Sir Tristram, so that when several months had passed by and Sir Tristram did not return to Tintagel, he said to himself: Of a surety, Tristram must now be dead in the forest, and, as there is no one nigher of kin to him than I, it is fitting that I should inherit his possessions.

But as Sir Andred could not inherit without proof of the death of Sir Tristram, he suborned a certain wicked lady who dwelt in the forest; and he one day brought that lady before King Mark, and she gave it as her evidence that Sir Tristram had died. And so Sir Andred seized upon the possessions of Sir Tristram.

And when the news was brought to Belle Isoult, she swooned away. Thereafter she mourned continually for Sir Tristram and would not be comforted; for she was like to a woman who hath been widowed from the lover of her youth.

But meanwhile Sir Tristram dwelt with the swineherds for over a year. Then one day Sir Launcelot came riding through the forest, and he came to that place where Sir Tristram and the swineherds abode.

There Sir Launcelot made pause for to rest and to refresh himself. And it chanced that Sir Tristram lay asleep at the edge of the clearing. And Sir Launcelot asked who it was that lay there. To which the chief of the swineherds made reply: "Messire, it is but a poor madman whom we found in the forest."

Sir Launcelot knew not Sir Tristram, for the beard of Sir Tristram had grown down all over his breast, and he was very ragged. But Sir Launcelot beheld that the body of Sir Tristram was very beautiful and strong. Wherefore Sir Launcelot said, "Now I deem that this is no mere madman, but some noble knight in misfortune."

Therewith he touched Sir Tristram gently, and Sir Tristram awoke. And Sir Tristram knew Sir Launcelot not. Yet he felt great tenderness for that noble knight, and he smiled lovingly upon him.

Then Sir Launcelot said, "Fair friend, who art thou?" Whereunto Sir Tristram made reply: "I know not."

Then Sir Launcelot felt great pity, and he said: "Wilt thou go with me into the habitations of men? There I believe thy mind may be made whole again. And when that shall come to pass, I believe the world shall find in thee some great knight it hath lost."

Sir Tristram said: "Sir Knight, though I know not who I am, yet I know that I am not sound in my mind; wherefore I am ashamed to go amongst mankind. Yet I love thee so much that I believe I would go with thee to the ends of the world."

Then Sir Launcelot smiled upon Sir Tristram, and he bade the swineherds clothe Sir Tristram decently. And the two of them went away through the forest, Sir Launcelot proudly riding upon his great horse and Sir Tristram running lightly beside him.

Now Sir Launcelot purposed to take the madman to Camelot; but there were three knights of ill repute who were harrying the west coast of that land, and Sir Launcelot had sworn to seek them out. So he had first of all to go thitherward.

Now the castle of Tintagel lay upon the way that he was to take, and so he brought Sir Tristram to Tintagel. And he said to King Mark: "Pray you to grant me a favor: that you cherish this poor madman and keep him here, treating him kindly, until I shall return from my quest."

And King Mark said with great courtesy: "We will cherish and care for this man while you are away." For he did not recognize Sir Tristram, nor did any of his Court.

CHAPTER V: THE RED ROSE AND THE WHITE

Now while Sir Tristram abode thus at Tintagel, he was allowed to wander whithersoever he chose, for everyone thought that he was only a poor gentle madman. And Sir Tristram could not remember what this place was, yet it was strangely familiar to him.

Now of all those places whereunto he wandered, Sir Tristram found most pleasure in the pleasance of the castle where was a fair garden and fruit trees; for it was there that he and the Lady Isoult had walked together aforetime. Now one day Sir Tristram came wandering thus into that pleasance and he sat under the shade of an apple tree. And there came the Lady Belle Isoult into the garden with her lady, the Dame Bragwaine, and the hound, hight Houdaine. Then Belle Isoult said to Bragwaine: "Who is yonder man under the apple tree?" And Bragwaine replied: "That, Lady, is the gentle madman of the forest whom Sir Launcelot brought hither."

So the Lady Belle Isoult said, "Let us see what manner of man he is." And they went forward, the dog with them.

Then Sir Tristram turned and beheld the Lady Isoult for the first time since he had gone mad; and the lady was looking at him, but knew him not.

Then of a sudden, because of his great love for Belle Isoult, the memory of Sir Tristram came all back to him, and he knew who he was and all that had befallen him. And Sir Tristram was all overwhelmed with shame that he should be thus found by that dear lady; wherefore he turned away his face, for he perceived that she did not know who he was.

Now at that moment the dog, Houdaine, leaped away from the Lady Belle Isoult and ran to Sir Tristram and smelt eagerly of him. And with that he knew his master.

Then the two ladies beheld Houdaine fall down at the feet of Sir Tristram and grovel there with joy. And they beheld that he licked Sir Tristram's feet and his hands and face; and they were greatly astonished.

Then of a sudden Dame Bragwaine catched the Lady Isoult by the arm and she said: "Certes, Lady, that is Sir Tristram."

Therewith, at those words, the scales fell from Belle Isoult's eyes; and with a great cry of joy she ran to Sir Tristram and flung herself at his feet and embraced him about the knees. And she cried out: "Tristram! They told me thou wert dead!" And with that she fell to weeping with a fury of passion.

Then Sir Tristram got to his feet in great haste and he said: "Lady! Stay your passion! For behold, I am alone and unarmed in this castle, and if it be discovered who I am, both thou and I art lost."

Then, perceiving how that Belle Isoult was in a way distracted, he turned to Bragwaine and said to her: "Take thy lady hence and I will find means to come to her in private."

So Bragwaine and Sir Tristram lifted up Belle Isoult, and Bragwaine led her thence; for I believe that Belle Isoult knew not whither she went but walked like one in a swoon.

Now it chanced that Sir Andred had been in a balcony overlooking that pleasance, and so he also wist by now that the madman was Sir Tristram. Therewith he was filled with a great fear lest, if Sir Tristram should escape with his life, he would reclaim his possessions.

So he went to King Mark and said, "Lord, know you who that madman is whom Sir Launcelot hath fetched hither?" King Mark said, "Nay." But with that he fell to trembling, for he began to bethink him who that madman was. "Lord," said Sir Andred, "it is Sir Tristram."

At that King Mark smote his hands together and he fell to laughing and he said to Sir Andred: "Lo! God hath assuredly delivered that traitor into mine hands. For behold! he is unarmed. Go, Messire, with all haste, gather a force, seize him and bind him. Then let justice be executed upon him." And Sir Andred said: "Lord, it shall be done."

Therewith Sir Andred went and armed himself, and he gathered together a number of knights and led them to that pleasance; and there he found Sir Tristram sitting sunk in thought. And when Sir Tristram beheld those armed men, he arose to defend himself. But Sir Andred cried out: "Seize him ere he can strike!"

With that a dozen or more knights flung themselves upon Sir Tristram. And they bore him to the earth, and held him and bound his wrists together. And then they lifted him up and held him there, a knight in armor with a sword standing upon his right hand and another armed knight with a sword standing upon his left hand.

Then Sir Andred came and stood in front of Sir Tristram and taunted him, saying: "Ha, Tristram, how is it with thee now? Lo! thou shalt die no knightly death, but, in a little while, thou shalt be hanged like a thief." Then he laughed, and therewith he lifted his hand and smote Sir Tristram upon the face.

At that blow the rage of Sir Tristram so flamed up in him that his eyes burned as with green fire. And in an instant, so quickly that no man wist what he did, he turned upon that knight who stood at his left, and he lifted up both hands that were bound, and he smote that knight such a blow upon the face that the knight fell down and his sword fell out of his hand. Then Sir Tristram snatched the sword and he smote the knight upon his right so that he too fell down. Then Sir Tristram turned upon Sir Andred, and lifting high the sword with both hands tied, he smote him so terrible a blow that the blade cut through his épaulière and half through his body.

At that great blow the breath fled out of Sir Andred with a groan, and he fell and immediately died.

Now all this had happened so suddenly that they who beheld it stood staring. But when they beheld Sir Tristram turn upon them with that sword lifted high, terror seized them and they fled, yelling. Then, when they were gone, Sir Tristram set the point of his sword upon the pavement and the pommel against his breast, and he drew the bonds that held his wrists across the edge of the sword so that they were cut and he was free.

Then Sir Tristram looked about him for some place of refuge; and he beheld that the door of the chapel which opened upon the courtyard stood ajar. So he ran into the chapel and shut and bolted the door. But a great party of King Mark's people brought rams for to batter in the door. So Sir Tristram ran to a window of the chapel and looked out thence. And lo! twelve fathoms below him was the sea, and the rocks of the shore upon which the castle was built. Sir Tristram said, "Better death there than here," and he leaped out from the window ledge, and thence he dived down into the sea; and no one saw that terrible leap that he made. So he sank down deep into the sea, but met no rocks, so that he presently came up again safe and sound. Then, looking about him, he perceived a cave in the rocks, and thither he swam to find shelter for a little.

Now when they who had come against him had broken into the chapel they all ran in in one great crowd. But lo! Sir Tristram was not there. Then they were greatly astonished; but one of them perceived where the window of the chapel stood open, and therewith several of them ran there and looked out. And they wist that Sir Tristram had leaped out thence into the sea, and so they thought that he must now be dead. So thereupon they shut the window and went their ways.

Now when all this affair was over and night had fallen, Gouvernail sought out a knight hight Sir Santraille who was a friend to Sir Tristram. To him Gouvernail said: "Messire, I do not think that Sir Tristram is dead, for he hath always been a most wonderful swimmer and diver. But if he be alive, and we do not save him, he will assuredly perish when the tide comes up and covers over those rocks amongst which he may now be hidden."

So Gouvernail and Sir Santraille went to that chapel unknown to anyone, and they opened the window and leaned out and called upon Sir Tristram in low voices.

Then after a while Sir Tristram recognized Gouvernail's voice and answered them. Then Gouvernail and Sir Santraille got a rope, and lowered the rope down to the rocks, and Sir Tristram climbed up the rope to the chapel. And at that time it was nigh to midnight and very dark.

And when Sir Tristram stood with them, he said at once: "Messires, how doth it fare with the Lady Belle Isoult?"

To this Sir Santraille made reply: "Sir, the lady hath been locked into a tower, and she is a prisoner."

Then Sir Tristram said: "How many knights are there here who are my friends, and who will stand with me to break out hence?" To this Gouvernail said: "Lord, there are twelve besides ourselves."

Sir Tristram said: "Provide me with arms and armor and bring those twelve hither, armed. But first let them saddle horses for themselves and for us and for the Lady Isoult and for Dame Bragwaine. When this is done, we will depart from this place, and I do not think there will be any in the castle will dare stop us."

So it was done as Sir Tristram commanded, and then Sir Tristram and several knights of his party went openly to that tower where the Lady Isoult was prisoner and they burst open the doors and went in.

And Sir Tristram said to Belle Isoult: "Dear love, never again will I entrust thee unto King Mark's hands; for I have great fear that if he have thee he will work vengeance upon thee. So, love, I come to take thee away from this place; and never again, right or wrong, shalt thou be without the shelter of my arm."

Then the Lady Belle Isoult smiled very wonderfully upon Sir Tristram. And she said: "Tristram, I will go with thee whithersoever thou wilt, even to the grave, for I believe that I should be happy even there, so that thou wert lying beside me."

With that Sir Tristram kissed Belle Isoult upon the forehead, and then he lifted her up and carried her down the stairs of the tower and sat her upon her horse. And Bragwaine followed after, and Gouvernail lifted her up upon her horse. And all they of that castle were so amazed that no one stayed them. And they rode across the drawbridge and into the forest, betaking their way toward a certain castle of Sir Tristram's, which they reached in the clear dawning of the daytime.

And so Sir Tristram brought the Lady Belle Isoult away from Tintagel and into safety.

NOW TWO DAYS AFTER those things aforesaid had come to pass, Sir Launcelot returned unto Tintagel from his quest; and when he learned all that had happened, he went through the forest until he reached that castle whereunto Sir Tristram had taken the Lady Belle Isoult. And he besought them to come with him to Joyous Gard, where they might be more safe from the vengeance of King Mark. Wherefore they and their court did depart for Joyous Gard, where they were received with great honor and rejoicing.

So the Lady Belle Isoult abode for three years at Joyous Gard, dwelling there as queen paramount in all truth and innocence of life; and Sir Launcelot and Sir Tristram were her champions. And indeed I believe this was the happiest time of all the Lady

Belle Isoult's life, for she lived there in peace and love and she suffered neither grief nor misfortune in all that time.

Then one day came King Arthur to Joyous Gard, and a great feast was set in his honor. And after the feast King Arthur and Sir Tristram and Belle Isoult sat together in converse.

Then after a while King Arthur said, "Lady, may I ask you a question?" And at that Belle Isoult said, "Ask thy question, Lord King." "Lady," said King Arthur, "answer me this: is it better to dwell in honor with sadness or in dishonor with joy?"

Then Belle Isoult began to pant with great agitation, and she said, "Lord, why ask you me that?" King Arthur said: "Because, Lady, I think your heart hath sometimes asked you the selfsame question." Then Belle Isoult cried out: "Yea, yea, my heart hath often asked me that, but I would not answer it." King Arthur said: "Neither shalt thou answer me, for I am but a weak and erring man as thou art a woman. But answer thou that question to God, dear Lady, and then thou shalt answer it in truth."

Therewith King Arthur fell to talking of other things with Sir Tristram. And Belle Isoult said no more. But three days after that she came to Sir Tristram and said: "Dear Lord, I have bethought me much of what King Arthur said, and this hath come of it, that I must return again unto Cornwall."

Then Sir Tristram turned away his face so that she might not see it, and he said, "Methought it would come to that."

So it came about that peace was made betwixt Sir Tristram and King Mark, and Belle Isoult and King Mark, and King Arthur was the peacemaker.

Thereafter Sir Tristram and the Lady Belle Isoult returned unto Cornwall, and there they dwelt for some time in seeming peace. But in that time the Lady Belle Isoult would never see King Mark nor exchange a word with him, but lived entirely apart from him in her own part of the castle; and at that King Mark was struck with such bitterness and hatred that he was like to a demon in torment. So he set spies to watch Sir Tristram, for in his evil heart he still suspected Sir Tristram of treason. But those spies could find nothing that Sir Tristram did that was amiss.

Now one day Belle Isoult could not refrain from sending a note beseeching Sir Tristram to come to her; and though he misdoubted what he did, yet he went as she desired.

Then came those spies to King Mark and told him that Sir Tristram had gone to the bower of the Lady Belle Isoult.

At that the vitals of King Mark were twisted with an agony of hatred. And he went quickly to that part of the castle where the Lady Belle Isoult inhabited; and he went very softly through a passage to where was a door with curtains; and he parted the curtains and peeped within. And he beheld that the Lady Belle Isoult and Sir Tristram sat at a game of chess, and that they played not at the game but that they sat talking together very sadly; and he beheld that Dame Bragwaine sat in a window to one side. And King Mark trembled with a torment of jealousy. So he went very quietly back into the passageway. There he perceived a great glaive upon a pole two ells long. This he took into his hand and returned unto that curtained doorway. Then he parted the curtains silently and stepped into the room. And the back of Sir Tristram was toward him. Then King Mark lifted the glaive on high and he struck; and Sir Tristram sank without a sound.

Yes, I believe that that good knight knew naught of what had happened until he awoke in Paradise.

Then Belle Isoult arose, overturning the table of chessmen. She made no sound of any sort. But she stood looking down at Sir Tristram, and then she kneeled down beside his body and touched the face thereof as though to make sure that it was dead. Therewith, as though being assured, she fell down with her body upon his; and King Mark stood there looking down upon them.

All this had passed so quickly that Dame Bragwaine hardly knew what had befallen; but now she fell to shrieking. At this, several knights of the court of Sir Tristram came running in and beheld what had happened. Then all stood aghast at that sight.

But one very young, gallant knight, hight Sir Alexander, came to where King Mark stood looking down upon his handiwork as though entranced with what he had done. Then Sir Alexander said, "Is this thy work?" And King Mark answered, "Ay!" Then Sir

Alexander cried out, "Thou hast lived too long!" And drawing his dagger, he drave it into the side of King Mark, and King Mark groaned and sank upon the ground, and died where he lay.

Then those knights lifted up the Lady Belle Isoult; but, lo! the soul had left her, and she was dead. For I believe that it was not possible for one of those loving souls to leave its body without the other quitting its body also, so that they might meet together in Paradise.

And so they two were buried with the graves close together, and it is said by many that there grew a rose tree up from Sir Tristram's grave, and down upon the grave of Belle Isoult; and it is said that this rose tree was a miracle, for that upon his grave there grew red roses, and upon her grave there grew pure white roses. For her soul was white like to thrice-carded wool, and his soul was red with all that was of courage or knightly pride.

And I pray that God may rest the souls of those two as I pray He may rest the souls of all of us who must some time go the way that those two and so many others have traveled before us. Amen.

Now here followeth more about Sir Launcelot. And here followeth also the history of Elaine the Fair, and of how Sir Launcelot came to know her.

PART IV—ELAINE THE FAIR

CHAPTER I: SIR LAUNCELOT BATTLES THE WORM OF CORBIN

ONE EVENING, WHEN SIR LAUNCELOT was riding errant about the countryside in search of adventure, darkness began to fall when he was far from any town or castle or shelter. The earth melted here and there into shadow; and Sir Launcelot was hungry, and he wist not where he might find refreshment.

So, thinking of this, he was presently aware of a light shining in the gray of the twilight, and thitherward he directed his way, and he came to where there was a merry party of strolling minstrels gathered around a fire. Some of them were clad in blue and some in yellow and some in red. And all were eating with great appetite a savory stew of mutton and lentils seasoned with onions and washed down with lusty draughts of ale and wine.

These jolly fellows, beholding Sir Launcelot, gave him welcome and besought him to eat with them, and Sir Launcelot was right glad to do so. So he dismounted and turned his horse loose to browse, and he sat down with those minstrels.

Then, after they all had supped their fill, several of the minstrels brought forth lutes, and anon one sang a rondel in praise of his sweetheart's eyes, and another sang a song of battle, and still another sang a song in praise of pleasant living; and Sir Launcelot listened to their music with great pleasure.

So with good cheer the night passed away until the great moon, like to a bubble of shining silver, floated high in the sky above their heads. Then perceiving it to be midnight, Sir Launcelot bestirred himself and said: "Good fellows, I thank ye with all my heart for the entertainment, but now I must go upon my way."

To this the chief of the minstrels said: "Sir Knight, we would fain that you would remain with us tonight and would travel with us tomorrow, for indeed you are the pleasantest knight that ever we met."

At this Sir Launcelot laughed, and he said: "Good fellows, I give you gramercy. Ye are indeed a merry company, and were I not a knight methinks I would rather be one of your party than one of any other. But lo! I am a knight and I must e'en go about my business. Ne'ertheless you may haply do me one service, and that is to tell me whether anywhere hereabout is to be found an adventure such as may beseem a knight of good credit to undertake."

Upon this one of those minstrels spake: "Messire, I know where there is an adventure which, if you achieve it, will bring you such great credit that I believe Sir Launcelot himself would not have greater credit than you."

At this Sir Launcelot laughed again. "What then is that adventure?" he asked.

"Messire," quoth the minstrel, "you are to know that some ways east of this place there is a large fair town hight Corbin; and the king of that country is King Pelles. Now one time Queen Morgana le Fay was on a visit to Corbin, and she grew angry with King Pelles because of an imagined slight. Thus it was that when she quitted the Court, as she and her attendants passed by the market-place she perceived where there lay a great flat stone. Then Queen Morgana le Fay cried out: 'Beneath that stone there shall breed a great Worm and that Worm shall bring sorrow and dole to this place! For that stone shall be enchanted so that no man may lift it. And beneath that stone the Worm shall live; and ever and anon it shall come forth and seize some fair young virgin of this town and shall bear her away to its hiding place and there devour her for its food.'

"So it was as the Queen said, and now that Worm dwelleth at Corbin, and ever bringeth sorrow to that place. So if any champion shall achieve the death of that Worm, he shall have done a deed worthy of Sir Launcelot himself."

"Friend," said Sir Launcelot, "that were indeed a worthy quest for a knight. As for me, I am so eager to enter upon that quest that I can hardly stay my patience."

With this saying, Sir Launcelot rose, mounted his horse and took his leave of the minstrels.

He rode toward the eastward through the moonlit night, and by and by he entered a great forest land. And somewhile after that the summer day began to dawn and all the birds began to chirp in every thicket.

And when the sun had risen very high in the heaven Sir Launce-lot came out of the forest into open country; and then, a great way off, he beheld a fair walled town set upon a hill with a shining river at its foot. When he had come close to the town he met a party of townsfolk with several pack mules laden with parcels. These Sir Launcelot bespoke, saying, "I pray ye, fair folk, tell me, is this Corbin?" Thereunto they replied, "Yea, Sir Knight, this is." Sir Launcelot said, "Why are ye so sad and downcast?" Whereunto the chief of that party—a man with a long white beard—made reply: "Sir Knight, have you not heard how we are cursed in this town by a Worm?"

"Sir," quoth Sir Launcelot, "I have indeed heard of this Worm that bringeth you so much woe, and I purpose, if God's grace be with me, to destroy that vile thing."

Now the hearts of those who heard Sir Launcelot were filled with hope, and they followed him as he rode into Corbin, crying out the news of his coming. And a great multitude gathered, lifting up their voices in loud acclaim and blessing him as he rode.

So, upborne by that multitude, Sir Launcelot went steadfastly toward the marketplace, in the midst of which lay that great stone. And when he had reached the place, the people stood afar off, and Sir Launcelot went forward alone to the slab of stone. And he looked down upon the slab and beheld that it was very wide and so big that three men might hardly hope to lift it.

Now you are to remember that Sir Launcelot wore a ring which the Lady of the Lake had given him when he quitted the Lake; and that ring was of such a sort that he who wore it might dissolve all magic directed against him. Wherefore Sir Launcelot put aside his sword and his shield and he seized the slab in both hands. And he bent his back and lifted, and lo! the bands of enchantment that lay upon the stone were snapped, and the slab stirred. Therewith Sir Launcelot bent again and heaved with all his might. And lo! he lifted the stone and rolled it over upon the earth.

Then he looked down into the hole beneath and he beheld two green and glassy eyes that looked up at him. And as Sir Launcelot gazed a huge worm began to crawl out of the hole, and it was covered all over with livid scales. And the Worm lifted the forepart of its body to the height of a tall man and gaped dreadfully with a mouth an ell wide, and all glistening with rows of teeth. And the Worm had as many as a thousand feet, and each foot was armed with a great claw like the claw of a lion, but as hard as flint, and venomous with poison. And the Worm hissed at Sir Launcelot. And its breath was like the odor of Death.

And when the people of the town saw that dreadful Worm appear, they shrieked aloud. But Sir Launcelot seized his sword in both hands, and he ran at the Worm and lashed at it a blow that might easily have split an oak tree. But the scales of the Worm were like adamant for hardness, wherefore the stroke of the sword glanced aside without harming the creature.

Then the Worm hissed again in a manner very terrible, and it strove to catch Sir Launcelot into the embrace of its claws. But Sir Launcelot sprang aside and he smote the Worm again and again, yet he could not cut through its scales. And at every blow the Worm hissed more terribly and sought to catch Sir Launcelot.

Thus for a time Sir Launcelot avoided the Worm; but by and by he began to wax weary with leaping from side to side, weighed down as he was with his armor. So at last it befell that the Worm catched Sir Launcelot in the hook of one of its claws, and in a moment it had embraced Sir Launcelot in several hundred of its claws so that his body was well-nigh hidden in that embrace. And the Worm tore at Sir Launcelot and strove to bite him with its teeth. And it cut with its claws through Sir Launcelot's armor and into the flesh of his left shoulder and through the flesh of his thigh to the bone.

Then Sir Launcelot put forth all his strength and tore free from the clutches of the Worm. And catching the haft of his sword in both of his hands, he stabbed with his sword into the gaping mouth of the creature and down into its gullet. At that, the Worm roared like a bull in torment, and it straightway rolled over upon the ground, writhing and lashing its entire body.

And Sir Launcelot, looking down upon the lashings of the Worm, beheld where there appeared to be a soft place nigh to the belly, and he plunged his sword twice and thrice into that soft spot, whereupon, lo! thick blood gushed forth. And presently the Worm ceased to bellow and lay rustling its dry scales upon the earth in its last throes of life.

Then Sir Launcelot stood leaning upon his sword, panting and covered with blood. And the people fell to shouting aloud beyond measure, and they gazed upon Sir Launcelot in wonder. And then they sent for a litter and they laid Sir Launcelot upon it and bare him into the castle of Corbin. And attendants eased him of his armor, and a leech searched his wounds and bound them up. And after that they bare Sir Launcelot to a fair soft couch spread with snow-white linen and laid him thereon, and he was at ease and much comforted in body.

Then there came King Pelles to visit Sir Launcelot. And King Pelles was a very noble, haughty lord, with a beard and hair like to the mane of a lion, and he was clad in a robe of purple studded with jewels. Upon the right hand of King Pelles there came his son, Sir Lavaine—a very noble young knight—and upon his left hand there came his daughter, the Lady Elaine the Fair.

Then Sir Launcelot looked upon the Lady Elaine and it seemed to him that she was the most beautiful maiden that ever he had beheld. For her hair was soft and yellow and shining; her eyebrows were curved and very fine; her eyes were very large, and her cheeks were like roses for softness of blush.

Such was the Lady Elaine, and Sir Launcelot was amazed at her beauty, and at the tender grace of her virgin youth.

Then King Pelles spake, saying: "Messire, what thanks shall we find fit to give you who have freed this land from its curse?"

"Lord," said Sir Launcelot, "give thanks to God whose tool and instrument I was." "Messire," quoth King Pelles, "I have not forgot to give thanks to God. Ne'ertheless seeing the instrument which He hath used, I pray you tell me who you are."

"Lord," said Sir Launcelot, "you must forgive me if I tell you not my name. For there is supposed to be shame upon my name, wherefore you may call me le Chevalier Malfait."

"Well," quoth King Pelles, "it shall be as you will, and with us you shall be known as le Chevalier Malfait until it pleases you to assume your proper name."

Now Sir Launcelot did not recover from his hurt as soon as he had supposed he would. For the venom of the Dragon had got into his blood, wherefore even after a twelvemonth he still remained in the castle of King Pelles at Corbin, albeit he was by that time quite healed in his body.

Meantime, and for all that while, there was great wonder at the Court of King Arthur whither Sir Launcelot had gone and what had become of him.

CHAPTER II: A TOURNAMENT AT ASTOLAT

Now WHEN Sir Launcelot had been at Corbin over a year, King Arthur proclaimed a great tournament to be held at Astolat. And the King sent word of this tournament throughout the land. And so King Pelles at Corbin ordained that his Court should make ready to go to Astolat to that passage of arms.

Then Sir Launcelot was troubled, for he said to himself, I fear me that if I go unto Astolat there may be someone there who will know me. For he was still bitterly affronted that his kinsmen had chid him so greatly for riding in the cart as aforetold. And until full justification had been rendered unto him, he was unwilling that any of his former companions should behold him. Yet as he was now one of the Court of the King of Corbin he was bound to obey whatsoever that king should command him. So when the time came Sir Launcelot made him ready to go with the others to

Astolat, but he planned not to take part in the knightly tournament.

Now the Lady Elaine was not very well pleased with this, for she held Sir Launcelot in great admiration above all other men, and she would fain have had him stand forth with the other knights. So one day whilst they two sat together in the garden of the castle the Lady Elaine spake to Sir Launcelot saying: "Fair sir, will you not take part in this noble tournament the day after tomorrow?"

To this Sir Launcelot replied, "Nay, Lady."

She said to him: "Why will you not, Messire? Methinks with your prowess you might win yourself great credit."

Then after a little Sir Launcelot said to her: "Lady, do you dis-remember that I call myself le Chevalier Malfait? That name I have assumed because my friends and my kinsmen deem that I have done amiss in a certain thing. Now since they are of that opinion I am greatly displeased with them, and I would fain avoid them. At this tournament there will be many of those who knew me afore-time; wherefore I am disinclined to take part in the battle."

After this they were silent for a little, and then the Lady Elaine said: "Sir Knight Malfait, I would I knew who you really are." At that Sir Launcelot smiled and said: "Lady, I may not tell you at this present."

So at that time no more was said concerning this matter, but ever the mind of the Lady Elaine rested upon that thing—to wit, that Sir Launcelot should take part in that tournament. So at another time she said: "Sir Knight Malfait, I would that thou wouldst suffer me to purvey thee a suit of strange armor so that thy friends might not know thee therein, and that thou wouldst go to the tournament disguised in that wise. And I would that thou wouldst wear my favor at that tournament so that I might have glory in that battle because of thee."

Then Sir Launcelot sighed, and he said: "Lady, I must tell you that never have I worn the favor of any lady, having vowed my knighthood to one who is a queen. Ne'ertheless, I would freely lay down my life at your bidding. So in this case I will even do as you ask me."

Thereat the Lady Elaine smiled upon Sir Launcelot, and both

her joy and her great love stood revealed in that smile. Quoth she: "Assuredly I shall gain great honor at thy hands. For I believe that thou art indeed one of the greatest knights in the world."

Now the Lady Elaine went and obtained armor for the use of Sir Launcelot; and after this had been accomplished, she came to Sir Launcelot's chamber, and her brother Sir Lavaine was with her. And the lady bore in her hand a sleeve of flame-colored satin richly bedight with pearls. And she said to Sir Launcelot: "I beseech you to take this sleeve, Sir Knight, and wear it as a favor for my sake."

Then Sir Launcelot smiled very kindly upon the Lady Elaine and he said, "Will this give you pleasure?" and she said, "Yea." Then Sir Launcelot smiled again and said, "It shall be in all things as you will have it." So he took the sleeve, and he wound it about the crest of his helmet, and the sleeve formed a wreath about the helmet like to a wreath of fire.

Then Sir Lavaine said: "Sir Knight Malfait, I beseech you that you will take me with you unto this tournament as your knight-companion."

Then Sir Launcelot said: "Friend, I will gladly accept thee as my companion in arms."

And Sir Launcelot said to the Lady Elaine: "Lady, mine own shield and all mine armor were given to me by a wonderful lady who is not of this world. Now I beseech you for to take them to your bower and to hold them in trust for me." And the Lady Elaine said: "It shall be as you say."

So the next day Sir Launcelot and Sir Lavaine betook their way to Astolat with the Court of King Pelles. And at Astolat they lodged with a certain old and worthy knight hight Sir Bernard.

Now the habitation of Sir Bernard was a fair house over against the castle of Astolat where King Arthur and his Court were staying. And there was a high garden belonging to the castle, and the garden overlooked the garden of Sir Bernard. That day it chanced that King Arthur was walking back and forth in that garden where the air blew cool over the flowers and grass. As the King so walked he chanced to look down into the garden of Sir Bernard's house, and at that time Sir Launcelot was walking privily in the garden for to refresh himself.

The King was much astonished to see Sir Launcelot in that place, and at first he was of a mind to send word to Sir Launcelot, bidding him to come to him. But afterward he bethought him that mayhap Sir Launcelot did not choose to be known to anyone at that time. So King Arthur said to himself: Well, let be! Tomorrow, I dare say, Sir Launcelot will declare himself in such a wise as shall astonish a great many knights who shall battle him. Wherefore let him e'en declare himself in his own fashion.

IT IS TRUE THAT in these days one may not hope ever to behold a sight like to the field of battle at Astolat, when that tournament proclaimed by King Arthur was about to be fought. For upon that morning—which was wonderfully bright and clear and warm— the entire green meadow was covered over with a moving throng of people of all degrees. And here were gay attires and colors and the fluttering of silk and the flash of shining baubles, and the whole world appeared to be quick with life and motion.

Yet little by little that multitude took seat; and so it came to pass at last that the field was cleared for battle.

Then the marshal of the tourney blew his trumpet, and straight-way there entered upon that wide meadow two companies of knights. Then, lo! how the sunlight flashed upon shining armor! How it catched the bannerets so that they twinkled at tips of lances like to sparks of fire! How war-horses neighed for love of battle! How armor clashed as those goodly knights brought themselves into array!

Upon the one end of the meadow there gathered the knights-champion of King Arthur; and their chiefs were the King of Scots and the King of Ireland. And the knights of that company numbered two hundred and ten.

Upon the other end of the meadow there assembled those who were to withstand the party of King Arthur; and their chiefs were the King of North Wales and the King of Northumberland. And though there were no knights of the Round Table in that company, yet there were many champions of great renown. And that party numbered two hundred thirty and two.

Now near to a certain part of the field of battle the forest came close to the meadow. Here, beneath the shade of the trees, Sir Launcelot and Sir Lavaine took stand and looked out upon those two parties of knights. The eyes of Sir Lavaine shone like sparks, and his breath was thick and stifled when he breathed, for this was the first great battle in which he had ever taken a part. He said to Sir Launcelot, "Messire, upon what side do we take part in this battle?" And Sir Launcelot said: "Let us wait awhile and observe the issue, and when we behold that one side is about to lose then will we join with that side." And Sir Lavaine said, "Sir, thou speakest with wisdom."

Then the herald blew his trumpet and the two parties rushed the one upon the other in an uproar of iron and cracking of wood. Then all the air was full of dust and splinters and scraps of silk and of plumes. Anon, out of a thick cloud of dust there arose the shouts of men, the neighing of horses, and the crash of blows. At times, some knight would come forth out of the press reeling in the saddle and all red from some wound. At other times, a party of esquires would run into that cloud, presently to come forth again bearing with them a wounded knight.

And for a while no one could see how the battle went. But after a while the dust lifted a little, and those who contended became fewer upon one side than upon the other. And those who looked upon that battle beheld that the party of King Arthur was pushing their opponents back, little by little, toward the barriers upon their side of the field.

Then Sir Launcelot said to Sir Lavaine: "Now let us take side with that side which is so sore bested."

So Sir Launcelot and Sir Lavaine rode out from the forest, and they set their spears and they drove forward full tilt into the thickest of the press.

In this charge and in other charges that he made in that onset, Sir Launcelot smote down Sir Brandiles, and Sir Sagramore, and Sir Dodinas, and Sir Kay, and Sir Griflet, and he smote down all those good knights of the Round Table with one spear ere that spear burst asunder. And Sir Lavaine smote down Sir Lucian and Sir Bedivere with one spear in that charge and then that spear also was burst. And then Sir Launcelot got him another spear and Sir Lavaine did likewise and they two charged again. And in this assault Sir Launcelot smote down four more knights, and Sir Lavaine smote down two, and then those second spears were burst. So at that each drew his sword and smote right and left so that in a wonderfully short pass they had smitten down still more knights.

By now all who looked upon that field were aware of how terrible a battle it was that the knight of the red sleeve fought, wherefore they shouted with loud acclaim. And the Lady Elaine the Fair wept and trembled for joy. And King Arthur said to those about him: "Saw ye ever a better battle than that?" And they said, "Nay, never so great a battle!"

And it stands recorded that all in all in that battle Sir Launcelot struck down thirty knights, and that sixteen of those were knights of the Round Table. And Sir Lavaine struck down fourteen knights and six of those were knights of the Round Table. And beholding how Sir Launcelot and Sir Lavaine fought, their party took great heart and added strength to strength and drave their enemies back across the meadow against the barriers of their side and so the battle was won.

But Sir Launcelot paid a price; for toward the end of the battle five knights of the Round Table joined to attack him; and in that charge the spear of one smote Sir Launcelot in the side, and thrust deep, and the head of the spear brake and remained in the side of Sir Launcelot. So now that the battle was over Sir Launcelot sat wounded nigh to death, and an exceeding faintness overclouded his spirit.

To him came the King of North Wales and the King of Northumberland, and these said to him: "Sir, God bless you, for without your aid and that of your companion this day had certes been lost to us. Now we pray that you will come with us to King Arthur so that you may receive the prize you so worshipfully deserve."

Then Sir Launcelot spake in a very weak voice. And he said:

"Fair lords, if I have won credit in this I have paid a price for it, for I am sore hurt. Now I pray that you will suffer me to depart from this place, for I would fain go where I may have aid and comforts."

So they suffered him, and he rode very slowly away from that place, and Sir Lavaine rode with him.

CHAPTER III: THE HERMIT OF THE FOREST

AFTER SIR LAUNCELOT and Sir Lavaine had ridden a mile or two into the woodland, Sir Launcelot let droop his head and he groaned with great dolor. "Woe is me!" he said. "I suffer much pain." And therewith he would have fallen from his horse had not Sir Lavaine catched him and upheld him. Then Sir Launcelot turned his eyes, all faint and dim, upon Sir Lavaine, and he said: "Oh, gentle knight, you must bear me away to the westward. After a while you shall find a path that runs across your way. Take that path toward the right and you will come to the hut of a forest hermit. Bring me to that holy man; for if anyone can cure me he can do so."

So Sir Lavaine, weeping, made a litter of young trees and he bound the litter to the horses. Then he lifted Sir Launcelot from his horse and laid him upon the litter as though he were a little child. Thereafter he took the foremost horse by the bridle, and so they traveled on. And by and by night descended and the moon arose. At last in the moonlight they came to a little chapel built up against the rocks of a cliff. And Sir Lavaine smote upon the door; and therewith the door was opened and there appeared an aged man with a white beard. And that man was the Hermit of the Forest afore spoken of in these histories.

Then when that reverend hermit beheld where Sir Launcelot lay in the litter, he came to him. And, perceiving him to be alive, he aided Sir Lavaine to lift the wounded man and to bear him into the hut and to lay him upon a soft couch of moss. Then the hermit searched Sir Launcelot's wound and plucked out the spear point and bathed the wound and bound it with bandages. And after that

Sir Launcelot fell into a sleep so profound that it was like to the slumber of a little child.

Now that same night a great feast was held at Astolat. And King Arthur looked all about but he beheld no sign of Sir Launcelot, wherefore he said to the King of North Wales: "Where is that worthy knight who was with you today—he who wore about his helmet a flame-colored sleeve?" To this the King of North Wales replied: "Lord, that champion proclaimed himself to be sore wounded and craved our leave to withdraw; and we know not whither he hath gone."

Then King Arthur was much grieved and he said: "That is sad news, for rather would I lose half of my kingdom than that death should befall that champion." So said King Arthur, for he wist that champion of the red sleeve must be Sir Launcelot. Yet he would not say who he was, for he perceived that Sir Launcelot would fain conceal his name.

But when that feast was over, King Arthur took Sir Gawaine aside, and he said to him: "Sir, I would that you would seek out that knight of the red sleeve and bring him aid and succor."

Sir Gawaine said: "Lord, I pray you tell me; who is that knight?"

"When you have succored him then you will know who he is," said King Arthur.

So Sir Gawaine withdrew from the Court to seek that wounded champion. And he remembered him that the knight's companion in arms was Sir Lavaine, the son of King Pelles. So Sir Gawaine rode forth to where King Pelles had taken up his lodging, and he was brought before the King. And the Lady Elaine was with King Pelles, and Sir Gawaine, when he beheld her, was amazed at her beauty.

Then Sir Gawaine said to King Pelles: "Fair Lord, can you tell me where I shall find that knight who was with your son?" King Pelles said, "Alas! we have heard that he was wounded, but I know not where he is." Sir Gawaine said, "Lord, I pray you tell me who he is." To this King Pelles made reply: "Messire, I know not who that knight is saving only that he calls himself le Chevalier Malfait and that he came to us somewhat more than a year ago."

And Sir Gawaine said: "Then I pray you tell me who was the lady who gave her sleeve unto him, for she may know who he is."

Then the Lady Elaine said: "Messire, I gave my sleeve to him, yet neither do I know who he is."

Sir Gawaine said: "Have you naught that you may know him by?" Whereunto the Lady Elaine made reply: "Sir, he confided his armor and his shield to me that I might hold them in safekeeping for him."

Then Sir Gawaine said, "Let me see that shield." And the Lady Elaine sent her attendants and they brought the shield to her. Then Sir Gawaine unlaced the leather from the shield, and lo! the shield shone all dazzling bright, and the device upon it was a knight kneeling to a lady, and by that Sir Gawaine knew that it was the shield of Sir Launcelot.

Thereupon he turned him to the Lady Elaine the Fair and he said: "Lady, it is no wonder that this knight should have done so well in battle. For this is the shield of Sir Launcelot of the Lake. So I wish you much joy of that honor that hath come to you; for never before this hath Sir Launcelot worn the favor of any lady to battle."

When the Lady Elaine knew that it was Sir Launcelot to whom she had given her sleeve, she had much joy that she should have been so honored. And yet when she bethought herself how she had set her regard upon him who regarded no lady in the light of love she was filled with a sort of terror because she forecast that nothing but sorrow could come to her who had placed her heart in his keeping.

But the spirit of King Pelles was greatly uplifted with the thought that Sir Launcelot should have been a knight of his Court, and he said: "Messire, this is a wonderful thing that you tell us."

"Lord," said Sir Gawaine, "I do indeed give you great joy of this honor; for I must tell you that yours is the only Court in the world in which Sir Launcelot has ever served as champion, saving only the Court of King Arthur."

With that, Sir Gawaine departed from that place to return to the King's Court which was still at Astolat, there to bring them news that it was Sir Launcelot who had fought in that battle.

But when that news came to Queen Guinevere she was filled full of indignation. For Sir Launcelot had vowed vows of service unto Queen Guinevere, and she upon her part had acknowledged him as her knight-champion. Wherefore, finding he had worn the favor of another lady, she was filled with a most consuming anger. And after a while she sent for Sir Bors de Ganis, who was kin to Sir Launcelot, and she said: "What is this your kinsman hath done, Messire? Who ever heard of any knight who would swear his faith to one lady and yet wear the favor of another? So I say Sir Launcelot is forsworn and is no true knight. And I bid you find him and bring him hither that he may answer me to my face for this unknightly faithlessness."

Then many things came into the mind of Sir Bors, wherefore he did not choose to look into the Queen's face, but only bowed and said: "Lady, it shall be as you command."

Thereafter the Queen went into her closet and locked herself in. And she wept amain; and as she wept she communed with her soul, saying: "My soul! My soul! Is it anger thou feelest or is it aught else than anger?"

Now MEANWHILE the Lady Elaine the Fair took great grief concerning the fate of Sir Launcelot. For he lay wounded she knew not where. So upon a day she came to her father, King Pelles, and pleaded that he let her go and seek for Sir Launcelot.

Then King Pelles was very sorry for the Lady Elaine and he embraced her and gave her permission.

So the Lady Elaine the Fair went in search of Sir Launcelot, and her father sent with her an escort of knights and damsels and attendants. These betook their way to Astolat and made inquiry, and there they found a woodchopper who had seen Sir Launcelot and Sir Lavaine when they had entered the forest; and the woodchopper had heard one knight entreat the other to bear him to the cabin of a certain hermit. So the Lady Elaine and her company traveled to the hut of the hermit.

As they drew near they heard the neighing of horses. Then there came one and opened the door of the hut and stood gazing at the

Lady Elaine, shading his eyes from the sun. And Elaine beheld that it was Sir Lavaine, wherefore she cried, "My brother!" Then Sir Lavaine cried in great amazement, "My sister, is it thou?" and therewith he ran to her and she stooped from her horse and kissed him.

Then she said to Sir Lavaine, "How is it with him, doth he live?" Whereunto Sir Lavaine said, "Yea, he liveth, albeit he is weak." She said, "Where is he?" And Sir Lavaine said, "Come." So he lifted Elaine down from her horse and he led her into the hut and there she beheld Sir Launcelot where he lay and lo! his face was white like to wax and his eyes were closed.

So the Lady Elaine went to Sir Launcelot and she kneeled down and the tears ran down her face. Therewith Sir Launcelot opened his eyes and he beheld her and he smiled upon her and said, "Is it thou?" She said: "Yea, Messire." He said, "And have you come hitherward only for to find me?" Whereunto she said, "Yea." Sir Launcelot said, "Why have you taken so great trouble as that on my account?" And at that she bowed her head and said softly, "Certes, thou knowest why."

Then Sir Launcelot said no more but lay gazing upon her. But after a while he sighed deep and said: "Lady, God knows I am no happy man. For even though I may see happiness within my reach, yet I cannot reach out my hand to take it. For my faith lieth pledged in the keeping of one and that one can never be aught to me but what she now is. And it is my unhappy lot that whether it be wrong or whether it be right I would not have it otherwise."

Now the Lady Elaine wist that Sir Launcelot spake of Queen Guinevere. And Elaine wept and said, "Alas, Launcelot, I have great pity both for thee and for me." And at that Sir Launcelot sighed again and said, "Yea, it is great pity."

Then after a while the Lady Elaine came out from where Sir Launcelot lay, and she gave command to her escort that they should abide at that place until the wounded knight was healed.

And by the end of a month Sir Launcelot was healed of his infirmities. And they traveled by easy stages back to Corbin, and there Sir Launcelot was received with great rejoicing.

It hath been told how that Queen Guinevere bade Sir Bors for to go seek Sir Launcelot. Now one day Sir Bors had news that Sir Launcelot was at the Court of King Pelles; so he went thither.

When Sir Launcelot beheld Sir Bors, such joy seized upon him that he ran to Sir Bors and embraced him with great passion.

Then presently Sir Bors took Sir Launcelot aside and he said to him, "Sir Knight, I bear a message from Queen Guinevere and it is that you return immediately to the Court of King Arthur and present yourself to her."

After Sir Bors had thus spoken, Sir Launcelot turned him away. Then after a considerable while he said, "Sir, would you return to Camelot if you were me?" Sir Bors said, "That I cannot tell." Then after another while Sir Launcelot cried out: "Nay, I will not go; for though my heart lieth there and not here, yet I hold the happiness of another in my hand and I cannot cast it away."

"Then," quoth Sir Bors, "I will return and tell them at the Court that your honor binds you here."

So Sir Bors returned to the Court of King Arthur, and there he delivered his message, and thereat the Queen was like one whose heart had been broken. And she withdrew into her bower and no one saw her for a long time.

Now after Sir Bors had departed from Corbin, Sir Launcelot was very heavy and sad. And this the Lady Elaine observed, and her spirit was troubled. So she sent for Sir Launcelot and said to him, "Launcelot, I know what is in thy heart. Thou wouldst fain return to the Court of King Arthur."

"Lady," said Sir Launcelot, "it matters not what may be my inclination at present, for above all inclinations it is my will that I remain at this place."

Then Elaine looked at him and said: "Not so, Messire, for I cannot bear to see you dwell with us thus in sadness. Wherefore, I command that you return to the Court of King Arthur."

Then Sir Launcelot turned away from her, for he wist that there was joy in his face, and he would not have her see that joy. Then with his back turned he said: "Lady, if that be your command I must needs obey, but it shall be only to go for a little while and then to return." So for a little no more was said, but the Lady Elaine ever gazed upon Sir Launcelot's back, and after a while she said, "Ah, Launcelot! Launcelot!" Upon that Sir Launcelot turned him about and cried, "Elaine, bid me stay and I will stay!" But she said, "Nay, I bid thee go."

So the next day Sir Launcelot departed for Camelot, and though he thought a great deal of the Lady Elaine, yet he could not but look forward with joy to coming back again to the Court of the King and beholding the Queen and his knights-companions once more.

Now when Sir Launcelot reached Camelot the news of his coming spread like fire and everywhere was heard the noise of rejoicing. But Sir Launcelot spake to nobody but came straight to Queen Guinevere and he stood before her and he said, "Lady, here am I."

Then Queen Guinevere gazed at him with great coldness though her soul was tossed and troubled with passion. And she said: "Sir Knight, one time I sent my word to thee by a messenger and thou heeded him not. Now it matters not that thou comest."

Then Sir Launcelot's heart was filled to bursting with bitterness, and he cried: "Lady, thou beholdest me a miserable man. For I have left all my duty and hope of happiness and have come to thee. Hast thou not then some word of kindness for me?"

But the Queen only hardened her heart and would not answer.

Then Sir Launcelot cried in despair: "Alas! what is there then left for me? Now even thy friendship is withdrawn from me!"

Then Queen Guinevere's eyes flashed like fire, and she cried out: "Sir Knight, I bid you tell me this—is it true that you wore as a favor the sleeve of the Lady Elaine at Astolat?"

Sir Launcelot said, "Yes, it is true."

Then Queen Guinevere laughed with flaming cheeks and she said: "Well, Sir Knight, I see that you are not very well learned in knighthood not to know that it is dishonorable for a knight to swear faith to one lady and to wear the favor of another. Yet what else may be expected of one who knoweth so little of the duties of knighthood that he will ride errant in a hangman's cart?"

So spake Queen Guinevere in haste, her words being driven onwards by her passion. But when she had spoken those words she would have recalled them; and she could do nothing but gaze into Sir Launcelot's face in a sort of terror. And she beheld that his face became red and redder. And he strove to speak but at first he could not and then he cried out in a choking voice, "Say you so!" and then again he cried, "Say you so!"

Therewith he turned, staggering like a drunken man. And there was a tall window behind him, and straightway he leaped out of that window into the courtyard beneath, where he fell with a loud and dreadful crash. Then he leaped up, all bloody, and ran away like one gone wild. And after that, he leaped upon his horse and thundered away.

Now the word of all this was talked about the Court almost as soon as it had happened. Thereat the kinsmen of Sir Launcelot were filled with indignation, and most of all Sir Bors, for he said: "Lo! this Lady sends me to bring my kinsman to her, and when he cometh then she treats him with contumely!" But Queen Guinevere, not knowing of the indignation of the kinsmen of Sir Launcelot, sent for three of them to come to her, Sir Ector and Sir Lionel and Sir Bors.

When these three had come to her they found her weeping, and she said, "Messires, I have done amiss."

To this they said nothing lest from anger they should say too much. Yet the Queen beheld their anger, wherefore she spake with pride, saying: "Messires, I ask you not to forgive me, but I would fain ask Sir Launcelot to do so. Now as your Queen I lay this command upon you, that you straightway go in quest of Sir Launcelot and bring him to me so that I may beseech his forgiveness."

So spake Queen Guinevere, and those knights, though they were angry with her, yet they could not but obey her command.

So began the quest for Sir Launcelot, and in time there went forth also Sir Gawaine and Sir Ewaine and Sir Percival of Gales.

Now when Sir Launcelot had quitted the presence of Queen Guinevere he rode furiously away, he wist not whither and cared not. Thus he drove onward until he reached the forest, and he rode through the forest until his horse was all in a lather. Still he drove ever forward, traveling all that night until he came to the hut of the Hermit of the Forest. Here Sir Launcelot leaped down from his horse, and he burst violently into the dwelling place of that good man. And Sir Launcelot cried out in a violent voice, "God save you!" and therewith he fell forward and lay with his face upon the floor.

Then the hermit beheld that Sir Launcelot was in a fit. So he eased Sir Launcelot of his armor and he loosed his shirt. And he laid Sir Launcelot on his cot and there he lay for the entire day. But toward the sloping of the afternoon he opened his eyes and gazed about him, and he said, "Where am I?" The hermit said, "Thou art with me," and he further said, "What aileth thee, Sir Launcelot?"

But to this Sir Launcelot answered naught but ever looked about him as though bedazed. By and by Sir Launcelot said, "I know not what it is that hath happened." Then Sir Launcelot fell once more into a deep slumber. And as he slept the hermit sat beside the pallet. And he gazed very steadfastly upon Sir Launcelot, and was greatly grieved to see him in that condition.

Now about the middle of the night the hermit fell asleep where he sat and shortly after that Sir Launcelot awoke. And in his madness Sir Launcelot took of a sudden a great fear of the hermit, so that the only thought in his mind was to escape from him. For by now he was completely mad. Wherefore he arose and went very softly out from that place.

And after he had come outside he sped into the forest, and he fled for all the rest of that night. And when the dawn had come he crouched down and hid himself in a thicket.

After that Sir Launcelot abided in the forest for a long while. All that time he gathered the wild fruit of the forest for his food, and he drank of the forest fountains, and that was all the food and drink that he had. And after a while the clothes of Sir Launcelot were all torn into shreds by thorns, and his hair grew down into his eyes and his beard grew down upon his breast so that he became in all appearance a wild man of the forest, all naked, and shaggy, and gaunt like to a starving wolf.

And then one day Sir Launcelot encountered a wild boar, and was wounded by the boar in the thigh, and he lost much blood from the wound.

Indeed death was very close to Sir Launcelot that day. And then suddenly there was but one thought in his mind and that thought was to return to Corbin. For even through his clouds of madness, Sir Launcelot wist that there a great love awaited him and that if he might reach that place he might have rest and peace.

So Sir Launcelot made his way toward Corbin, and he traveled thitherward several days. And one morning at the break of day he entered the town by a postern gate. And he made his way slowly through the streets, and the town was still asleep. So he came unseen to the marketplace and there sat him down upon that slab of stone beneath which the Worm had made its habitation.

So when the people of the town awoke they beheld him sitting there all naked and famished, gazing about him with wild looks.

And many stared, and then laughed and jeered at Sir Launcelot. And anon some of those began to cast stones to drive him away. So, at last, one of those stones struck Sir Launcelot, and at that his rage flamed up, whereupon he leaped up and ran at those who were tormenting him.

Upon that, some screamed and fled away, but others stoned Sir Launcelot all the more, until at last a stone smote him upon the head and he fell to the earth.

Then they within the castle, hearing the uproar, flung open the gate and came charging out. Thereupon the multitude scattered, leaving Sir Launcelot lying where he was. Then they of the castle gazed upon Sir Launcelot, and they beheld what a noble frame he had, and they took pity. So the captain of the guard said: "Alas, that such a man as this should come to such a pass. Let us bear him into the castle where he may have care."

So they brought Sir Launcelot into the castle of Corbin.

Now it chanced that the Lady Elaine the Fair happened to be

at her window, and looking down into the courtyard she beheld where several men-at-arms bare a wounded man into the castle. As they passed beneath where she was, the Lady Elaine looked down upon the countenance of the man. Then she beheld his face with the sun shining bright upon it, and at that, recognition struck through her like the stroke of a knife, whereat Elaine clasped her hands and cried aloud: "My soul! My soul! Can it be he?" And she ran to King Pelles to tell him what she had seen. Then King Pelles was amazed beyond measure and he said: "Daughter, stay thy weeping and I will go and examine into this."

So he went to the cell where his men had placed Sir Launcelot and he looked long upon Sir Launcelot as he lay there. And he looked at the ring which the wounded man wore upon one finger, and indeed the ring was the same as the one that Launcelot had always worn. So King Pelles knew that that was indeed Sir Launcelot who lay there.

Immediately King Pelles bade those who were in attendance to lift Sir Launcelot and bring him to a fair large room. So they did, and they laid Sir Launcelot upon a couch of down. And King Pelles sent for a leech to search Sir Launcelot's hurts. And all that while Sir Launcelot lay in that deep swoon like to death and awoke not.

And Sir Launcelot slept in that wise for three full days, and when he awoke the Lady Elaine and her father alone were present. And lo! when Sir Launcelot awoke his brain was clear of madness and he was himself again, though weak, like to a little child.

Then Sir Launcelot said, speaking very faintly, "Where am I?" and the Lady Elaine wept and said, "Lord, you are safe with those who hold you dear." Sir Launcelot said, "What has befallen me?" She said: "Lord, thou hast been bedazed in thy mind and hast been sorely hurt. But now thou art safe."

He said, "Have I then been mad?" And to that King Pelles said, "Yea, Messire." Then Sir Launcelot groaned, and he covered his face and he said, "What shame!"

Then, weeping, the Lady Elaine said, "No shame, Lord, but only very great pity!" and she kissed his hand and washed it with her tears. And Sir Launcelot wept also, and by and by he said, "Elaine, meseems I have no hope or honor save in thee," and she said, "Take peace, Sir, for in my heart there is both honor for you and hope for your great happiness." And so Sir Launcelot did take peace.

Then after a while Sir Launcelot said, "Who here knoweth of my madness?" and King Pelles said, "Only a few in this castle, Messire."

Then Sir Launcelot said: "I pray you that this be all secret, and that no word concerning me goes beyond these walls." And King Pelles said, "It shall be as you would have it."

Now after a fortnight had passed, Sir Launcelot was fast becoming cured in body and mind. And one day he and the Lady Elaine were alone in that room where he lay and he said, "Lady, meseems you have had great cause to hate me." At this she smiled, and said, "How could I hate thee, Launcelot?" Sir Launcelot said, "Elaine, I have done thee great wrong in times gone by." She said, "Say naught of that." "Yea," he said, "I must say this, that I would that I could undo that wrong which I did thee by my neglect. But what have I to offer thee in compensation? Naught but mine own broken life. Yet that poor life and all that it holds dearest I would fain offer thee if only it might be a compensation to thee."

Then the Lady Elaine looked very intently at Sir Launcelot and she said: "Sir Launcelot, thy lips speak, but that which matters is that thy heart should speak."

Then Sir Launcelot smiled and he said: "I have looked well into my heart ere I spake to thee, and it is my heart that speaks. In my heart meseems I find great love for thee and certes I find all honor and reverence for thee therein. Now tell me, Lady, what can any heart hold more than that?" And Elaine said, "Meseems it can hold no more."

Then Sir Launcelot took her by the hand and drew her to him, and he kissed her upon the lips and she forbade him not. So they two were reconciled in peace and happiness.

So when Sir Launcelot was altogether healed of his sickness, they two were married. And after they were married, King Pelles gave to them a very noble castle for to be their dwelling place and that castle was called the castle of Blayne.

That castle stood upon a beautiful island in the midst of a lake of water as clear as crystal. And the island was covered with many orchards of beautiful trees. And there were gardens and meadows and there was a town so fair that when one gazed across the lake he beheld such a place as one may see in a shining dream. And he dwelt there in seeming peace and contentment.

Yet was it indeed peace and contentment? Alas, that it should be so, but ever and anon he would remember him of other days of deeds of glory, and ever and anon he would bethink him of that beautiful Queen to whom he had one time uplifted his eyes, and of whom he had no right to think in that wise.

Then his soul would cry out: Let us go hence and seek that glory and that other's love once more! Then Sir Launcelot would ever say to his soul, Down, proud spirit, and think not of these things, but of duty.

CHAPTER V: THE RETURN TO CAMELOT

So TWO YEARS went by. Then at last Sir Ector, one of the three kinsmen who sought Sir Launcelot, learned where he was, and came to the castle of Blayne, and taking Sir Launcelot aside he finally delivered Queen Guinevere's message.

Then indeed was Sir Launcelot more torn and troubled than ever. He sent Sir Ector away, and he went to a certain chamber of the castle where he was alone and there he communed with his spirit, and these communings were very bitter and sad.

Anon came the Lady Elaine to that place and looked into Sir Launcelot's eyes, and she said, "Launcelot, what ails thee?" He said, "My kinsman hath given me a message from Queen Guinevere, and she commands that I appear before her."

Then the Lady Elaine took Sir Launcelot's head into her embrace and she said, "Alas, love, then thou must return unto the Court of King Arthur, for it is thy duty. After that thou mayest return hither, and I pray God that thy staying away from this place may not be for very long."

Then Sir Launcelot said: "Elaine, I will not go to King Arthur's Court unless it be that thou goest with me. If thou wilt not do that, I will disobey the Queen's command and will stay forever here with thee."

Then the Lady Elaine smiled sadly and she said: "Ah, Launcelot, I am sorry for thee and for thy doubts. But as thou wilt have it so, I will go with thee." Therewith Sir Launcelot kissed her as with a great passion.

So three days after that time they departed from the castle of Blayne. With them also traveled Sir Lavaine, the Lady Elaine's brother, and their court of esquires and ladies and demoiselles. And when they drew nigh to Camelot (which same was upon the fourth day after they had left) Sir Launcelot sent a herald before them to announce their coming.

So it befell that when they came in sight of Camelot, many knights and esquires came forth to meet them. These gave loud acclaim, crying, "Welcome!"

This welcome they gave on behalf of King Arthur, for the King was glad beyond measure to have the champion who was so dear to his heart return to him once more. So, rejoicing, they all progressed toward the King's town.

And all they who had thus come forth from the town looked with great curiosity upon the Lady Elaine and all were astonished at her beauty and her grace; wherefore they said to one another: "Certes, even Queen Guinevere herself is not more beautiful than yonder lady."

So they came to the King's castle, and there they found King Arthur and Queen Guinevere, crowned with golden crowns, sitting in state to receive them. So Sir Launcelot and Lady Elaine kneeled down before them. Then the King arose and descended from his throne and gave them great welcome.

And all that while the Queen's face was smiling like to a beautiful mask. And ever she gazed at the Lady Elaine, beholding how that lady was exceedingly beautiful and gentle. And as the Queen gazed upon Elaine she hated her with great bitterness, yet ever she hid that hatred beneath a smiling countenance.

So it was that the next day after that day, Queen Guinevere sent for the Lady Elaine and said to her: "Lady, I have it in mind to do thee a singular honor, and this is that thou shouldst be in personal attendance upon me. To this end I have purveyed thee a room next to mine own chamber in mine own part of this castle, and there thou and thy attendants may lodge so that ye shall be near to my person."

Thus spake the Queen, for so, under pretense of doing honor to Elaine, she purposed to separate Sir Launcelot from his lady. Though why she should do this she could not rightly tell even to her own heart.

Now at this time the Lady Elaine was in very tender health, wherefore, after a day or two, she began to repine at being thus separated from Sir Launcelot; and she wept a great deal and ate and slept little.

Now there was with the Lady Elaine a lady hight Dame Brysen. This was a very old and sedate lady who had been the Lady Elaine's nurse and attendant ever since Elaine had been a little babe. Now Dame Brysen wist that Elaine was like to fall sick unless she had sight of her lord. So Dame Brysen went to Sir Launcelot and said: "Sir, if you find not some opportunity to see your lady, she will fall ill." Sir Launcelot said: "How may I see her?" Dame Brysen said: "Come to me this night in a certain passage of the castle during the midwatch and I will bring you to her."

So that night Sir Launcelot came to that place and Dame Brysen took him to Elaine. And when Elaine beheld Sir Launcelot she could scarce control her joy, and she catched him in her arms and held to him like as one sinking in deep waters. And Sir Launcelot soothed her and comforted her. So at last she took good cheer and smiled and laughed. And Sir Launcelot remained with her for a long while; and he did not quit that place until day dawned.

Now there was a damsel of the Queen's court who acted as a spy upon Sir Launcelot. So when the next morning had come, this damsel went to the Queen and told her how Dame Brysen had brought Sir Launcelot to the Lady Elaine, and when the Queen heard that news she was very wroth, and she cried out: "Where is that false traitor knight, Sir Launcelot! Bring him hither!"

So anon came Sir Launcelot to the Queen, and then all those who were there withdrew. So Sir Launcelot stood alone before the Queen and he said, "Here am I."

Then the Lady Guinevere looked for a long time upon Sir Launcelot. Anon she said, in a voice that was very harsh: "Is it true that thou camest to this part of the castle last night?" and Sir Launcelot said, "Yea, Lady." Then the Queen ground her teeth together, and she said, still in that same voice: "Traitor! how didst thou dare to come hither without my permission?"

Sir Launcelot looked very long then into the Queen's face, and at last he said: "In what way am I a traitor, to thee or to anyone? Is not my duty first of all toward that lady to whom I have sworn my duty? What treason did I then do in cherishing her who is sick and helpless in this place where thou keepest her prisoner?"

After that the Queen and the knight-champion stared very fiercely at one another. Then by and by the Queen's eyes fell, and she cried out: "Ah, Launcelot! Launcelot! May God have pity upon me, for I am most unhappy!" Therewith she covered her face with her handkerchief.

Sir Launcelot wist not what to do, albeit his heart was rent with love and pity. And he came close to her and he said: "Lady, Lady! You tear my heartstrings with your grief!" Therewith he sank upon his knees before her, and he took her hands and strove to draw them away from her face. And after a while she let him withdraw her hands, and then he held them imprisoned in his own. Yet ever she kept her face turned away; and thus she said: "Launcelot! Launcelot! Art thou not sorry for me?" He said: "Yea, Lady, I am sorry for thee and for myself. For God knoweth I would abide by my duty, and mefeareth thou wouldst have me do otherwise." Then the Queen said: "Launcelot, what is duty when we measure it with the measurement of happiness and unhappiness?" And Sir Launcelot said, "Lady, for God's sake, forbear."

Now as Sir Launcelot said those words he became of a sudden

aware that someone was in that room. So he looked up and behold! there stood the Lady Elaine, and her face was as white as death.

Then Sir Launcelot was overwhelmed with confusion and with pity. So he arose from his knees and stood there before Elaine with folded arms and with his gaze downcast. Then the Queen likewise beheld Elaine, and her face flamed red and she arose haughtily and she said: "Lady, this is well met, for I was about to send for you. Now tell me, was it by your will that this knight came last night to this part of the castle?" and the Lady Elaine said: "Yea, Lady, it was."

Then with anger the Queen said: "Then you have broken an ordinance of the King's Court, and for this I command you that you quit this place with all expedition."

And Elaine looked very proudly upon the Queen and she said: "Lady, I shall be glad to depart, for this is a place of great unhappiness to me. But tell me, Lady, ere I go: What would you say of one who took from another who harmed her not, all the happiness and joy that that other had in her life? And what would you say if that one who would so rob the other had for herself a lord who was the most noble and worthy knight in the world?"

At this the eyes of the Queen shone very wild like to the eyes of a hawk. And she strove to speak, and it was as though the words strangled her. And she said, "Go! You know not what you say!"

Then the Lady Elaine turned with great dignity and went away. And then the Queen, turning to Launcelot, said: "Messire, I command you, that though your lady shall depart, yet you shall remain here at this Court." Then she also went away, and for a while Sir Launcelot remained, standing alone like to a statue of stone.

So the next day the Lady Elaine quitted the Court of King Arthur, riding in a litter. And her countenance was very calm and steadfast. Yea, I believe that at that time her soul itself was altogether cheerful and content. For once, when Sir Lavaine spake with great anger, she chid him, saying: "Brother, let be. What matters it? Could you but see into the future as I do, you would know that it mattereth little indeed that such things as this befall us in this brief valley of tears."

Thus they journeyed by easy stages for two days, what time they came to a fair priory set in the midst of fertile fields of corn. And the white walls of the priory and the red roofs thereof shone against the deep blue sky. And the road whereon they traveled went beside a placid river; and there were willows upon the one hand and smooth fields of ripening grain upon the other.

Now at that time the Lady Elaine was suffering great pangs of sickness, wherefore she said to those attending her: "Dear friends, it is well that we have come to this place, for I am very sick. Wherefore I pray you let me rest in this priory till God shall have dealt with me as He sees fit." Upon that command they bare the Lady Elaine into the priory.

Meantime Sir Launcelot abided at the Court of the King, very heavy of heart. For his soul was dragged this way and that. And he could not tell whether he did altogether ill or somewhat well in remaining at the King's Court.

Yet ever he said to himself: So soon as I can escape from this place with courtesy to the Queen, I will follow Elaine. Wherefore had he wist that she was lying so sick at the priory, it may be believed that he would have flown to her upon the wings of the wind.

But Sir Launcelot knew not how it was with his lady, and so God was even then preparing a great punishment for him.

CHAPTER VI: MERLIN'S PROPHECY

MEANWHILE, OF THOSE KNIGHTS who went forth in quest of Sir Launcelot, two had not yet returned to the Court of King Arthur. And those two were Sir Gawaine and Sir Bors de Ganis. So it was that one day Sir Gawaine was alone, riding through the forest at the season when all the trees were green and bosky and when the days were warm and balmy. Stopping then in a pleasant shady place, he took his midday meal and rested until the sun should shed a less fervid heat.

Then it was that he became suddenly aware of a bird with

plumage of gold that sat upon the ground at a little distance, regarding him with eyes that were very bright and shining.

Now Sir Gawaine's heart leaped strangely in his breast, for he remembered that he had once heard that Lady Nymue of the Lake had just such a golden bird. So, leading his horse, Sir Gawaine drew near the bird. Then the bird took wing and flew with shrill chirping to a distance and settled again upon the ground. And when Sir Gawaine approached it again, again it took wing and flew chirping to a distance. And Sir Gawaine wist that he was meant to follow it.

So ever it flew and Sir Gawaine followed, and thus it conducted him a long way until, at last, it brought him out of the forest and to a dreary valley, naked and bare, and covered all over with stones and rocks. And in the center of the valley there was a cloud of thick mist in the shape of a pillar. And that cloud of mist moved not in any way but remained fixed in its place as if it were a pillar of stone.

Then Sir Gawaine beheld that golden bird perched high in a tree. And he saw that it had folded its wings to rest, wherefore he knew that the bird must have conducted him to this place for some purpose. So Sir Gawaine went down into the valley and drew near to that pillar of mist and stood and looked upon it.

Now ye are to know, that some years before this time, the Enchanter Merlin, who had so helped King Arthur in his early years, had been himself bewitched by an enchantress. This enchantress had caused for Merlin to be cast into a magic sleep, and then she had caused him to be imprisoned in this sleep under a great coffer of stone. And this coffer she had concealed with the same pillar of mist which Sir Gawaine now looked upon.

Thus it was that as Sir Gawaine stood looking upon the pillar of mist, a voice issued of a sudden out of the midst of the cloud saying, "Gawaine! Gawaine! is it thou who art there?" And Sir Gawaine was astonished beyond all measure that a voice should thus address him from out of the midst of the pillar of cloud.

But he answered, "Who art thou who callest upon Gawaine?"

Then the voice replied: "I who speak to thee am Merlin. Here for twelve years have I been lying asleep, enclosed in a coffer of stone, yet once in every six years I awake for one hour of life and at the end of that hour I relapse into sleep again. This is my time for waking, and so hast thou been brought hither that thou mightest hear that prophecy that I have to utter. And this is my prophecy:

"The Sacred Grail that has been lost to the earth for so long shall be brought back to earth again. And now he who shall achieve the quest of that chalice is about to be born into the world. Now when that babe is born he shall be taken away by that knight who is most worthy to handle him, and he shall be hidden by that knight until his time hath come.

"You, who are a sinful man, may not have that babe in your keeping, but there is one who hath but little of sin and he may do so. So do you thus as you are commanded: Follow that golden-winged thing that hath conducted you hither and it will lead you to where you shall find Sir Bors de Ganis. He is most worthy in all of the world for to handle that babe and hide him until his time shall be come.

"Bid Sir Bors to follow that golden bird with you and it shall bring you both to where you shall find that wonderful infant.

"Thereafter, when that babe shall have been taken away by Sir Bors, go you and proclaim to all men that when eighteen years have passed, then shall the knights of the Round Table depart in quest of the Holy Grail. And when that Grail hath been recovered, then soon after shall come the end of the Round Table.

"And this is the prophecy of the Grail which you have been brought hither to hear."

So spake that voice. Sir Gawaine listened for a while, but it spake no more. Then Gawaine cried: "Merlin, what may I do to free thee from the enchantment that lieth upon thee?" And he waited for a reply, but no reply was vouchsafed him. And Gawaine called repeatedly upon the name of Merlin, but at no time did Merlin answer him. Then Gawaine went forward with intent to enter that cloud of mist, but lo! it was like to a wall of adamant. Then Gawaine was aware that the golden bird was flitting hither and thither nearby, as though it were restless to depart. So once more Gawaine called upon Merlin, saying, "Farewell, Merlin," and it appeared to him that he heard a voice, very faint as though from a dream that is fading, and beseemed that voice said, "Farewell."

Thereafter Gawaine mounted his horse and turned him about and departed from that place. And never more after that time was the voice of Merlin heard, for no one saving Sir Gawaine ever found that valley with its pillar of cloud.

So Sir Gawaine followed the golden bird, and ever it led him in a certain direction. So, about the middle of the following day, he came forth into an open place of the forest and there beheld the hermitage several times mentioned in these histories. And as Sir Gawaine approached, the door of the hut opened and the hermit appeared; and perceiving Sir Gawaine he cried out: "Welcome, Sir Gawaine! Sir Bors awaits thee; for it hath been told him in a dream that thou wouldst meet him here."

So Sir Gawaine entered the cell of the hermit and there he beheld Sir Bors kneeling at prayer. And when Sir Bors had finished his orisons he arose and he turned with great joy and took Sir Gawaine into his arms; and either embraced the other.

After that the hermit brought them food and they ate, and meantime Sir Gawaine told Sir Bors concerning the prophecy of Merlin. Then Sir Bors became all enwrapped as with a certain exaltation of spirit, and he cried out: "How wonderful is this miracle that thou tellest me! Let us straightway go forth and perform the bidding of this prophecy." Accordingly they arose and they gave thanks to the good old hermit. Thereafter they went forth and mounted their horses. And straightway the golden bird appeared once more and flew chirping before them.

So they followed the bird until at last, toward the sloping of the afternoon, they came forth out of the forest and into a fertile valley where there was a fair priory with white walls and red roofs. So Sir Bors and Sir Gawaine entered this pleasant valley; and then the golden bird chirped very shrill, and straightway flew high into the air and disappeared. Thereupon those two champions knew that this must be the place where they should find that young child of which Merlin had spoken. So they went forward toward the priory with a certain awe, as not knowing what next of mystery was to happen to them.

So as they approached that holy place, there came forth Sir Lavaine, the brother of the Lady Elaine. And they beheld that the face of Sir Lavaine was very sad as he gave them greeting, saying: "Messires, ye come none too soon." And he said, "Dismount and come with me."

So Sir Bors and Sir Gawaine dismounted; and Sir Lavaine brought them to a small cell of the priory, very bare and white as snow. In the center of the cell there lay a couch and upon the couch there lay a still figure, and Sir Bors and Sir Gawaine beheld that it was the Lady Elaine. Her hair lay spread out all over the pillow, shining like to pure gold, and her face shone very white. Her eyes gazed ever straight before her; and it was as though her looks were fixed upon something very strange that she beheld a great distance away.

Then Sir Lavaine, whispering, said, "Come near and behold," and thereupon Sir Bors and Sir Gawaine came close to the Lady Elaine. Sir Lavaine lifted the coverlet and they beheld that a new-born babe lay beside the lady. Then they wist that that babe was the child of Sir Launcelot and the Lady Elaine; and they wist that this was the babe of whom Merlin had spoken. For the child was wonderfully beautiful, and it was as though a certain radiance of light shone forth from its face; and it lay perfectly still.

So Sir Bors and Sir Gawaine kneeled down beside the bed and set their palms together, and for a while all was very silent. Then suddenly the Lady Elaine spake in a voice very faint and remote. And she said, "Sir Bors, art thou there?" and Sir Bors said, "Yea, Lady."

Then she said: "Behold this child, for this is he who shall achieve the quest of the Holy Grail. So he shall become the greatest knight that ever the world beheld. But though he shall be the greatest champion-at-arms that ever lived, yet also he shall be gentle and meek and without sin, innocent like a little child. And because he is to be so high in chivalry and so pure of life, therefore his name shall be called Galahad." And she said again, "Sir Bors, art thou there?" and he said, "Yea, Lady."

She said: "My time draweth near, for even now I behold the shining gates of Paradise, and soon I shall quit this troubled world. Nevertheless, I leave behind me this child, and his life shall enlighten that world from which I am withdrawing." Then she said for the third time, "Sir Bors, art thou there?" And Sir Bors wept, and he said, "Yea, Lady, I am here."

Then the Lady Elaine said: "Take thou this child and bear him hence unto a certain place. Thou shalt know that place because there shall go before thee a bird with golden plumage. Leave the child at that place, and tell no man where that place is." And she said, "Hearest thou me, Sir Bors?" And Sir Bors, still weeping, said, "Yea, Lady."

Then she said: "Go and tarry not, for the ending is near. Wait not until that end cometh, but go immediately and do as I have asked thee."

Then, still weeping, Sir Bors arose, and he took the child and he wrapped it in his cloak and he went out thence and was gone.

THAT SAME DAY the Lady Elaine died about the middle watch of the night.

Then Sir Gawaine said, weeping, "Let me go and fetch Sir Launcelot of the Lake." But Sir Lavaine, speaking sternly, said: "Bring him not, for he is not worthy. But as for you, do you depart, for I have yet that to do I would do alone. Go you and return unto the Court of the King. But I charge you to say nothing unto anyone there concerning the birth of the child Galahad, nor of how this sweet, fair lady is no more."

So Sir Gawaine departed from that place, leaving Sir Lavaine alone with his dead. And there came several of those of the priory to that cell, and they lifted up that still figure and bore it away to the priory chapel, and there they chanted a requiem. And Sir Lavaine kneeled for a long time in prayer beside the bier. Then when morning had come he arose, and going to the people of the priory, he said, "Whither is it that this river floweth?" They said,

"It floweth past the King's town of Camelot, and thence onward to the sea."

Sir Lavaine said, "Is there a boat at this place that may float upon the river?" And they said, "Yea, Messire, there is a barge and there is a deaf-and-dumb man that saileth that barge."

So they took him to the bargeman. And the bargeman was a very old man with a long white beard. So Sir Lavaine made signs to him, asking him if he would ferry him down the stream, and the bargeman made signs in answer that it should be as Sir Lavaine desired.

After that Sir Lavaine gave command that the barge should be draped with white samite and that a couch of white samite should be established upon the barge. So when all was in readiness there came forth a procession from the chapel, bearing that still and silent figure, and they brought it to the barge and laid it upon the couch. Thereafter Sir Lavaine took his station in the bow of the barge and the deaf-and-dumb man took his station in the stern. Then the bargeman trimmed the sail and the barge drew slowly away from that place, many watching its departure.

And the barge floated gently down the smooth river, betwixt banks of rushes and rows of pollard willow trees. And all about them was the pleasant weather of the summertime, and everything was abloom.

Then anon they drifted past open meadowlands, with fields and uplands all trembling in the hot sunlight. And after that they came to a more populous country where were small villages with here and there a stone bridge crossing the river.

So ever they floated onward until at last they came to the town of Camelot. And as they passed by the town walls, lo! a multitude of people came to the walls and gazed down upon that barge. And the people whispered in awe, saying: "What is this and what doth it portend? Is this real or is it a vision?"

But ever that barge drifted onward, and so, at last, it came to a landing place of stone steps not far from the castle of the King. There the dumb bargeman made fast the barge to the landing stage, and so that strange voyage was ended.

Now at that time King Arthur and many lords and ladies sat at feast in the castle, and amongst those was Sir Launcelot and Queen Guinevere. So as they sat thus, there came one of a sudden running into the hall as in affright. And he said: "Lord, here is a wonderful thing. For down by the river there hath come a barge to the landing stairs, and in the barge there lieth a dead lady so beautiful that I do not think her like is to be found in all the earth. And a dumb man sits in the stern of the boat, and a knight sits in the bow with his face shrouded in his mantle."

Then King Arthur said: "This is indeed most singular. Now let us all go and see what this portendeth."

So the King arose, and he went out, and all who were there went with him.

Now Sir Launcelot of the Lake bethought him of the Lady Elaine and of how she was even then in tender health, wherefore he repented him that he was not with her. And he said to himself: Suppose that she should die like to this lady in the barge? So his feet lagged because of his heavy thoughts, and he was near the last who came to the riverside.

Now there were many townsfolk standing there, but upon King Arthur's coming all those made way for him, and so he came and stood upon the upper step of the landing stairs and looked down into the boat.

And he knew that it was the Lady Elaine who lay there; and he looked upon that dead figure in a sort of terror, and then he said, "Where is Sir Launcelot?"

Now when the King so spake, they who stood there made way, and Sir Launcelot came through the press and stood also at the head of the stairs. Then of a sudden he beheld with his very eyes that thing which he had been thinking of; for there beneath him lay in truth the dead image of his dear lady.

Then it was as though Sir Launcelot had been struck with a shaft of death, for he neither moved nor stirred. But ever he stood there gazing down into that boat as though he had forgotten that there was anybody else in the world saving only himself and that dead lady.

Then a great hush fell over all, and at that Sir Lavaine lifted the hood from his face and looked up and beheld Sir Launcelot. Then Sir Lavaine stood up and cried out in a great harsh voice: "Ha! art thou there, thou traitor knight? Behold the work that thou hast done!"

So said Sir Lavaine, but it was as though Sir Launcelot heard him not, for he stood as though he were a dead man. Then he awoke, as it were, to life, and he clasped his hands across his eyes, and cried out, "Remorse! Remorse! Remorse!"

Then he shut his lips, and thereupon turned and went away. And at the castle he ordered his horse and mounted it and rode away; and he bade farewell to no one, and no one was there when he thus departed.

So for a long time Sir Launcelot rode he knew not whither, but after a while he found himself near the cell of the Hermit of the Forest. And he beheld the hermit, that he stood in front of his cell feeding the wild birds; for the little feathered creatures were gathered in great multitudes about him, and a wild doe and a fawn of the forest browsed nearby, and all was full of peace and content. But at the coming of Sir Launcelot, all those wild creatures took alarm and fled away. For they wist, by some instinct, that a man of sin and sorrow was coming thitherward.

And Sir Launcelot leaped from his horse, and ran to the hermit and flung himself down upon the ground before him. And the hermit was astonished and said, "What ails thee, Sir Launcelot?" Whereunto Sir Launcelot cried out: "Woe is me! I have sinned very grievously and have been punished and now my heart is broken!"

Then the hermit lifted Sir Launcelot to his feet and brought him into his cell. And Sir Launcelot confessed everything to the hermit—yea, everything to the very bottom of his soul, and the good, holy man hearkened to him.

Then after a while the hermit said: "Messire, God telleth me that if thy sin hath been grievous, so also hath thy punishment been full sore. Wherefore meseemeth I speak what God would have me say when I tell thee that though neither thou nor any man may undo that which is done, yet there is this which thou or any man mayest do. Thou mayest bathe thy soul in repentance as in a bath of clear water, and having so bathed thou mayest clothe thyself as in a fresh raiment of new resolve. So thou mayest stand once more upon thy feet and look up to God and say: 'Lo, God! I have sinned and done great evil, yet I am still Thy handiwork. So, though I may not undo that which I have done, yet I may, with Thy aid, do better hereafter than I have done heretofore.'"

Then Sir Launcelot wept, and he said, "There is comfort in thy words."

After that he abode for three days in the cell of the hermit and then he went forth again into the world, a broken yet a contrite man, and one full of a resolve to make good the life that God thenceforth intended him to live.

Now it only remaineth to be said that, after the departure of Sir Launcelot from the King's Court, they brought the dead figure of the Lady Elaine to the minster at Camelot and there high mass was said for the peace of her soul. So for two days that figure lay in state in the minster, and then it was buried and a monument of marble was erected to the memory of that kind and loving spirit.

Thus the history of Elaine the Fair cometh to an end. And here followeth the story of Sir Galahad, which same includes the recovery of the Grail and its exaltation into Paradise.

PART V—GALAHAD

CHAPTER I: THE SEAT PERILOUS IS FILLED

𝕰IGHTEEN YEARS PASSED BY in the kingdom of Arthur after the death of Elaine, and they were years of peace and greatness and fulfillment. Forty-nine knights sat at last at the Round Table, and King Arthur rejoiced.

Now one day Sir Launcelot sat at Court with many lords and ladies of high degree. And suddenly there entered that place a maiden clad in a robe of white with a crimson girdle. This maiden called out in a high, clear voice, "Sir Launcelot of the Lake—which knight is he?"

To this Sir Launcelot made reply, "I am he." The maiden said, "Sir Launcelot, I bid thee follow me." Quoth he, "To what purpose?" She said, "Thou shalt see."

So Sir Launcelot arose and followed her. And outside were two horses standing, one a white palfrey, the other a black stallion; and the maiden mounted the palfrey, and Sir Launcelot mounted the stallion, and so together they rode away from Camelot.

They traveled all day, till toward eventide they came to a quiet valley, fruitful with orchards and fields of wheat. And in the midst of the valley there stood a nunnery, with white walls and green trees all about it. Above the nunnery was the radiant sky, very blue and full of floating clouds.

Quoth the maiden, "Thither is where I am taking thee." Thus, anon, they came to that pleasant convent. Here the gate was opened to them by a youthful esquire, who assisted them to dismount and took their horses.

After that the maiden led Sir Launcelot to the convent chapel.

Here Sir Launcelot beheld an abbess and three nuns kneeling before the altar; and he beheld that beside these ladies there were two knights kneeling.

Anon they who kneeled arose, and Sir Launcelot beheld that the two knights were Sir Bors de Ganis and Sir Lionel. Then Sir Launcelot said to them, "Messires, what brings you hither?" To this Sir Bors replied, "Sir, to each of us came a fair maiden who brought us to this place. Since our coming we have been waiting for thee." Sir Launcelot said, "For what purpose have I been brought hither?" And Sir Lionel said, "Thou shalt see."

Upon this the Lady Abbess turned to one nun who stood beside her, and with that the nun left them. Then in a little while she returned, bringing with her a youth of eighteen years of age, very tall and fair, and clad all in white silk. The Abbess said to Sir Launcelot, "Sir, this is thine own son, hight Galahad, and his mother was the Lady Elaine the Fair."

Then Sir Launcelot cried out, "How is this? I knew not that I had a son. I beheld the Lady Elaine upon a certain black and terrible day, lying dead in a boat at Camelot; but I knew not that she left a son behind her!" Said the Abbess, "Ne'ertheless she did so, and this is that son. He hath lived with us since the time of his birth when Sir Bors fetched him hither; but now hath the time come that he is to be knighted, and thou hast been sent for that thou mightest make him a knight." Quoth Sir Launcelot, "I know of no joy that would be greater than that."

So that night Galahad watched his armor in the chapel. And when the morning was come, Sir Bors and Sir Lionel bathed him and clad him in a robe of white, and they brought him to Sir Launcelot, and Sir Launcelot made him a knight, according to the custom.

Now, after this ceremony, Sir Launcelot besought Sir Galahad that he would accompany them to the Court of King Arthur (for Sir Launcelot desired that Sir Galahad should be manifested to the entire world of chivalry).

But to this Sir Galahad replied, "Sir, I cannot yet go to the Court of the King, for all is not yet accomplished to prepare me for that going. Anon, however, I shall come thither; meantime, do thou wait for me at King Arthur's Court." So Sir Launcelot and Sir Lionel and Sir Bors departed from that convent, and they returned to Camelot.

But they said nothing to that Court concerning the knighting of Galahad, for it was not yet to be known to the world that there was such a one as Galahad, and that he was Launcelot's son.

So it befell Pentecost Day, what time the Feast of the Round Table was held.

And early in the morning when the water carriers went to the river to draw water, they beheld beside the river a great block of red marble, cubical in shape; and in that cube of stone there was thrust a sword. The hilt of the sword was studded all over with precious stones, and the blade of that sword shone like lightning for brightness.

Then they who beheld the wonder hastened to the King and told what they had seen. So the King with his Court went down to the river. And when they had come to that place they beheld that there were words written around about the blade of the sword. So King Arthur read:

> "This sword is for the greatest knight in the world and for him who shall win the Holy Grail."

Then he read:

> "Whoso draweth forth this sword from the stone, to him shall that sword belong."

Then King Arthur said to Sir Launcelot, "Messire, thou art the greatest knight in the world, and perhaps thou shalt win the Holy Grail. Let me see thee draw forth that blade."

Quoth Sir Launcelot, "Lord, I fear me that I shall not be able to win the Grail, for I am a sinful man. So I would fain not endeavor to draw forth this sword."

Then King Arthur turned to Sir Gawaine, and he said, "Sir, let me see thee attempt that sword."

So Sir Gawaine laid hand to the hilt of the sword and drew

strongly upon it, but the sword did not move a hairbreadth in the marble.

Then the King said to Sir Percival, "Try thou."

So Sir Percival drew upon the sword very strongly, but neither could he move it so much as the breadth of a hair.

After that no other lord chose to attempt the sword, but all avoided it. So, thereafter, they all withdrew from that place and went away, marveling at the miracle.

Thus that day of marvels began, and by and by came the time of the Feast of the Round Table.

Now all they of the Round Table were gathered about that board and every man sat in his place, and behind every knight stood a young knight to serve him. Thus, as they all sat there, there came, of a sudden, a commotion at the doorway, and after that there appeared at the doorway an old man clad in white. That old man was the Hermit of the Forest, and with him he brought a tall, fair young knight and that knight was Sir Galahad. At that time Sir Galahad was clad in flame-colored armor and a long mantle of flame-colored cloth, but he bore no shield, nor was there a sword within the scabbard that hung at his side.

The old man lifted up his voice, saying, "Lords, here by the grace of God come I amongst you with him who is to be the greatest knight that ever the world beheld. Also, he is to be the one who shall achieve the Holy Grail. So I have brought him hither to this place."

King Arthur answered him: "Holy Sir, if thou sayest sooth, then this is a very marvelous thing. But we shall put it to the test. Yonder is the Seat Perilous wherein no one of the Round Table hath dared to seat himself. Let this youth take there his seat, for that seat is for him who is without sin. Also, down beside the river there is a strange sword in a cube of marble. Let him draw that sword and then shall we believe in him."

The old hermit said, "Sir King, it shall be done as thou desirest." So the old man led Sir Galahad to the Seat Perilous. Here he took his seat, and lo! no harm of any sort befell him. Then, anon, Sir Launcelot reached forward and drew aside the silken coverlet that hung at the back of the seat upon which Sir Galahad sat, and, behold! there were these words estamped upon the back of the seat in letters of gold:

Sir Galahad

Then a great shout went up from all the knights of the Round Table, for thus was the Seat Perilous achieved, and so was the Round Table completed.

Then King Arthur said, "Lo! this youth is he for whom we have been waiting. Let us now take him to the sword in the marble stone."

So they all arose and conducted Sir Galahad to the marble stone. And Sir Galahad set hand to the sword and drew it forth very easily, and where the sword came forth it left no mark upon the stone. Then Sir Galahad thrust the bright-shining blade into his scabbard, and it fitted to the scabbard, and so he was armed.

Thereafter King Arthur kissed him upon either cheek, and said, "Hail, Sir Galahad! For thou art to be the crowning glory of my entire reign." And he said, "Come, let us go up to the castle that I may present thee to the Queen."

Then Sir Galahad said, "I cannot go with thee now, O Lord. For one cometh here, and with her I must go. I go first to seek for the shield of Balan, who slew his brother Balin unwittingly at the time of Uther-Pendragon. Through him the Holy Grail was lost to the earth, so that I must recover first his shield. Then must I go to search for the Holy Grail, for that is my mission here in life. Likewise I have this to tell thee, that two of those knights here present shall win the Grail along with me; but who those two shall be I may not relate to you."

And even as Sir Galahad ceased speaking there appeared a damsel clad in white, riding upon a white palfrey, and by her hand she led a coal-black charger of great size. So Sir Galahad mounted upon the black charger, and he saluted King Arthur and Sir Launcelot and Sir Bors and Sir Lionel, and he rode away from that place, leaving them all in great wonder and amazement.

So, when he had gone, King Arthur said to his Court, "This is certes a very wonderful visitation, for this youth came to us like an angel from Heaven. Let us now go and hear the mass ere we return to the Hall of the Round Table."

So as they were going to the mass, Sir Gawaine said to Sir Launcelot, "Messire, this is a sad day for thee, for now there is a greater knight than thou in the world." Sir Launcelot answered, "Not so, Messire, for, wit you, that this is mine own well-beloved son. Wherefore I, being his father, may well surrender unto him that glory which I cannot carry with me into Paradise."

And thus all the world became acquainted with the fact that Sir Galahad was the true son of Sir Launcelot.

Now, after the mass was over, all they of the knights of the Round Table retired to the Hall of the Round Table. Then, when all were seated, King Arthur said, "Lords of the Round Table, all ye have heard what Sir Galahad hath said; to wit, that two of you should achieve the Grail with him. Now it doth seem to me that several among you should go forth in search of that Holy Chalice. For, by not going, those two may miss the chance of achieving that great glory."

In answer, all those who were there arose, and each man drew his sword and held up the handle before his eyes as a crucifix. And each man swore upon that crucifix that he would presently depart and search for the Holy Grail.

Then King Arthur was filled with sorrow, for many of his knights he would have kept with him at his Court. And he was grieved because he foresaw that many of them should die upon the quest.

But Sir Launcelot said to the King, "Comfort you, my Lord, for though the Round Table may indeed perish thus, yet, ere it be dissolved, what greater glory can there be to you than that the knights of your Round Table should achieve the Grail? And what greater honor can there be than that we should endanger our lives in that quest?"

Quoth King Arthur, "That which thou sayest, Launcelot, is true, yet do I grieve. For though I may take glory that my knights shall achieve the Holy Grail, yet is the sorrow very great to me that this Round Table should be dissolved. Alas, and alas, that it should be so!"

Thus the knights of the Round Table went forth in quest of the Grail—fifty of them in all. All of those who thus went had adventures, and many of them lost their lives and did never return. But of those of whose adventures this history telleth there are only Sir Percival, Sir Bors, and Sir Galahad.

Sir Galahad rode away from Camelot following after the maiden clad all in white. They wended their way onward for a long distance into the forest until finally the maiden said, "Sir Galahad, I must here leave you. But go you upon yonder path, and thither thou wilt find thy shield."

Then lo! she was gone and Sir Galahad rode forward alone. He soon came to a monastery and here he smote upon the gate. Then the porters opened the gate to him and gave him welcome. So he entered the courtyard, and they conducted him to the hall of the monastery, and there he beheld the Abbot of that place, and he said to him, "Sir, I pray you tell me, is there at this place a shield?" The Abbot replied to him, "Aye, sir, there is here a strange and miraculous shield, and it hangeth behind the altar."

So he led Sir Galahad to the chapel and he led him behind the altar, and there he beheld the shield. And it was white and shining, as it were of brightly polished silver. And upon it was marked a red cross, very bold in its marking.

And with the Abbot's permission, Sir Galahad took the shield and hung it about his neck. Then he gave the Abbot thanks, and mounting upon his horse he rode away. Anon, he met a tall and noble-appearing knight, clad in white armor. This knight said to him, "Sir, whence come you?"

To this Sir Galahad made answer, "Sir, I came from a monastery yonder, where I got me this shield." Quoth the White Knight, "Art thou Sir Galahad?" and Sir Galahad replied, "Yea, I am he."

Then the White Knight said to him, "I pray you, sir, to allow me to ride along with you, for I have been awaiting you this long while." And Sir Galahad replied, "So let it be."

So the White Knight rode along with Sir Galahad. And he spoke to Sir Galahad as follows:

"In the old days of Uther-Pendragon there were two knights who were twin brothers. One of these knights was hight Balan and the other was hight Balin.

"Now there were in the far-off city of Sarras two very great marvels: one of these was the spear with which the blessed side was wounded at the time of the crucifixion, and the other was the chalice into which the blood was drained from that deep and pitiful wound.

"Now Sir Balan was in the city of Sarras, and he was attacked by enemies one day when he was unarmed. So he fled away and escaped into the chapel of the castle, where those two holy relics—to wit, the spear and the chalice—were kept. Hither the enemies followed him and would have slain him, only that Sir Balan seized upon that holy spear and ran with it against them.

"But as Sir Balan stood beholding his enemies retreat, there came to him a voice as from Heaven, saying, 'Balan! Balan! what hast thou done?'

"And there came, as from beneath, a deep and hollow rumbling. And the rumbling grew louder and louder, until it became a great earthquake. Then the castle reeled, and fell, one stone upon another, so that all who were within it were buried beneath the ruins, saving only that Sir Balan was not killed. At the same time the spear and the chalice disappeared from that place, and they have never been seen from that time—saving only in visions.

"Now one day Sir Balan came to a river, and beheld there a knight guarding the ford. Then Sir Balan attempted to pass the ford, but the knight would not allow him to do so, wherefore they came to battle with one another. They fought for an entire morning; but at last Sir Balan gave to his enemy a deadly blow that brought him to the earth. Then he rushed off his helmet to make an end of him, but when he beheld the face beneath, he saw that it was the face of his twin brother, Sir Balin. Then he cried out in horror, 'Alas! is it thou, Balin, whom I am about to slay? Lo! I am thy brother Balan!'

"Then Balin, feeling that he was near to death, wept. And he forgave his brother Balan. Then he died. And anon came several White Friars from a monastery that was nearby, and these took Balan to the monastery and there he also died, for he too was wounded, and his heart was broken.

"But ere he died he drew upon his shield a great cross in his own blood. And he told the friars of that place to keep that shield until he should come who was to achieve the Holy Grail and to return it unto Sarras. He predicted of it that no one should be able to wear that shield saving only that one for whom it was intended; and he predicted that it should never be pierced by the point of any weapon forged by the hand of man. It is that shield of Sir Balan which thou carriest, Sir Galahad."

Then Sir Galahad said, "Sir, I would that I knew who thou art." But to this the White Knight only smiled and made reply, "Only this I may say, that I am he who hath had that shield under continual surveillance until now, and now I find that it hath fallen into hands for which it was intended."

Thus these two knights traveled together until the setting of the sun. Then the roadway divided, and at that place the White Knight said to Sir Galahad, "Messire, I must leave thee. Continue upon that way and anon thou wilt come to a chapel where thou mayest lodge for the night."

So saying, the White Knight rode down the path into the woods, and Sir Galahad entered upon the other path. But Sir Galahad turned his head to look after the White Knight ere he should reach the forest, but lo! he was not there, nor was anything to be seen, saving only the trees and the red light of the sunset that lay upon the ground.

After that Sir Galahad continued upon his way until, anon, he heard the ringing of a bell. So Sir Galahad spurred forward and in a little while he beheld the Hermit of the Forest, ringing the bell for vespers.

So he came to that place that was very quiet and innocent, for he beheld that many birds sat perched upon the branches of the trees, and that a wild doe and its fawn were also there. For these creatures loved the Hermit of the Forest. And the Hermit of the Forest beheld Sir Galahad and gave him welcome, and he prepared a lodging for him.

Now leave we Sir Galahad there to follow the other parts of this story.

Now of all the knights of the Round Table Sir Percival was the purest, save for Sir Galahad, and save perhaps for Sir Bors. He was also a most puissant knight, very strong and with great beauty of countenance. In his childhood and youth he had dwelt alone among the mountains with his mother, and thus he had grown to manhood in great innocence. He had known but little of the world until, at nineteen, he had left the mountains to win his knighthood at King Arthur's Court.

All this had happened in bygone years; and Sir Percival was now a well-tried knight who had undergone many adventures.

Now when he set out on the quest of the Grail he traveled for some time with Sir Launcelot; then he rode upon his way alone. And his way led him one day through a waste of land where nothing grew, but where great quantities of stones were scattered over the earth. Here he rode for some time; and then the horse which he rode slipped his foot upon a round stone, and the stone turned under the horse's foot so that it strained its shoulder. Presently, anon, the horse began to limp, and every minute it limped worse. So Sir Percival dismounted, and he walked and the horse limped behind him.

Anon he left that stony waste and came to a country where green things grew. Here he beheld a fair damsel sitting beside a fountain of water, and the damsel was clad all in red. This damsel had with her a palfrey and a great black horse.

Quoth Sir Percival, "Ha, maiden, that is a fine horse that thou hast there. I would that thou wouldst sell me that horse; for mine own, as thou seest, is lame." The maiden said, "Sir, are you not Sir Percival of Gales?"

Then Sir Percival was astonished, and he said, "Yea, damsel, that is my name." "Then," quoth she, "I cannot accept money from you for this horse. But you may take him for your own, and leave your lame horse here. For wit you I have been sent with this horse that you might have it."

Then was Sir Percival astonished. But he thanked the damsel, and he handed her the reins of his horse. Then he put his foot in the stirrup and mounted the black horse.

After that the horse bowed its head and rushed away to the southward with great speed like the wind. Nor could Sir Percival control or guide it, for the horse held the bit between its teeth. And Sir Percival said to himself, Is this beast a horse or is it a demon?

By and by Sir Percival began to catch glimpses of the sea across the uplands like bright silver against the distant horizon; for by this time night had fallen. And anon he could hear the roaring of the sea beating upon a place where there were rocks. Then, reaching this spot where the water churned amongst the rocks, the horse stopped all of a sudden, panting and trembling and all in a lather.

Then Sir Percival dismounted, and as soon as his foot touched the earth the black horse vanished. And Sir Percival stood there, wondering.

Anon he beheld a boat coming across the water from a great way off. Then Sir Percival perceived that there was a beautiful lady in the boat, and that there were seven beautiful damsels attendant upon her. And this lady was clad all in red, and her hair was red, the color of gold, and it was enmeshed in a net of gold.

Thus that boat came to the beach, and Sir Percival came forward and assisted the lady to disembark. And the lady said, "Hail, Sir Percival, and give thee peace."

Quoth Sir Percival, "Who are ye who know me and I know not you?" To the which the lady replied, "We are Fay; therefore we know many things that you wit not of."

Then that lady bade her attendants to set up a pavilion and they did so, and in the pavilion they set a table of gold. Then Sir Percival and the lady seated themselves at the table, and certain of the damsels brought to them all manner of dishes, and Sir Percival and the lady ate together. Then others brought wine, and this wine was very powerful and sweet, and Sir Percival and the lady drank together. Then the lady grew very fond toward Sir Percival, and she put her arms about his shoulders. With this the wine swam in Sir Percival's head. And he said, "Lady, tell me—what is this, and why am I here?" To this she answered, "Percival, thou glorious knight! this is the pavilion of Love, and I am the spirit of Venus who inhabits it. So yield thou to that spirit and take thou the joy of life whiles thou mayest."

Therewith she reached her arms again to Sir Percival and he took her into his arms, and he kissed her upon the lips and the fire from her lips passed into his heart and set his soul aflame.

Then, in that moment, he knew not why, he suddenly bethought him of his quest for the Grail. Then it was as though a wind of ice struck across the flame of his passion, and he cried out in a loud voice, "God! God! why should I sin in this wise?" And therewith he drew upon his forehead the sign of the cross.

Then in an instant the lady shrieked very loud, and all about him was confusion.

And Sir Percival looked, and behold! the lady smote her hands together, and in that instant she disappeared, and all her attendants disappeared, and the pavilion and the table disappeared, and the boat in which she had come disappeared, and Sir Percival found himself alone upon the seaside.

Then Sir Percival kneeled and he set his hands together and he prayed. And he said, "O God! how hast Thou saved Thy servant by means of a thought? For the thought of that which was holy hath purged my sin. How shall I thank Thee for this?" So he prayed for a long time. And when he stood up he beheld that the full moon was shining.

Anon he beheld in the distance an object that approached rapidly. And this object also was a boat, and there was a couch within it, covered with white linen.

Then Sir Percival said, "What is this? Is there a sin also in this, or is it without sin?" And he said, "If this be sin, let it declare itself," and he marked the sign of the cross upon his forehead. But there followed not any malignant sign, and the boat remained where it was. Then Sir Percival perceived that it was intended for him to enter that boat, and he did enter it. Then the boat moved away from the shore rapidly and smoothly. And it ran past the sharp and treacherous rocks, and so out onto the surface of the sea beyond.

Here all was stillness and peace, and there was no sound whatsoever to mar that stillness, but only the moon and the stars shone above in the sky with a wonderful radiance.

So Sir Percival laid him down upon the couch and anon he slept a deep and dreamless sleep.

Now leave we Sir Percival lying in that boat, and turn we to the story of Sir Bors de Ganis.

Upon a certain day Sir Bors rode into the forest, and by and by he came to the chapel of the Hermit of the Forest. So he abided that night with the hermit, and the next morning he besought the hermit to confess him. And the hermit shrived Sir Bors, and he beheld that the soul of Sir Bors was extraordinarily free from sin. And the hermit said, "Sir, if valor and purity of life may so recommend a man that he may win the Grail, then will you certainly behold it with your eyes and touch it with your hand."

To this Sir Bors said, "Sir, that which you tell me is exceedingly comforting to me, for so would I rather achieve a sight of the Grail than anything else in the world. Now, I pray you, tell me if there is anything else that I may do that may better fit me to find that Holy Chalice."

Quoth the hermit, "You shall finally purify yourself by fasting upon bread and water until you have beheld the Grail. And you shall lay aside your armor and shall ride forth in leathern doublet and hose."

So Sir Bors laid aside his armor of defense, and in doublet and hose he rode forth into the world. And whensoever he came to a roadside cross, he kneeled down before it and recited a prayer. So Sir Bors rode forward for many days, and toward evening of one day he found himself in a strange, wild place. He knew not where he was, for there was a wide stretch of dark and dismal land upon all sides of him. And very little grass grew upon that land, but many thornbushes. And anon a carrion crow would spring from the earth and fly heavily away against the gray and dismal sky.

Here he came to a crossroad and as he approached that crossroad he was aware of a solitary knight who was waiting there. This knight was clad in white armor, and he sat upon a white horse, and he said, "Greeting, Sir Bors, whither goest thou?"

Then Sir Bors said, "Messire, who art thou who knowest me and I know not thee?"

The White Knight said, "It matters not who I am, but I know you well, and I know that you seek the Holy Grail. Sir Galahad shall achieve that Grail, and you and Sir Percival, who is the next purest knight to him, shall find it with him. So come now with me."

And Sir Bors said, "I will do so."

So after that they two rode together side by side. And anon the sun sank and the moon arose. And ever they rode in silence all bathed by the white moonlight, their shadows, black and obscure, following them.

Anon Sir Bors heard a roaring, and he said, "What is that sound?" The White Knight said, "That is the sea breaking upon the beach. Thither it is we go."

So they came to where there was a cove of the sea, and at that place there was a beach of pure white sand. Here Sir Bors beheld that a boat rested against the shore, and in the boat was a couch, and on the couch there was a knight lying asleep. And Sir Bors perceived that that knight was Sir Percival.

Then the White Knight said to Sir Bors, "Sir Bors, enter yonder boat, for so only shalt thou find the Grail."

So Sir Bors dismounted from his horse and he entered the boat, and with that Sir Percival awoke. And when Sir Percival perceived Sir Bors he gave him greeting, and Sir Bors greeted Sir Percival. Then the White Knight gave the boat a thrust from the shore, and the boat immediately sped away. And as Sir Bors and Sir Percival gazed back they could yet see the figure of the White Knight seated upon his horse as still and motionless as though he were carved in marble stone. And though neither of them knew it, yet that knight was the spirit of Sir Balan who had returned to lead those knights-champion to find the Grail.

Then anon that white figure faded into the dimness of the moonlight and was gone, and all about them lay the sea, very strange and mysterious and yet full of motion, and on the crests of waves the moonlight ever wavered this way and that as though it were liquid silver.

CHAPTER II: THE GLORY OF THE GRAIL

AND NOW TURN WE to the further adventures of Sir Galahad.

Now, Sir Galahad had ridden far since he had obtained his shield. Then one evening, after the sun had set, he found himself in a wide moorland, and he wist not where he should sleep.

So at last the moon arose, shining very brightly, and by the light thereof Sir Galahad perceived before him a small chapel. And he said to himself, Here will I lodge me for the night.

So Sir Galahad rode up to the chapel and he smote upon the door. Anon there came the recluse to whom that chapel belonged, and he bade Sir Galahad to enter. So Sir Galahad entered. And anon there came another knock, and when the recluse opened the door, he beheld a beautiful lady clad in white; and the lady was mounted upon a cream-white jennet, and the saddle of the jennet was of crimson leather. And the lady said to the recluse, "Sir, I pray you tell me, is there within a knight hight Galahad?"

This heard Sir Galahad, and he said, "Lady, I am Galahad. What would you have of me?"

She said, "Sir, I pray you ride with me and I will lead you to such an adventure as you have never had." Quoth he, "Where is that adventure?" She said, "I cannot tell you more than that."

So Galahad mounted his horse, and immediately he was mounted the lady rode away, and Sir Galahad followed her. So they rode across the moorland together. And all around them lay the silent whiteness of the moon. And the shadows of each followed them across the moorland, very black and mysterious.

They traveled in silence. And thus, by and by, they reached a high part of the moorland, and of a sudden Sir Galahad beheld the sea. And the moon shone upon the sea so that it looked like a shining stretch of silver.

Then they rode down to the sea, and there Sir Galahad beheld a boat lying in the moonlight. And as they two approached the boat, Sir Galahad perceived that the boat was all draped with white linen, and he perceived that there were two men within the boat. And in the moonlight Sir Galahad perceived that one was Sir Percival, and that the other was Sir Bors de Ganis.

Then Sir Galahad sprang down from his horse. And he sprang into the boat and kissed each of those two upon the cheek, and they kissed him upon the cheek in return. And Sir Galahad said, "What do ye here?" To the which they replied, "We wait for thee." And they said, "What lady is that with whom thou hast come hither?" He replied, "I know her not, but she hath brought me here."

Then they beheld that the lady had also dismounted from her horse. And she came close to the boat, and she said, "I come to give you information: You shall sail away from this place, and by and by you shall find another boat of a very magnificent sort. That boat is the *Ship of Solomon*, and it is waiting for you. In it you will find the Grail established, and the ship will take you whither the Grail belongeth. So enter the *Ship of Solomon* freely, and it shall convey you to the city of Sarras where the Grail belongeth." Then turned she to Sir Galahad, and she said, "And to thee, Galahad, am I permitted to say this thing: that it is given to thee that when thou willest thy soul shall depart from thy body, and it shall ascend with the glory of angels into Paradise at thy command. And now fare you well."

Thereafter the lady turned and rode away.

Then that boat in which they were moved swiftly away from the shore, and they sailed until the day dawned; and then they perceived before them another and a larger ship. And that ship was built all of sandalwood, and was tinted with vermilion and ultramarine, and was glorified with gold.

Then Sir Percival said, "This must be the *Ship of Solomon*."

So they departed from their own boat and entered the *Ship of Solomon*, and as soon as they had done so the boat in which they had sailed disappeared. Then they descended below the deck, and they beheld a table of carved silver, and against the table there leaned the spear and upon the table was a purple velvet cloth, spread over something that stood upon the table. And from beneath it there shone a brilliant light, and that light was emitted by the Grail.

Sir Galahad went to the table and lifted the cloth; and lo! beneath it was the Holy Chalice. And it blazed with a light like that of the sun—very splendid and effulgent—so that they could scarcely look upon the splendor thereof.

Then they all three kneeled down before the Grail, and set their palms together, and gave all honor and glory to its splendors.

So the *Ship of Solomon* sailed very swiftly for all that day, and near eventide it approached a great city that stood upon a rocky hill. And that city was the city of Sarras. And anon the boat ceased its voyage beside a wharf that was there.

Then Sir Galahad said, "Let us convey this Holy Chalice to the minster, for, certes, this is where it belongeth."

So they three took up the silver table by three of its corners, and they bare it toward the town.

Now the history of these things telleth that at the town gate there sat a cripple begging. They said to him, "Come, help us bear the fourth corner of this table." He said, "How can I? Lo, I have been a cripple for thirty years." Sir Galahad said, "Ne'ertheless, arise and come." Then the man arose, supported by his crutches, and he laid hands upon the table of the Grail. Then, no sooner had he touched that table, than the strength flowed into him; his joints became supple, and he was no longer a cripple. Then he cried out, "Lo! I am healed!" And with that he skipped and leaped in his strength.

Now the news of this healing became known; so that when they entered the town, great crowds gathered and followed them. Thus they came to the minster, and the Bishop of that minster was there,

and seeing them enter he said, "What have you there?" Sir Galahad replied, "Sir, this is the Holy Grail upon this table."

And Sir Galahad lifted the velvet covering of the Grail, and lo!
the glory of the Grail blazed forth and illuminated the entire
interior of the minster. And all they who beheld the Grail and
that sudden illumination bowed down and uttered prayers.

So the Grail and the spear were placed before the high altar, and
there they remained unveiled; and the glory of them illuminated
all the coadjacent spaces with brightness.

So the Grail remained exposed in that city for three days, and at
the end of that time the three knights were praying before the high
altar, when of a sudden they heard a voice from on high, saying,
"Hail, ye heroes! For ye have recovered that Grail which now is
to be translated from earth to Heaven."

With that voice there came two hands, very white and shining,
and they took the Grail, and there was no body to be seen with
those hands. And there came two other hands and took the spear.
So those four hands lifted the Grail and they lifted the spear, and
they bare those two holy relics aloft. And they ascended, as it were,
through the roof of the minster and were gone in a burst of glory
that lingered and then faded away into darkness.

Then there sounded from on high, to the ears that were un-
stopped to hear that sound, a great anthem as of thanksgiving, and
they three heard that music, but no other who was there heard it.
And they were aware that it was the rejoicing of Heaven over the
return of those relics, wherefore they were filled with ecstasy.

Then was the spirit of Galahad exalted, and he cried aloud,
"There is nothing remaining for me to live for. So now let me
depart in peace."

Thereat with those words the soul was drawn out of his body,
and those two knights who kneeled beside him beheld his spirit
ascend into glory, and at the same time they heard, with a louder
tone, the peal of heavenly triumph as the spirit of Galahad was
received into glory. Then the brightness faded from their eyes.
And in the dark and empty minster they looked at the body of
Sir Galahad, and behold! it was dead.

So passed Sir Galahad, and he was yet not twenty years of age. So with high ceremony they buried the body of Sir Galahad there in the minster.

And after this was done Sir Percival said to Sir Bors, "Here shall I remain and take holy orders and live and die as a monk. But return you, Sir Bors, to the Court of King Arthur, and tell the Court concerning all those things that have befallen."

So the next day Sir Bors kissed Sir Percival, and both wept. Then they parted company and Sir Percival remained at that place and became a monk, and Sir Bors departed thence, returning back again to Camelot.

There he arrived at the ending of a year and a day, and all they who were there made great joy over his return. And Sir Bors told them all the circumstances of the finding of the Grail, and how it had been elevated at Sarras, and of how Sir Galahad had died.

And King Arthur had that history written down in three great books, and one of those books was established at Salisbury, and another at Camelot (which same is Winchester), and the third at Carleon upon Usk; and from these three volumes the story of the Grail has descended to us of the present day.

Now shall be told the history of the passing of Arthur and many of his splendid and glorious knights. With it comes the conclusion of this book, for no more shall then remain to be written.

PART VI—THE PASSING OF ARTHUR

CHAPTER I: SIR MORDRED'S TREACHERY

NOW AFTER THE QUEST of the Grail was ended, all those knights who had not died in that quest, or who were able to return, did return to the Court of King Arthur. But at Court it was not as it once had been. For as time went by it seemed as if more and more there was bickering at Court, and dissension, and partisanship. And much of this dissension centered about the Queen and about Sir Launcelot. For there had ever been those who disliked the Queen, as well as those who liked her; and there had ever been those who were jealous of Sir Launcelot, as well as those who were his friends.

And now some of those who disliked the Queen, and who were jealous of Launcelot, began to plot very openly to cause their downfall. And they began to maintain that the Queen possessed an evil soul, and that Sir Launcelot was her dishonorable lover.

Of this party were two of the brothers of Sir Gawaine, thus nephews of King Arthur; to wit, Sir Mordred and Sir Agravaine. These knights in time spoke very boldly, saying that Sir Launcelot practiced treachery with the Queen against the King's high honor. And one day Sir Agravaine said, "Well it is that Sir Launcelot is the greatest knight now living on the earth, yet he is not greater in his strength than several knights who might come against him at once."

And many knights listened. And Sir Mordred said, "We shall spy upon Sir Launcelot and, when next he visits the Queen in her apartments, we and several others will fall upon him and seize him and hale him before the King for trial."

This said Sir Mordred openly, but in private he said to Sir Agravaine, "Sir Launcelot is guilty of thou knowest what treason. Now what I really purpose is this: that we slay Sir Launcelot in the Queen's apartments. For once he is dead the King will forgive us and believe the Queen to have been guilty, but if Sir Launcelot is alive he will never forgive us. Ha, brother, a dead lion is less dangerous than a living fox."

In this Sir Agravaine agreed with him; so after that they set watch upon Sir Launcelot to take him when next he should visit the Queen. But Sir Launcelot was warned by one who overheard them, and for that while he did not visit the Queen in her apartments.

So one night Sir Mordred called to him a page of the Queen's court, and he said to him, "Lanadel, go you to Sir Launcelot and tell him that the Queen would fain speak with him in her bower." Thereupon the page delivered that message to Sir Launcelot, and Sir Launcelot, suspecting no evil, went secretly to the Queen's apartments.

And Sir Mordred watched at the entrance of the Queen's apartments until he beheld Sir Launcelot enter them. Upon that he ran to Sir Agravaine, and said to him, "Brother, Sir Launcelot is in the Queen's chamber."

So those two called about them certain knights who were at enmity with Sir Launcelot, and they said to them, "Gentlemen, let us hasten and take that traitor knight who is even now in the Queen's bower."

Now those knights whom they called upon were eleven in number, and two of them were sons to Sir Gawaine. These knights, together with Sir Agravaine and Sir Mordred, went to the apartments of the Queen.

And the ladies of the Queen beheld them coming, and wist that they came for no good purpose. Wherefore these ladies ran screaming and bolted the door. Then they ran to the Queen's apartments and they found that Sir Launcelot was there and they cried out, "Lady, your enemies are upon you!"

By this time those knights were at the door, and Sir Agravaine knocked and cried in a thunderous voice, "Launcelot! Thou traitor knight! Why liest thou behind locked doors in the Queen's apartments? Come forth and render an account to us!"

These words were uttered so powerfully that they echoed throughout the castle, and when they struck upon the Queen's ears, she fell as white as ash and sank back upon a couch, placing her hand above her heart.

And Sir Launcelot cast his eyes around him from side to side, but he could see no armor for defense and no way of escape. Thereupon he wrapped his cloak about his arm, and he took his sword in his hand, and he said to those who were beating upon the door, "Messires, cease your uproar and I will come forth." Then he opened the door a little, but not very far, setting his foot against it.

At that a tall and powerful knight, Sir Colgrance, struck a terrible strong blow at Sir Launcelot. This blow Sir Launcelot put aside with his sword and immediately delivered a blow in return, and in that blow he smote Sir Colgrance upon the head so that Sir Colgrance fell down and died.

Then Sir Launcelot seized Sir Colgrance's body and dragged it into the room, and immediately he bolted the door as before. And he said to the Queen, "Lady, here hath Providence delivered armor into my hands. I prithee aid me to arm myself."

So the Queen and her ladies assisted Sir Launcelot to clothe himself in Sir Colgrance's armor. Then Sir Launcelot flung wide the door. And he strode out amongst his enemies like to a lion into the midst of a pack of dogs. And first he smote Sir Agravaine, and Sir Agravaine cried out very terribly and fell down dying to the earth. And then Sir Launcelot smote to the right hand and to the left; and of those eleven knights who were with Sir Agravaine and Sir Mordred he slew nine, including the two young sons of Sir Gawaine. And he smote Sir Mordred upon the shoulder so that he sheared a great slice from the bone, so that anon he and the other two knights fled in tumult from that place. Then he turned him and re-entered the Queen's chamber.

And he said to the Queen, "Lady, my love for thee hath ever been my curse, and now it hath brought us to this end. For in our defense I have slain a nephew of the King and two of the sons of

Sir Gawaine. So now the King will be my foe, and so I must quit this place for aye. But I cannot leave thee, Lady, for without me thou wilt be defenseless. So I prithee prepare thyself for a journey. I will gather about me a number of mine own friends, and we will take thee away from this place."

Then the Queen wept bitterly, and she said, "Ah, Launcelot! Alas! is this then the end?" And he said, "Aye, Lady." Therewith he went forth and left her.

So Sir Launcelot went to Sir Bors, and he told Sir Bors all that had befallen, and when he had told it Sir Bors sent for Sir Ector and for Sir Lionel and for a great number of other knights, and Sir Launcelot told unto them what he had told to Sir Bors.

All those knights held up their swords with their handles before them, and they said, "Herewith and upon this holy sign of the crucifix do we swear that we will ride with and aid Sir Launcelot of the Lake, and assist him to bring this lady to Joyous Gard, and we will there aid and defend him and her with our bodies until the last extremity."

Then came one running to Sir Launcelot, and said to him, "Sir, the Queen biddeth thee to come to her in haste, for they are taking her into custody."

So Sir Launcelot and his knights mounted, and rode with all speed to where the Queen was. And as they approached, Sir Launcelot beheld the Queen surrounded by an armed escort which the King had sent.

Then the Queen beheld Sir Launcelot and she called to him, saying, "Sir Launcelot, make haste!" And she reached out her arms toward him.

Then Sir Launcelot emitted a great and bitter cry. And therewith he and his friends drew their swords and they rushed into the throng smiting from right to left and from left to right. And those who were thus assaulted smote back. But the knights of King Arthur were driven back.

And Sir Launcelot catched the Queen up and seated her on his saddle before him. Then he shouted, "Let us away and escape while there is yet time!"

So with that they all spurred away from that place, cleaving their way before them and taking Queen Guinevere with them. And they rode away from that city, and they ceased not to ride until they had come to Joyous Gard.

Now COME WE TO the beginning of the end of this great and glorious reign of King Arthur of Britain. For so Sir Launcelot stepped between the Queen and the King, and having done so there was no recession for him from that act. For after that he was ever bound to protect the Queen and to cherish her if he could do so; and King Arthur was bound to bring his Queen back to her duty again if he could do so.

So King Arthur armed himself and he summoned those knights and princes, earls and barons who were still allied to him. This he did very reluctantly, for he wished not to wage war with Sir Launcelot and his knights.

Then King Arthur led his army to Joyous Gard. And Sir Gawaine rode upon his right hand. For though Sir Gawaine had ever loved Sir Launcelot, he could not forgive Sir Launcelot for having killed his brother and his two sons. And the army was so vast and multitudinous that it covered all the hills and valleys as it advanced. And red clouds of dust hung over it so that the bright and tranquil light of the sun was obscured by those clouds. And great flocks of carrion crows accompanied the army, for they smelt the blood of many carcasses as from afar. So this army came and settled about Joyous Gard, and it was like an army of locusts that had settled at that place.

And Sir Launcelot and Sir Ector stood upon the parapet of Joyous Gard, and they looked out upon the multitude that encompassed them; and Sir Ector's heart failed him and he said to Sir Launcelot, "Behold, oh brother! would it not be better to compromise with the King and to surrender the Queen?"

Quoth Sir Launcelot, "How talk you of compromise, Messire? Wit you not that to surrender the Queen would be to dishonor ourselves?"

That night the Queen also spoke to Sir Launcelot, and she said,

"Launcelot, why do you suffer for me? Surrender me unto King Arthur and with that this war will cease."

Then Sir Launcelot groaned, but he said, "Lady, I will not surrender you until I am sure that your safety is ensured. Let first the King assure your safety and then we shall consider whether or not you shall return to him."

Then the Queen burst out weeping and she cried, "Oh, woe is me that I have brought so much trouble upon this world!"

Now the army of King Arthur made many assaults upon Joyous Gard. And somewhiles they made breaches in the walls; but ever those breaches were rebuilded at night. And King Arthur lost many hundreds of men; but the defense of the castle lost many scores, and those scores were of greater loss to them than the hundreds that King Arthur lost. For those hundreds could be replaced by other hundreds, but the scores could not be replaced by other scores. Then the friends of Sir Launcelot wist not what they should do, for ever they were growing weaker with each assault, but the armies of King Arthur were not growing weaker.

At this extremity there came the Bishop of Rochester to King Arthur, and his purpose was to make peace betwixt these parties. The Bishop found King Arthur sunk in grief. For already three and twenty knights of the Round Table had lost their lives in this war, and King Arthur grieved for them very sorely.

Then the Bishop stood before the King, and the King looked at him with eyes dimmed with weeping. And the Bishop said, "Lord, let this quarrel cease between you and Sir Launcelot, and let there be peace in the land."

The King said, "Sir, this war was not of my forming, but of Sir Launcelot's; he took the Queen away from me. Let him then deliver the Queen to me and there shall be peace betwixt us."

The Bishop said, "They will not deliver the Queen to thee, Lord, excepting thou wilt declare upon thine honor that no harm shall befall her. And a pledge must also be given for the safety of those knights who have guarded the Queen."

Then the King sat with his fist upon his forehead, and at last he said, as in a smothered voice, "Well, then, let the Queen be delivered to me at Camelot, and I upon my part shall promise that no harm shall be done to her life, or to the lives of those knights who have taken her."

So the Bishop took that message to Joyous Gard, and they in the castle were very glad of it. And Sir Launcelot said to the Bishop, "Let the King return to Camelot, and I will bring the Queen to him in three days' time."

So the King withdrew his army from that place and he returned to Camelot. And upon the third day Sir Launcelot brought the Queen to Camelot. And King Arthur sat in state upon his throne to receive the Queen, and so Sir Launcelot and the Queen came to the foot of the throne, and Sir Launcelot kneeled and the Queen stood before King Arthur.

Quoth Sir Launcelot, "Dread Lord and King, here I bring to you your Queen as I have promised to do. And, Lord, I pray you that you will take her to your heart, and will cherish her there as you one time cherished her."

Then King Arthur frowned, and he said, "Messire, one time you were my friend and the best beloved of all my knights, but that time is past and gone, never to return. Wit you not that that which hath been done can never be undone? Look you, Messire, here beside me is this throne, which is empty. So it shall remain, for never again shall Queen Guinevere or any other queen occupy it, for I hereby renounce her utterly. She hath withdrawn herself from my Court and my bed and so she shall forever remain withdrawn from them.

"I have pledged myself that no harm shall come to her through me; but herewith I give her over to the Church. There she shall remain a recluse until the day of her death."

So said King Arthur, and at a motion of his hand the Lord Bishop of Rochester came forth and led the Lady away, and she was weeping very bitterly.

So the Bishop took the Queen to the Convent of Saint Bridget at Rochester, and there she remained the Lady Abbess of that convent even to the day of her death many years later.

Anon the King said to Sir Launcelot, "Messire, your own doom

I will not announce to you; but I will relegate the annunciation of that doom to my nephew, Sir Gawaine. For the injury which you did to him is a thousand times greater than the injury which you did to me."

Then Sir Gawaine smiled bitterly upon Sir Launcelot, and he said, "Messire, this is the doom that I pronounce. No harm shall befall you in life or in limb. But you must quit this kingdom. And also I pronounce the doom of banishment against those who have been associated with you in these late affairs."

Said Sir Launcelot, "Sir, that is a bitter sentence; for here in this island have I lived all my life, and of it I love every stock and stone. But if I be outlawed, I will go to live in France. So come, my lords, and let us be gone to that country."

So Sir Launcelot and all those lords who were with him departed for France, where, with much sorrow and repining, they took up their lodging at the castle of Chillion.

And King Arthur seized upon all their earldoms and estates, and some of these he bestowed elsewhere and some of them he held for the crown.

CHAPTER II: THE THRONE IS CHALLENGED

WHEN THOSE KNIGHTS had departed for France, Sir Gawaine urged King Arthur that he should follow them to that kingdom and attack them there. King Arthur said, "Sir, why should I do this thing? Is not Sir Launcelot now punished for all he has done? Let him live and die in peace."

But Sir Gawaine said, "Sir, I cannot surrender my rights in this case. For Sir Launcelot slew my brother and my sons, and either his blood or my blood shall answer for this."

Now by this time King Arthur was growing toward being an old man, and he was much broken by sorrow, wherefore at last he agreed with Sir Gawaine to sail to France and to attack Sir Launcelot at Chillion. So King Arthur entrusted the government of Britain to his nephew, Sir Mordred (who was brother to Sir

Gawaine), and he and Sir Gawaine departed with a great army for France.

So this army appeared before the castle of Chillion, and they besieged it. And so there were many battles around Chillion and many lost their lives. And though the knights of King Arthur lost more lives than did the knights of Sir Launcelot, yet they could better afford to lose those lives because new knights were constantly coming from Britain, but no new knights were coming to the army of Sir Launcelot.

Now at that time there was a very learned physician in the camp of King Arthur, and one day Sir Gawaine sent for this learned man, and he said to him, "Sir, can you not produce for me a lotion that shall render me free from all wounds of any sort?"

Quoth the wise man, "Sir, this is impossible. But I can give to you a medicine that will give you, from the ninth hour of morning until the prime of noon, the strength as of ten men." Sir Gawaine said, "Provide me then with that medicine."

So the wise man gave that medicine to Sir Gawaine, and it was as that physician had promised, for from the ninth hour of the morning until the prime of noon, Sir Gawaine was uplifted in body to the strength of ten men.

So the next morning, Sir Gawaine paraded under the walls of the castle, and he called out, "Sir Launcelot, come forth and do me battle. For this satisfaction thou owest to me for slaying my kindred."

But Sir Launcelot would not come forth to do him battle. For Sir Launcelot still loved Sir Gawaine and he loved King Arthur; and because of this love Sir Launcelot would not fight in that part of the battle where Sir Gawaine or King Arthur was.

But when the next morning had come, Sir Gawaine came again and paraded back and forth, and ever he cried out, "Sir Launcelot, thou wicked knight! Come forth and do me battle!"

Then Sir Ector came to Sir Launcelot, and he said, "Kinsman, suffer me to go forth and do battle in thy behalf; for this man shameth us by this challenge."

Then Sir Launcelot wept, and he said, "Thou shalt not go, for wit you that I loved this man better than mine own blood; but if thou art killed, then will I be without my brother. So rather than have thee fight him, I myself will go forth."

And at that Sir Launcelot put on armor and mounted his horse, and he rode forth to meet Sir Gawaine. And he gave him greeting, and said, "Sir Gawaine, I have tried to avoid this battle, for I fear me either you or I shall be slain. And I would not slay you for the love that was of old betwixt us; wherefore I would not do battle with you if that battle could be avoided."

Quoth Sir Gawaine, "What prate you of love, Sir? For wit you that even if ever I loved you, yet all that love is now transformed into hate. Wherefore either you or I shall die by the hand of the other."

Then Sir Launcelot sighed. And with that sigh he closed his helmet, and withdrew to that part of the field which was to be his place of battle.

Then both knights shouted to their horses and sprang to the charge, galloping against one another with a noise like thunder. So they met and smote one another in the center of the other's shield. And before that shock the spear of each was split into many small pieces. Then each knight drew his sword, and each rushed at the other furiously.

But though Sir Launcelot smote with all of his strength, yet Sir Gawaine smote with the strength of ten. So Sir Launcelot was driven backward and around and around in small circles; and he was altogether astonished at the strength of Sir Gawaine.

And Sir Launcelot had so much ado to defend himself that he made no attack, but only a defense with sword and shield. And anon the blood began to flow from him, so that the ground on which he fought was all red with blood; and in all that while Sir Gawaine had hardly any wounds at all.

Yet by and by it reached the prime of noon, and still Sir Gawaine had not struck down Sir Launcelot. Then that strength of ten that he had from the medicine began to wane away as the flame of a candle flickers and wanes away when the wax is consumed. So anon Sir Launcelot felt that the attack of Sir Gawaine was no longer so furious as it had been. Therewith he redoubled his own battle. And he drave Sir Gawaine backward before him, for Sir Gawaine could not now stand before the fierceness of Sir Launcelot's attack.

Then from weariness the shield of Sir Gawaine began to fall low, and Sir Launcelot ran in upon him, and whirling his sword, he smote Sir Gawaine upon the neck upon the left-hand side. And the blade of Sir Launcelot's sword sheared through the armor and through the neck and breast of Sir Gawaine. Then Sir Gawaine sank slowly down upon his knees and there rested, with his hand upon the earth. And the blood poured down his arm and wet the earth beneath him.

Then Sir Launcelot rushed the helmet off Sir Gawaine's head, and he cried, "Sir Gawaine, yield or I will slay thee!"

Quoth Sir Gawaine, "Messire, already thou hast slain me. For thou hast given me my death wound."

Then Sir Launcelot wept and he said, "Sir, say not so. Now I pray thee that thou wilt forgive me for this wound and for all else that I have done against thee!"

But Sir Gawaine looked at the blood that ran in streams down his arm, and he said, "I will not forgive thee, Launcelot. For thou hast slain me as thou hast slain my sons, and upon thee I voice my curse and their curse as well."

Then Sir Launcelot knelt weeping before Sir Gawaine, and Sir Gawaine said, "Get you hence, Sir Knight, for my friends are coming."

Then Sir Launcelot looked and he beheld the knights of King Arthur coming in that direction. So he mounted his horse and rode away to the castle. And when those knights, Sir Gawaine's friends, came to where Sir Gawaine lay, they laid him upon a litter, and they bare him away to his tent, and anon the chirurgeon came to him to search his wounds. But when the chirurgeon beheld that great wound in his neck, he sent for King Arthur, and he said, "This man cannot live, but must die."

Then King Arthur hid his face and for a while he said nothing. Then he went to the bedside of Sir Gawaine, and he said to him,

"Sir, keep up your heart." To this Sir Gawaine made answer, "My heart faileth not, but my life hangeth fluttering upon my lips, and soon it must pass from me." And he further said, "Sir, wit ye of this, your own case is as bad as mine. Return you again to Britain as fast as you are able, for I trust not Sir Mordred, albeit he is my brother. For he hath ever had a dark and gloomy spirit. And he hath ambition for the throne, and now that you have lost so many good knights at this castle, he will certes seize upon your throne. Wherefore I pray you to return to Britain as soon as may be."

King Arthur said, "Sir, these are imaginings upon your part. For Sir Mordred is a knight of the Round Table, and is bound to me in fealty."

Sir Gawaine said, "Lord, I lie now very close to death and all things appear extraordinarily clear to mine eyes. Sir Mordred hath no love for any soul save himself. Wherefore, I fear me he will sacrifice you to his desires. Lord, I shall not live until tomorrow morning, wherefore, I charge you, bury me in haste, and depart straightway for England."

So that night in the second hour after midnight, Sir Gawaine drew his last breath and died. And after he had passed, King Arthur wept and he said as follows:

The Lament of King Arthur

"So passeth this dear and faithful friend. There is not of all those who are left anyone whom I love so well as I loved him. For though he was passionate in his angers, yet to me he was always loving and full of dutifulness and kindliness.

"He was the companion of my youth. When I had come to my throne, he was among the first who came and laid his hands between my palms. Also he was one of the first of all those of the Round Table to take his seat at that table. But now he is gone and I am left alone, like the tree in the forest that hath been struck by lightning. Yea, like that tree my foliage is withered and now I stand stark and bare against the sky. For my Queen, who was the lover of my youth, is estranged from me, and I shall never behold her more. My Round Table, that was otherwise the chiefest glory of my reign, is broken and scattered; and my throne itself totters to its fall.

"All these are sad and woeful happenings, but the saddest and most woeful of all is that this knight hath died. Would that I had died in his stead! What worse hath Fate in store for me than this that he is dead?"

So King Arthur mourned for Sir Gawaine. And then the next morning he was aroused very early from his couch of grief by a messenger from Britain, and his message was this: that Sir Mordred had seized upon the throne and the crown of Britain, and was holding them for his own.

Then King Arthur gave command that the siege of Chillion should be raised, and that after Sir Gawaine was buried they should all return again to Britain.

So THE NEWS CAME to Britain that King Arthur was returning. And when that news was conveyed to Sir Mordred, he hastily collected such of his army together as were there at hand, and he took that army with him to Dover; his intent being to prevent the King from landing if he could do so.

So as King Arthur approached the shore at Dover, he beheld that there was a considerable army drawn up on the beach. At length he perceived Sir Mordred in the forefront, and he wist that that army was there to do battle with him. Then he groaned and said, "Is there yet more blood to be shed? Well, then, it must be shed, for never will I give up my throne unless I give it up with my life."

So as the boats drew near to the shore, those who were in them leaped into the water and waded to the shore. And the army of Sir Mordred came down to the water, and a great battle was fought there at the edge of the water, so that the water was all discolored red with the blood of those who were slain.

But yet Sir Mordred did not prevent that army from landing, for ever more leaped from the boats, and so at last the army of Sir

Mordred was forced back, and King Arthur's army landed. Then King Arthur took possession of that part of Britain; and Sir Mordred withdrew to Baremdown, and he gathered about him all of his followers who had hitherto been tardy in coming to him. So Sir Mordred had a very considerable army, and he stationed that army upon a rise of land where were three hills. For so he could charge down those hills against his enemies, whilst they must charge up those hills against him.

So came King Arthur, and when he perceived the dispersion of Sir Mordred's army, he arranged his army into three divisions.

Then he charged his army up those hills against his enemy, and he charged again and again, but still he could not gain the crest of those hills. But then when he charged for the fourth time, this time he took the center hill, and with that the army of Sir Mordred broke and fled. And the army of Sir Mordred took up its station not far from Salisbury.

So King Arthur won the battle of Baremdown, but with sad and bitter loss. For many knights fell in that assault and amongst them was Sir Ewaine, who was mortally hurt.

CHAPTER III: KING ARTHUR'S VISIONS

NOW WHEN KING ARTHUR heard that Sir Ewaine was hurt, he went to where the wounded knight lay in his pavilion. And Sir Ewaine's face was very pale, and the dew of death stood upon his forehead. And Sir Ewaine said, "Art thou there, my King?" And King Arthur kneeled beside Sir Ewaine and said, "Ewaine, it is I."

Then Sir Ewaine said, "Sir, I beseech thee to send for Sir Launcelot. For Sir Launcelot is the best of thy knights and he has with him several knights that are very strong. These will come to thine aid if thou wilt ask them, and so thou wilt overthrow Sir Mordred. But if thou dost not send for Sir Launcelot then it may be that Sir Mordred will overthrow thee."

Quoth King Arthur, "How shall I send for him? And by what right shall I ask him to come to mine aid?"

Quoth Sir Ewaine, "Give me parchment and ink." So they brought parchment and ink, and they propped Sir Ewaine up upon his bed. Then Sir Ewaine wrote a letter to Sir Launcelot. And this letter King Arthur sent to Sir Launcelot in France.

There Sir Launcelot summoned his knights and read that letter to them, and he said, "Messires, who will go with me to Britain and do battle for the King?"

And those knights said, "I will go!"—"And I!"—"And I!"— until they all agreed to go fight for King Arthur.

Now return we to King Arthur again. For there was he left kneeling beside the couch of Sir Ewaine. And presently Sir Ewaine said, "Good my Lord, are you there?" For Sir Ewaine's eyes were now darkening in death. And King Arthur said, "Yea, I am here." And Sir Ewaine said, "Hold my hand." So King Arthur held the hand of Sir Ewaine. So Sir Ewaine lay for a little, breathing deep draughts of death; and by and by he lay still, for his spirit had passed from him.

King Arthur arose, weeping, and went forth from that place. And that day Sir Ewaine was buried at the minster and many honors were paid to him.

Then King Arthur gathered his army together and he pursued Sir Mordred in the direction of Salisbury. And the next day he came to that place where Sir Mordred was, and there he halted his army.

That night King Arthur lay in his pavilion and he slept very deeply. And anon while he slept he had a dream.

He dreamed that he sat upon his throne, and that his throne was established upon a monstrous wheel. And anon the wheel rose above the rim of the earth, and he beheld the sun shining in all its glory, and the sun glittered upon him and he felt all the joy and delight of that sunlight. So the wheel reached its apex, and then it began to descend. And it descended below the rim of the world, and so the sunlight left the King.

And King Arthur dreamed that he looked beneath him, and he beheld that the wheel was descending more and more swiftly to a great pool. And this pool was filled with blackness and with blood, and behold there was no bottom to it. And by then the throne of

King Arthur was inclining very greatly toward that pool, and the King felt that he was slipping from his throne, and at that his soul was filled with terror. So he screamed loudly, "Save me!" At that several attendants ran into his pavilion, crying out, "Lord, Lord! what aileth thee? Awaken!" And with that King Arthur awoke.

And he sat up and gazed about him in amazement, and he said, "I dreamed a dream, and it was a dreadful dream." And he said to those in attendance upon him, "Do not go from me yet, for that dream hath affrighted me."

So they all sat near to him and by and by they wist that he slept again. Then they withdrew.

But King Arthur did not sleep, though it was a manner of sleep, for he beheld all the things about him as though he were partly awake. And in this state he beheld a vision. For he saw the flap at the doorway of the pavilion that it moved, and anon it was raised and Sir Gawaine entered. And the face of Sir Gawaine was very calm and cheerful. Then King Arthur dreamed that he said to Sir Gawaine, "Sir, how is this? Was it not then you whom we buried in France?"

Sir Gawaine said, "Nay, Lord, that was not I, that was but my shell. This is I myself, and I have come from Paradise to charge you that great danger lieth before you, and if you do battle tomorrow-day you will assuredly perish. Wit you that Sir Launcelot will in a little while come to your assistance. Wherefore I pray you make such terms with Sir Mordred as you may, but do not join battle with him yet."

Then the figure of Sir Gawaine melted slowly from his sight, and King Arthur sat up upon his couch and he beheld daylight, for the sun had risen.

Then King Arthur was much perturbed in spirit, for he wist that what he had beheld was no dream, but a vision of prophecy. So he called to him his knights, and also the wisest of his counselors. When these were come he told to them the vision, and he said, "Sirs, is it better to treat with these our enemies today than to do battle with them?"

Then all those agreed with him and said, "That which thou sayest is true. Do not fight with Sir Mordred today, but treat with him." So King Arthur chose him two bishops and two knights, and those four he sent as ambassadors to Sir Mordred. And he said to them, "Spare not your promises of land and of estate, but make a treaty for a month and a day; for by that time we will know how Sir Launcelot standeth toward us."

So those envoys went to Sir Mordred, and it was arranged that Sir Mordred and King Arthur should meet upon the next day, at a place betwixt the two armies. And it was arranged that each of them should sign a treaty, and that there should be peace in the land at least for a month and a day.

Now the place where this meeting was to be held was a certain gentle valley. Upon one extremity of the valley one could behold the distant ocean, and upon the other extremity the plains of Salisbury, and the two armies were gathered upon the hills looking down upon the middle of that valley. And in the center of that valley there was a pavilion erected. And King Arthur came with six knights and Sir Mordred came with six knights, and these twelve knights stood some short distance away from one another, and King Arthur and Sir Mordred entered the pavilion. There upon the table lay the treaty to be signed, and those two drew near to sign it.

Now it was understood that none of those twelve knights who had come with King Arthur and Sir Mordred should draw a weapon of any sort. For King Arthur did not trust Sir Mordred, and Sir Mordred did not trust King Arthur. But whilst those knights stood talking to one another, it chanced that an adder lay hidden in a bush. And one of Sir Mordred's knights stepped back and trod upon the adder, and the adder stung him in the heel. Then that knight, without thinking of those commands that had been laid upon him, drew his sword to slay that adder. And when the knights of King Arthur beheld this and beheld the bright blade gleam in the sunlight, then they too drew their swords crying, "Treason!" And the knights of Sir Mordred also drew their swords.

And upon that outcry Sir Mordred rushed out from the tent,

crying, "I come! I come!" Then King Arthur also rushed out from the tent and he beheld his six knights at battle with the six knights of Sir Mordred, and he beheld his army and Sir Mordred's army rushing toward them. And the beat of the hoofs of those approaching armies was like to the sound of thunder ever coming nearer. And the cloud of dust behind those armies was like the smoke of a conflagration. Thus those armies rode rapidly down the slopes and toward them, and King Arthur ran to his horse and mounted nimbly thereon, and he spurred back to join his army.

So those two armies met with a shock that might have been heard a league. And many knights fell in that assault, and the horses pressed upon them with their hoofs and many died beneath that pressure. And then came the yeomen afoot, and these ran hither and thither and slew many who yet lived.

So that fierce battle continued for all that day, and in it were slain twelve thousand men. But as night descended the army of Sir Mordred broke and fled, and King Arthur was left the victor.

But when King Arthur sat his horse in the midst of the battlefield, he wept so that the tears ran in streams down his face. Yea, he tasted those tears in his mouth and they were salt to his taste.

For of all those knights who had once surrounded the Court of King Arthur and had made it so glorious there were hardly any left. And of all the knights of the Round Table, there were not twelve who were yet alive. All others had perished, and the ground was sown thick with them as the seashore is sown thick with the cobbles that lie upon it.

Now presently, as King Arthur sat there, Sir Bedivere joined him. And the moon arose very full and round and clearly shining. What time King Arthur and Sir Bedivere rode across the field of battle, and the King discovered many knights lying there who were friends and many other knights who were foes. For the sky was without any cloud at all upon it; and the light of the moon was as clear and bright as though it were daylight.

Now as King Arthur and Sir Bedivere progressed upon the field of battle, they were, by and by, aware of a knight who stood alone beside a bramblebush. And the knight stood very still, like to a statue of iron. And the light of the moon shone down upon him and upon his armor. And that armor was stained with red, for he had been wounded in several places.

So they came nearer to that knight, and they knew him to be Sir Mordred. And all about Sir Mordred there lay dead knights; for here Sir Mordred had made his last stand with several of his knights.

But the horse of Sir Mordred had been slain and Sir Mordred himself had been wounded in the thighs so that he could not escape with those of his army who had fled.

Then King Arthur said to Sir Bedivere, "Look you! Yonder is Mordred himself. Through him hath come all this later evil, wherefore he is meet for death at my hands." And the King said to Sir Bedivere, "Lend me thy spear and I will slay him."

Then Sir Bedivere said to the King, "Look you, Sir, how he stands looking at us, like a wounded hawk. Beware, Sir, and remember the dream that you had. So far have you escaped harm, but should you assail this man, who knoweth but that you may yet meet your death?"

But King Arthur said, "What is my life to me now, and what have I to lose in losing my life? Tide me life, tide me death, I will slay this man, so give me your spear, Messire."

Then Sir Bedivere gave his spear to King Arthur, and Sir Mordred drew his sword, and he came forward to meet King Arthur, and as he came he whirled his sword on high. And King Arthur drave his spurs into his horse and charged against Sir Mordred; and King Arthur's spear pierced the body of Sir Mordred and stood an ell out behind the back.

Then Sir Mordred felt that he had received his wound of death, wherefore he bethought him only of revenge against King Arthur. So he pressed up against the spear with all of his might, and when his body was against the burr of the spear, he swung his sword above his head, and he smote King Arthur upon the helmet.

In that blow was all the last desperation of Sir Mordred's life, and so the blow sheared through the helmet of King Arthur, and it sheared through the brainpan of the King and deep into the brain itself. Then King Arthur reeled upon his saddle and swayed. And he would have fallen only that Sir Bedivere catched him and held him up upon his saddle.

And Sir Mordred wist that he had given King Arthur his death wound, wherefore he fell down and he laughed and he said, "So I die, but ere I die I have finished my work." Therewith he breathed very deep, and his spirit left his body.

Sir Bedivere said to King Arthur, "Lord, are you hurt?" And King Arthur, breathing heavily, said, "Sir, this wound is the wound of my death as that knight declared. Take me hence to a shelter."

And Sir Bedivere said, "Lord, yonder is a chapel." And King Arthur said, "Take me thither and let me be at peace."

CHAPTER IV: CONCLUSION

So Sir Bedivere dismounted, and he took the horse of King Arthur by the bridle, and so he brought King Arthur to the chapel, and helped him into the chapel and laid him upon a bench.

Then King Arthur groaned very deeply, and he said to Sir Bedivere, "Remove my helmet, and search my hurt."

So Sir Bedivere removed the helmet of King Arthur and he beheld the wound upon his head that it was very deep and bitter. And Sir Bedivere wept; for he wist that of that wound King Arthur must die.

But King Arthur said, "Weep not, Sir Bedivere, but do straightway as I tell thee." And he said, "Beholdest thou Excalibur strapped about my loins?"

And Sir Bedivere said, "Yea, Lord."

King Arthur said, "Take that sword and carry it to the water and cast it into the water; then return thou hither and tell me what thou seest."

Then Sir Bedivere unbuckled the strap from about King Arthur, and he folded the strap around the blade of Excalibur and he took the sword and went away with it.

But when Sir Bedivere had come out into the moonlight, the moonlight shone very brightly down upon Excalibur; and Sir Bedivere said to himself, Why should I cast this splendid sword into the sea? Certes, the King raves! Rather will I keep this sword, to show to generations yet to come how great and splendid was the estate of King Arthur.

So Sir Bedivere took Excalibur and he hid it beneath the roots of a tree. Anon he returned to King Arthur, and he said, "Lord, I have cast the sword into the sea."

Quoth the King, "What sawest thou, Sir Bedivere?"

Quoth Sir Bedivere, "What should I have beheld, Lord? I beheld nothing but the waves beating upon the shore."

Then King Arthur said, "Ah, liar and despicable knight! Thou hast deceived me, who trusted in thee. For thou hast coveted the jewels upon the handle of the sword, and hast refrained from casting it into the sea."

Then Sir Bedivere said, "Lord, I repent me."

But King Arthur said, "Go now, and do what I bid thee do, and this time fail not. For my time draweth near and I have now but a little time to live."

So Sir Bedivere went forth again. And he took the sword from where it lay hidden. But when he again beheld it in the light of the moon, his purpose weakened within him, and he said to himself, Surely, it would be a sin to cast away this sword. For it is the most beautiful sword in all the world.

So Sir Bedivere hid Excalibur again and returned to the King, and the King said, panting, "Sir, have you performed that which I have commanded you?"

And Sir Bedivere said, "Yea, Lord."

Quoth the King, "What saw you in doing this thing?"

Said Sir Bedivere, "Lord, I beheld the moon shining on high, and the waves of the sea breaking against the beach; but naught else did I behold."

Then the King cried out, "Oh, woe is me! that all my authority hath departed from me with my strength! For here I lie hovering upon the edge of death, and now this knight who is my sworn knight and vassal will not do that which I bid him to do."

Then Sir Bedivere wept and he ran forth from that chapel. And he took the sword and ran down to the seashore, and when he had come there he whirled the sword several times about his head and cast it far out over the water. And Sir Bedivere beheld the sword that it flashed in the moonlight describing pure circles of light. So the sword descended to the water, and there emerged from the water an arm clothed in white samite. And the arm catched the sword and brandished it thrice, and then drew it down beneath the water.

All this Sir Bedivere beheld, and then he returned to King Arthur, and he said, "Lord, I did as you commanded me."

Quoth King Arthur, "And what did you behold?"

Said Sir Bedivere, "When I thus threw that sword into the sea, an arm clothed in white samite came out of that water. And the hand of the arm catched Excalibur and brandished it three times in the air and then drew it beneath the water. That is what I saw."

Said King Arthur, "Well hast thou served me! But the time groweth short. Take me upon thy shoulders and bear me to the shore at that place where thou didst cast Excalibur into the sea. There thou wilt find a boat with several ladies in it, for now I know that that boat will be there."

So Sir Bedivere stooped his shoulders. And he drew the arms of King Arthur upon either side of his neck. And Sir Bedivere lifted King Arthur and bare him out of that chapel and into the moonlight. And Sir Bedivere bare King Arthur down the cliffs to that place where he had cast the sword into the sea. And as he drew near he perceived that there was a boat drawn up to the shore at that spot where he had stood to cast the sword into the water. And Sir Bedivere saw that there were three queens and their attendants standing within the boat.

Two of those queens Sir Bedivere knew, for one was Queen Morgana le Fay and the other was the Queen of North Wales. But the third of those queens he did not know. Yet he saw that she was very tall and straight and that she was clad in garments of green; and her hair was black and glossy, and her face was exceedingly white, and her eyes were very black and brilliant. This lady stood at the tiller of that strange boat and she was the Lady of the Lake, though Sir Bedivere wist not who she was.

Then when Sir Bedivere came thitherward carrying King Arthur upon his shoulders, the ladies in the boat lifted up their voices in piercing lamentation.

And Queen Morgana le Fay and the Queen of North Wales arose and reached their arms for King Arthur; and Sir Bedivere gave King Arthur into their arms and they two took him—Queen Morgana by the shoulders and the Queen of North Wales by the knees—and they lifted him into the boat.

And they laid him upon a couch within the boat, and his head was pillowed upon the lap of Queen Morgana. And Sir Bedivere stood upon the shore and looked upon the face of King Arthur, and he beheld that it was white like to ashes.

And Sir Bedivere cried out, "My Lord and King, wilt thou leave me? What then shall I do? For here am I alone in the midst of mine enemies."

Then King Arthur opened his eyes and he said, "Ha, Messire, thine enemies are all put to flight, and in a little while Sir Launcelot comes who will be thy friend. But go thou back into the world and tell them all that thou hast beheld. For wit you that now I know that I shall not die at this place, but that I shall go in this boat and with my sister, Queen Morgana, to Avalon. There in the Vale of Avalon I shall live, and after many years I shall again return to Britain. And no man shall know of my return. But with that return shall come peace and tranquillity; and war shall be no more. So take that message back with thee into the world, for now I go to leave thee; and so farewell."

Then the boat trembled and moved away from the shore. And for a while Sir Bedivere saw it, and then he was not sure that he saw it, and then it vanished away into the whiteness of the moonlight, and was gone from his vision.

Then Sir Bedivere walked weeping away from that shore and he wept so that hardly could he see what next step he took. And when the morning was come he found himself near to a city. So he went to that city and he found that there was a great bustle of people coming and going.

So Sir Bedivere said, "Who is here?"

And they said to him, "It is the Archbishop of Canterbury."

Sir Bedivere said to them, "Take me to him."

So they took him to where the Archbishop was, and Sir Bedivere told the Archbishop of all that had happened. The Archbishop listened with great astonishment and he cried out, "What is this thou tellest me? Is King Arthur then gone?" And he said, "What next of kin doth the King leave behind?" Sir Bedivere said, "His nighest of kin is Sir Constantine of Cornwall, who is cousin unto Sir Gawaine."

The Archbishop said, "Him then shall we crown to be the next King. For so will he succeed in rightful line from the strain of King Uther-Pendragon."

And so it was done as the Archbishop said, for shortly after that Sir Constantine of Cornwall was crowned King of Britain.

So I HAVE TOLD YOU of the passing of Arthur, which in all the other histories of those things is told as I have told it. But of that which happened thereafter there are many separate histories.

But that history which hath been accepted of old by the people of England is this: that King Arthur was taken by those queens to Avalon, and that there he was salved so that he did not die.

And touching Avalon there is this to say—that it is the dwelling place of Queen Morgana le Fay, and that it is a strange and wonderful island that floats forever upon the sea to the westward.

There in that pleasant country is no snow and no ice; neither is there the scorching heat of summer; but all forever and for aye is springtime.

And the people are always happy, and live in peace watching their flocks, which are as white as snow, and their herds, whose breath smelleth of wild thyme and parsley.

There, people believe, yet liveth King Arthur, and ever he lieth sleeping as in peace. But it is believed by many that the time shall come when he will return once more to this earth, and all shall be peace and concord amongst men. Wherefore, let every man live at peace with other men, and wish them well and do them well, and then will King Arthur awake. Then will he return unto his own again.

NOW IT HATH ALREADY BEEN told how that Sir Launcelot of the Lake received the letter of Sir Ewaine, and of how he decided to come to the aid of King Arthur.

So Sir Launcelot and his knights to the number of two hundred and twelve came to England in ships and galleys, and they landed at Dover.

And when Sir Launcelot arrived at Dover there came to him a messenger and told him of that battle which had been fought near Salisbury, and of how Sir Mordred had been slain and King Arthur had died thereafter. And that messenger also told him how that Sir Constantine of Cornwall had been crowned King of Britain.

All this Sir Launcelot heard, and he wept a very great deal and those knights who were with him wept also. And Sir Launcelot cried out, "Ah, my dear noble Lord, King Arthur! Woe is me! For all is turned to ruin and to loss about us!"

So Sir Launcelot made his lament, and the tears flowed down his face. And he said to his knights, "Who of us can now serve under King Constantine as vassals?" They said to him, "None of us." Said Sir Launcelot, "Nor can I." Then he said to the messenger, "Where is now Queen Guinevere?" And he said, "Sir, she is the Abbess of the Convent of Saint Bridget at Rochester."

So that night Sir Launcelot took horse and he rode away alone, and he rode to the Convent of Saint Bridget. And he said to those who were there, "Let me have speech with the Abbess."

Then anon came Queen Guinevere. And when she beheld Sir Launcelot she cried out, "God save me! Is it thou?" And with that she felt around behind her as though in a blindness. And she felt that there was a form behind her and she sat down upon the form. Then she said, "Sir, what seek you here?" And Sir Launcelot replied, "I seek thee, Lady."

The Queen said, "Ah, Launcelot! It is vain for thee to seek me here, for ever my heart is here in this place and here it will always remain. For here have I bethought me of my life and of all the sinfulness that I have committed. And my Lord, King Arthur, is now ever first within my thoughts and within my heart."

Then Sir Launcelot cried out, "And I, Lady, is there naught in thy thoughts for me?"

She said, "Yea, Launcelot, there is great friendship and love for thee, but not that sort of love. So get thee back to Joyous Gard and there take thee to wife some fair and gentle lady."

Sir Launcelot said, "Lady, I can never wed any woman in this world but thee." And the Queen said, "Ah, Launcelot, that is a pity."

So speech between those two came to an end; and Sir Launcelot rode away. And anon he rode into the forest to the place where dwelt the Hermit of the Forest. And there he kneeled down before that hermit and he said, "Sir, I pray you to confess me and assoil me. For here henceforth and to the end of my days will I remain a hermit of the forest like as thou art."

So Sir Launcelot became a recluse of the forest with intent never more to be anything else. And in time he was joined by Sir Bors and six other knights.

So all those knights remained there within the forest and all of them assumed the holy orders of hermits. And they dwelt in great peace and concord, and they disturbed nothing that lived within the forest, so that the wild creatures of the forest presently grew tame to them. For they could lay their hands upon the haunches of the wild doe of the forest and it would not flee away from them for the wild thing wist that they meant it no harm.

Thus they lived there in solitude and they cultivated their plots of pulse and barley, and the fame of their holiness spread far and wide, so that many people came thither from the world for the sake of their prayers and benediction.

And so they lived there for five or six years. Then they left that forest as shall be told.

For now speak we of the passing of Sir Launcelot.

One morning all they who were there awoke very early and they went to their matin prayers. That morning was in the Maytime, and all the trees were in leaf and the apple trees were in blossom; and whensoever the soft warm wind blew, then did those blossoms shed their fragrant pink snow until all the grass around about was spread therewith.

And when they were assembled they beheld that Sir Launcelot was not there and they said, "Where is Sir Launcelot?" So Sir Bors went to the cell of Sir Launcelot and he beheld that Sir Launcelot was lying very peacefully upon his couch. And Sir Bors went to Sir Launcelot to arouse him, and he saw that Sir Launcelot was dead. And the hands of Sir Launcelot were folded upon his breast, and there was a smile of great peace upon his lips.

Then Sir Bors went to the door of the cell of Sir Launcelot and he called the others to come thither and they did so. And Sir Bors said, "God be praised that he died in such peace and tranquillity."

And all they, as they gazed upon Sir Launcelot, beheld that it was so, and that he had indeed died in great peace and tranquillity with his God.

And Sir Bors said, "Let us carry the body of this good knight to Joyous Gard. For so would he have it."

So they bare the body to Joyous Gard to be buried, and so, after many tribulations, the body of Sir Launcelot lay in peace and quietness at that place.

And those knights who were with him continued at Joyous Gard. And one of those knights always sat at vigil beside the tomb of Sir Launcelot and kept burning there seven waxen tapers. And so the tomb was always illuminated whiles those knights lived.

And the last of those knights to die was Sir Bors de Ganis, for Sir Bors was over fourscore years of age when he died. When the priest came thither one morning, he found Sir Bors sitting beside the tomb of Sir Launcelot, and Sir Bors had died. And one of those seven candles (which was the candle of Sir Bors) was not lit but was burned out. For so the life of Sir Bors had flickered out, even as the light of that candle had departed.

So with this endeth the history of the lives of those knights and so I have told it to you.

THUS HAVE I WRITTEN the history of King Arthur and of sundry of those knights that comprised his Round Table. For so may you see with what patience, what labor and what devotion those knights served their King, their Round Table and their fellows.

For those knights were very gallant gentlemen; and ever they brought aid to those who were in trouble; and ever they destroyed monsters and wicked men, and so made the world a better and a comelier place in which to dwell. And wit ye that no man can do better than that in this world: to bring aid to the afflicted, and a release from trouble to those who are in anxiety.

And now I thank God that He hath permitted me to finish this work, for wit ye that when a man undertaketh to write a history such as this, he knoweth not whether he shall live to complete that which he hath begun.

But so I have completed it, and for that I thank God who permitted me to complete it. Amen.

Howard Pyle
(1853–1911)

"PICTURES," SAID HOWARD PYLE, founder of the Brandywine School and father of twentieth-century American illustration, "are the creations of imagination, not of technical facility." Product of a Quaker upbringing in Wilmington, Delaware, Pyle combined the Quaker reverence for inward contemplation with a love of nature, especially the light and countryside of the Brandywine Valley, which was to remain his home and inspiration for much of his life.

Never a good student, Pyle was nevertheless an avid reader, devouring fairy stories, the plays of Shakespeare, and Malory's tales, later to be the basis for his four-volume masterpiece, *King Arthur*. *King Arthur*, the culmination of his career as an illustrator and author, was seven years in the making (1903–1910). It reflects both the carefully honed creative imagination of the artist and the mechanical skills of a craftsman who took care to understand and gear his finished product toward the best use of existing printing technology.

Creativity was something Pyle struggled for on his own, the standard art school curriculum of the time being to do endless copying (from copies!) of the "masters." No painting was done outdoors, because it was felt that nature was too "various." Art's purpose was to create the Ideal, and to that end studios were built to catch only the north light. Good painting meant technical exactitude, and nineteenth-century American art schools produced, for the most part, mediocre and derivative work.

Because of his dissatisfaction with such methods of training, Pyle began teaching. Refused by the Pennsylvania Academy of Fine Arts because of his unorthodox views, he went to the Drexel Institute of Art, Science, and Industry. In 1898, he convinced Drexel to finance a summer program for ten students in Chadds Ford, Pennsylvania, a tiny village on the Brandywine River about ten miles from Wilmington. The students spent ten hours a day six days a week outdoors, painting. By 1900, Pyle had quit Drexel and was running his school year round, on a tuition-free basis. With never more than ten dedicated artists at a time, Pyle was able to achieve a deep personal understanding of each student. As his student N. C. Wyeth said of him: "We received in proportion to that which was fundamentally within us." Besides Wyeth, Pyle trained such artists as Maxfield Parrish and Harvey Dunn, and in the process established the style and standards for twentieth-century American illustration.

Pyle was a man who loved activity, and throughout his teaching career he continued writing and illustrating his own work. He had six children, and there are stories of him sitting, surrounded by playing toddlers, correcting proofs, dictating to his wife, and holding an interview all at once.

In 1906, at age fifty-three, Pyle tried mural painting, a technique new to him. In 1910 he decided, with typical thoroughness and enthusiasm, to move the family to Italy where he could study the great frescoes of the Renaissance. On the passage over he fell ill, and he died in Florence less than a year later, at the age of fifty-eight.

Other Titles by Howard Pyle

Empty Bottles. Rochester, NY: Rochester Folk Art Press, 1975.

King Stork. (illus.) Boston: Little, Brown, 1986.

The Merry Adventures of Robin Hood. New York: Scribner's, 1946.

Otto of the Silver Hand. New York: Dover Press, 1967.

Sixth Merry Adventure of Robin Hood. New York: Dover Press, 1986.

The Story of King Arthur and His Knights. New York: Scribner's, 1984.

The Story of Sir Launcelot and His Companions. New York: Scribner's, 1985.

The Story of the Champions of the Round Table. New York: Scribner's, 1984.

The Story of the Grail and the Passing of Arthur. New York: Scribner's, 1985.

The Wonder Clock, or *Four and Twenty Marvelous Tales, Being One for Each Hour of the Day*. New York: Dover Press, 1970.